TRAPPED

TRAPPED

A RETRIEVAL, INC. NOVEL: BOOK 2

JB SCHROEDER

Two Feet
Press

11923 NE Sumner St, STE 843916
Portland, Oregon 97220

www.jbschroederauthor.com

Print Edition 1.0
ISBN-13: 978-1-943561-17-9

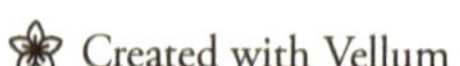 Created with Vellum

1

———————

Maria Lucia Rivera de Cruz scanned the single paragraph in the newspaper article for keywords first and found what she sought. *Mogul's son, returned home…*

Her body surged with relief. The animated sounds, smoky smell, and pressing heat of the outdoor market and over-warm afternoon returned to her ears, even as caution returned to her mind.

She dared a look past the hanging curtain where she'd tucked herself away from prying eyes and determined that she had a moment to read more thoroughly. Then she would tuck the paper into her weaved tote and discard it at the first opportunity she found. If it made it all the way home under vegetables and goods, she would simply burn it in the kitchens. She bent her head and focused.

Suddenly, a light brown hand with manicured nails clamped down to crinkle the page and yank it from her fingers. One crisp shake and all but the page she'd been reading from fell, flip-flopping erratically before settling in the dirt between them.

"What is so interesting that you must hide to read, sister?" Soft-spoken and polite, of course.

Lazaro Rivera Valdez was both her eldest brother and the patriarch of the family. Handsomely built, he was lean, of average height, and fine of face. He favored well-made clothes and a cane topped with a gold spider curled around a globe.

As always, their brother Jorge, who fell between Lazaro and Lucia in years, shadowed *el patrón*. Darker, stockier, and somehow always rumpled, he wore a menacing expression that seemed at home with the rough scar that marred his cheekbone. His wide mouth pressed tight in contrast to Lazaro's smooth, placid look. Lazaro's face, however, could never be trusted, as it was only a polished mask.

"*Nada*," Lucia replied coolly. "I sought shelter from the sun and was passing time with a newspaper." Lazaro did not tolerate lies, and this was the truth. He did not need to know that she'd sought this particular paper—despite the fact that it was marked June and the local Spanish one was current at the first week of January. But she must sacrifice herself—and safeguard the vendor she'd paid to save it for her—to some degree or she would not be believed. So she raised her chin. "News from the States."

Lazaro raised the paper and held it away from his body, the shiny wooden cane now tucked under his left arm. He would not be seen with reading glasses in public; it was a sign of age and weakness.

"Of course," he said with a tone that said he was not surprised. "The *L.A. Times*."

She'd long been fine-tuned to each of his nuances—a necessity—and she watched as his lips tightened almost imperceptibly. He could read English as well as she, yet he despised her time across the border. Even as a young man, he'd made no secret of his displeasure and disagreement with their father's plans.

She held her breath, hoping that he would let this go and look no further. That her dangerous secrets, kept carefully and close, would not come crashing down.

Lazaro scanned the page for only a minute before his eyes stilled.

Dios, no. He'd seen it. He'd remembered the name.

He snapped the paper then folded it and handed it to Jorge. "Keep this," he said, even as his right hand pulled the cane free.

Lucia forgot to breathe, as her eyes latched on to the arc of gold, wide and high, before a swift descent. Instinct had her arm raising to block the blow, but she was too late. Pain erupted near her temple, and instantly—mercifully—the world went black.

2

Three weeks later

IF GREAT SEX COULD HEAL ALL WOUNDS, CHARLIE Hart thought, then she and Mitch Saunders were well on their way to an incredibly healthy relationship. If not, well, they still had a lot of work to do.

"Never gets old, does it?" Charlie murmured, squeezing Mitch's hand, the only place they were still linked after a spontaneous and sexy midday tumble.

Mitch levered onto one elbow and pressed his lips to her collarbone. He met her eyes with a grin. "I'm counting on that never."

Charlie laughed, but the muscles of her neck and shoulders tensed.

He kissed her—she tasted both the salt of sweat and the tang of her own excitement—before he flopped onto his back.

She looked out the window at the gray winter sky and bare tree branches—standard fare for winter in Central

Pennsylvania. Charlie knew he wasn't fast-forwarding them to "until death do us part," but she couldn't help but feel the pressure. God… The Future. So friggin' loaded.

They were in his bed in his apartment today, though more often than not they spent nights at hers. When she first returned to Blakes Ridge, they'd shacked up out of necessity, because she had nowhere else to go. But she'd been solo and on the run for too long, and all that togetherness chafed. He hadn't been thrilled when she moved out a few months ago, but she needed her own place, her independence, and some room to breathe.

Breathing was hard a lot of times. Charlie was navigating—and in some ways very much enjoying—this first real relationship. Due to that bastard Thomas Weihle, she was also building a relationship with her mom, who was recovering from many years of illness. Little by little she was sorting out how to be part of her daughter's life. Mackenzie was only seven, so that included the girl's adopted parents, Pamela and Ray Hudson. Worst of all, she was fighting to remain Charlie Hart—when the legal system wanted her to relive her nightmare as Laura Macnamara.

She had no idea if she was doing any of it right.

She curled on her side, eyes raking over the hard planes of Mitch's body, trying to bring herself back to the present. He stretched and turned, then caught her eye. "Don't." His laugh was warm, and his cock twitched. "I gotta get moving."

"You can move right here." Charlie slid a hand down her stomach and tucked her fingers between her legs. A bad habit—or maybe not—she'd developed, keeping the focus on sex. Sex she could handle. She could separate from it when she felt too much—a trick she'd learned by necessity during years of abuse.

With Mitch, though, there was also the closeness and tenderness that came afterward—and even when they weren't naked. They had a connection she felt down to her bones. She never doubted his motives or her physical safety. With him there was no power play—at least not anymore. He simply gave.

But she didn't really know how to receive. Invariably, she got freaked out, all skittish.

Mitch's eyes heated, even as his brows lowered. Perceptive, especially when it came to her, he'd caught on to her game long ago. Still, he rolled toward her and slid a warm palm up her thigh.

Out of nowhere, his cell rang. "Shit." He squeezed her hip and then rolled, vaulting off the bed.

He was a detective and close to retiring, but she knew being a cop would always be part of him. She wiggled her toes inside her socks, glad for them now in the chilly room. Not exactly sexy, but she and Mitch had been in a hurry. Charlie didn't mind the hurry or the cop thing. She liked that he never shirked duty, that he took his commitments seriously, that he knew what to do in the worst situations, that he had morals and a strong sense of right and wrong.

Mitch snatched up the phone from the nightstand and sat on the bed, one knee up, back against the bare wall. Quite a view from her eye level.

There were a few grunted acknowledgments, and then Mitch yanked a pillow over his lap. "I wish I could help you, but I'm still with the force." He shut his eyes. "I can't take the case."

Charlie scooted out of bed. It wasn't his job this time. It was another brokenhearted, terrified parent who had found Mitch's private number. Another family praying he could help them find their runaway son or daughter.

He'd found Charlie—known locally as runaway Laura Macnamara—after six long years. Ever since, he'd been known as a man who didn't give up, a man who could do the impossible.

Mitch took the number of this caller and promised to let them know if anything changed. "I'm truly sorry," he said.

Charlie grabbed her t-shirt and panties from the floor and slid into both, before finding her cargo pants under Mitch's jeans. They were finally getting good and soft. She'd had to purchase a couple of new pairs from the nearest Army Navy store when she decided to stay in town. Her favorites were still in the apartment her dear friend Henrietta held for her in San Francisco. Henry had wanted to mail her things, but Charlie refused. She held on tight to the apartment and that faraway stuff. It felt like an out she could exercise at any time.

Mitch sat, elbows on knees, his palms pressed into his eyes. He blamed himself for his sister's death. The need to atone had him in a chokehold. Charlie understood only too well.

Her heart lurched, and she rounded the bed to go to him, popping her sweatshirt over her head on the way. She wasn't the only one with hard decisions to make and the future pressing in. "Not a missing dog this time, I guess."

He looked up and sucked in air, nostrils flaring. "No."

He didn't say more, partly, she thought, to spare her, and partly because it wasn't like she was helping matters. Because he didn't just want to leave the force and set up shop as a private investigator. He wanted Charlie to join him. She'd been a runaway, after all. She'd lived on the streets, understood the desperation, knew the tricks to stay hidden, and had a keen instinct when it came to threats and self-preservation.

But for the first time in her life, she finally had the opportunity to pursue an actual career—one of her own choosing, one that didn't require cash under the table. For now, she was buying time with another waitressing job— not as good as the one in San Francisco when she worked for her friend Cleo, but it was okay.

She was having trouble figuring out what she wanted to do, though. A lot of things had to factor in, like her mother, Mackenzie, Mitch… Still, she didn't want another decision made *for* her.

Mitch understood, but the clock was ticking.

The damn clock was always ticking, wasn't it?

3

———————

Ian Cross woke with a dread so terrifying that he refused to open his eyes. He had a mother of a headache, he was ten seconds from hurling, and his tongue was as dry and stiff as corrugated cardboard. His shoulders burned and the arm he was lying on felt half dead.

In short, he felt like pure hell—which meant only one thing.

He'd relapsed.

Except he couldn't even remember it to enjoy the high. Fucking hell.

If he opened his eyes it would be worse. Ian groaned, picturing a ratty couch—but no, he was lying on a hard surface. Probably some shit-caked floor surrounded by needles and losers and God knew what. He knew it would stink and tried not to breathe. If it was daylight, the brightness would just about kill him.

Just as well. He deserved it.

He'd rather be dead than have slipped.

"Fuck, fuck," he said.

"He's awake."

Ian tried to raise his hand to cover his eyes but couldn't. He shifted—testing—and discovered he was tied at the wrists, his arms wrenched behind him. *Oh God.* What the hell had he gotten himself into?

Ian's eyes shot open, only to see wrinkled linen slacks, bare ankles, and scuffed loafers pacing two feet in front of his nose. The first irrational and childish thought was that it was his dad—but no. Stephen Cross wore socks. Plus, this guy's skin was too dark.

Other possibilities, more probable, followed in short order. He'd traded sex for drugs—and the guy was a bondage perv or a total psycho. Or he'd been taken against his will to be sold into sex slavery. *Please, please no.* But he hadn't been using, so it made no sense!

Could this be a ransom thing because Dad was rich? Or—

Where *was* he, anyway?

His gaze darted around, past the shoes. On a plane? In a small rear cabin, maybe? The industrial-style carpet smelled new; the swivel-style captain's chairs appeared to be real leather. But the engines weren't screaming loud, so—

"*Sí.* On the ground. Where the hell is the transport?"

Christ. The man had spoken Spanish. Hungover as Ian was, he hadn't even realized he was translating it automatically. The shoes stopped, tips aimed at his nose.

Ian looked up past the sand-colored slacks to see a man with a stocky build, thick arms, and a brutish face with a puckered scar that curved from one cheekbone into the hairline at his temple. Black eyes bored into him with animosity. Maybe even hatred, although Ian was pretty sure he'd never met this guy before.

The man lowered a cell phone, traded it for a syringe, and squatted down.

"No," Ian said. He remembered now. He'd been in the garage, about to get in the car, when he felt a sharp prick in his neck and then beefy arms wrapping around him from behind.

"*Sí.*"

Ian reared back and tried to kick, but his legs were bound, too. The man grinned and drove an elbow into Ian's gut. Ian curled in pain.

The man put his forearm on Ian's upper arm and used his body weight to hold him still. Panic tore through him as the man fisted the syringe and stabbed the needle into Ian's neck.

What the ever-loving... Ian didn't even finish the thought before it all went dark again.

4

———

Monroe County District Attorney Gertrude Kolacsko resembled a plain brown mouse: small stature, fine bones, a tiny nose. Her suit was gray, her hair an unremarkable brown lying flat and straight. Even her glasses were plain, but Mitch knew from experience that when she whipped them off in the courtroom, watch out. Her eyes became weapons, her loud voice demanded attention, and her every gesture had purpose. She was smart, quick, and nearly always underestimated.

Mitch was damn glad Gerty was the one who'd be working to put Thomas Weihle behind bars for life. He wished there was the option of serving the bastard the death penalty on a silver platter, but between the governor's moratorium and the severity of the crime, it wouldn't happen. Far as he was concerned, the damn criteria was leaving out some of the worst crimes.

Gerty had been questioning Charlie for hours already. Mitch's presence was unusual. In fact, he was there only because Charlie had insisted. She didn't want him to hear any of her past for the first time in the courtroom, and she was adamant that she didn't want to tell any of it more than once. Gerty had narrowed her eyes, tapped her pen, and then shrugged, although she reserved the right to throw him out.

She just might need to. He'd sat off to the side, fetched coffee for them, and managed to keep his mouth shut. At this point, however, he'd just about reached his limit. A man couldn't hear about the sick shit Weihle had put a young girl—now the woman Mitch loved—through without wanting to throttle someone, or at least rail at the world. And he could see Charlie was having a hard time, too. The skin of her face was tight and pale, her mouth pinched, her hands clenched.

He got it—he himself had spent hours with Gerty earlier in the week to go over the details of the investigation into his sister Tiffany's disappearance and death, and his subsequent apprehension of Weihle. It was emotionally tough, so he'd been fried after—and he guaranteed it was far worse for Charlie. She'd suffered more than anyone. And the hours of endless prodding and rehashing couldn't help but dredge up a truckload of shit.

"Just one more question for today, and we'll call it quits," Gerty said, likely sensing the breaking point.

Charlie sucked in a breath and nodded, relief evident.

"Weihle says that you kissed him first—"

Mitch shot out of his chair. "You gonna believe a single word that sick fuck says?"

Charlie flinched, but Gerty just calmly crossed her arms. "You know damn well, detective, that what he says has no bearing on what I do or don't believe. Sit down or leave."

Mitch spun in a tight circle, hands pressed to his hair, and threw himself into the chair. This sucked.

Gerty leveled her gaze at Charlie. "It's my job to prepare us for every single thing the defense brings. I can't do that unless I know exactly what's what."

Charlie nodded and slid a glance to Mitch. He shook his head slightly, knowing she'd recall a heated conversation they'd had about this very instance. He also knew, despite the counseling and the law and a lotta years, that she still felt a tremendous amount of guilt.

Victim's guilt.

Gerty sat back in her chair, elbow on the armrests, a pen suspended between both hands.

"He's right," Charlie said softly. "Technically. I was nervous about meeting this boy at school."

"Name?"

"Billy Butler." She looked past Gerty, staring at the wall. "He sort of hinted that he could help me with that. That there was nothing to kissing, it only took practice."

A low growl erupted from Mitch. Both women ignored him.

"He back-pedaled right after he said it. Stupid me, I agreed to try it—kissing—with him, so I wouldn't look like a fool with Billy."

Gerty leaned forward and scribbled something on her notepad.

"He's going to say I asked for it, all of it."

"Yes," Gerty said.

"He's going to make everyone believe him." Charlie's voice cracked.

"He'll sure as hell try."

"He's a goddamn master manipulator," Mitch burst out as he towered over Gerty. "Those videos from his house? There are years' worth of footage of Charlie—from the time she was a little girl. He knew absolutely everything about her, probably before they ever had a single private conversation."

Abruptly, he spun, sinking to one knee in front of Charlie. He grasped her hands. They were ice cold.

"Guaranteed he knew *exactly* what to say to you, knew exactly how you'd respond, had been waiting patiently for this very situation so he could snag you. He had you all figured out before you ever set foot on his property. He steered every conversation you ever had. You were a child, honey, a kid. You couldn't possibly have had any idea how you were being played, couldn't have even imagined the ulterior motive he had in mind."

Charlie tried to pull her hands away, but he held fast. "The guilt you feel is misplaced. Weihle is the *only* one who did anything wrong."

Charlie wouldn't look at him, and his frustration doubled.

"Bravo, detective," Gerty said, her tone wry. "Mind if I borrow that for my closing arguments?"

He swore and shot a glare at the prosecutor, then rose and stomped to the door. He wrenched it open then banged it shut so hard it popped back open. He kept going but heard Gerty say, "He's right, you know."

That helped only marginally. Mitch burst out the front

door of the Monroe County Courthouse. He tried to suck air in and calm himself the hell down.

Charlie exited the building only a couple of minutes later.

"Listen, I—"

"I don't want to talk about it," she snapped. She held herself rigid and stalked toward where they'd parked his truck.

"Dammit," he muttered.

They rode in tense silence, Charlie's head turned toward the passenger window.

Mitch frowned, the coil of tension in his shoulders getting worse by the minute. Charlie had been backsliding on him little by little. When they'd been in California, searching for Tiffany, she'd assumed their time was limited. She'd thrown caution to the wind in order to soak up all he could offer. Then after Mackenzie and her mother had been saved, she was relieved and hopeful and willing enough to continue their relationship—mostly. Her walls had a tendency to pop back up now and then.

But now?

He had a death grip on the steering wheel and forced his fingers to ease up.

He wished he could just throw a line and reel her back to him. Hell, he wished he could put a ring on her finger and bind her to him by God, law, and witnesses.

But she wasn't having it, and for once in his life he didn't know what the hell to *do*. He sucked at following someone else's lead. Although he was trying. She'd asked for space. He'd found her a secure apartment in a safe neighborhood.

He'd purchased her a cell phone—more for his own piece of mind than her need—and then refrained from buying her anything but dinner. And most of all, he was trying damn hard not to push her on going into business with him.

Still, he was losing her. He could feel it.

Back in Blakes Ridge, he pulled up in front of her apartment and put the car in park. It didn't matter what he wanted, he reminded himself.

He kept his hands on the wheel. She was skittish enough on a good day, so he wasn't about to touch her now, after the brutal session with Gerty.

"I can't do this," she whispered, and shook her head, weariness evident in her posture.

Mitch's heart plummeted into his gut. She couldn't do what *this*? *This* him and her?

"I can't do this trial thing."

Mitch drew breath, relieved, even as he ached for her. "I know it's hard." He smoothed a hand over her layered white-blond hair and down to her neck. "There is no reason not to hold your head high in that courtroom. No one will be judging *you*."

She shook her head again, less dejected and more determined this time. "That's not true, and I don't want to go over it again and again. Even just talking to Gerty, it's..."

Big blue eyes—she still preferred the colored lenses she'd adopted over her natural brown—pleaded with him. Like he could change it. *If only.*

Charlie spoke again. "I want it in the past where it belongs."

"It will be if you do this. You have the power to put him away forever, to make sure he pays."

She pushed at his arm until his hand fell from her neck. "But at what cost to me, and to you? This is killing me, and it's nowhere near done."

"So speed up the meetings with Gerty. Give her two weeks to rehash everything and ask all the questions she wants and then that's it. Take a break."

"I need to be done *now*." She slammed her fist down on the seat.

"One week, then."

Charlie's lips tightened. "No. You don't understand. It's all of it. The past—it's the worst, but I'm about to implode."

"Okay, take a breath and try to calm down."

"Calm down? You did not just tell me to calm down." She shot him a dark look, but he already knew it'd been a stupid-ass thing to say. He just hated to see her like this.

"You've got no idea what it's like," Charlie said. "I'm used to being alone. *Alone*, Mitch. Responsible only for myself and that instant. I don't know how to do this." She waved her hand between them. "I don't know what the hell to do about my mother. How to support her—and still get what I need. I don't know how to handle the Hudsons, Mackenzie, anybody. And the guilt, *Jesus*." She pressed her fingers into her eyes.

"It'll all sort out," Mitch said. "You've got time."

"It's all I've ever wanted—everything. And I can't handle it. I'm fucking freaking out." Charlie threw open the truck's door. "I gotta get outta here."

Shit. He should have realized it was this bad. Mitch

shoved open his own door and sprinted across the parking lot to block her path. He squeezed her shoulders. "Charlie, please."

"Stop touching me, goddammit." She raised her arms, breaking his hold.

He opened his mouth, but nothing he could say was any good. He had no idea how to make it better. He doubted he even could.

"Just let me go." She burst past him and into her building.

This time, he let her.

5

———

This time when Ian woke, he was no longer trussed up on the floor of a private plane or bound and slamming against the metal bed of a dirty van breathing road dust and cigarette smoke. He still felt like shit, blistering headache and wicked nausea, although he was starving. Only a few months from eighteen years old, he was pretty much always starving, but this was worse. How long since he'd eaten?

This time he lay comfortably, somewhere cool and quiet. His mouth wasn't as dry, though his lips were chapped to hell. And there was a wet weight on his forehead. He smelled fresh air and sweet flowers, felt a light breeze, and heard an insane amount of chirping.

Ian cracked his eyes open and immediately spotted the source of the breeze: a big window. It had no glass, only bars like a jail cell and open shutters. Lush green treetops beyond. Bumpy stucco walls and minimal furniture, which included the bed he lay in—white sheets and a patterned blanket.

Like a hacienda-style resort. Not high end, but clean. Even the bars on the window had style, much like the decorative ones on many homes in California. Given his method of arrival, though, he'd bet they were built to hold. Damn.

He levered himself up and winced, sore all over. The clothes he'd been wearing—golf clothes—were gone. *Oh no,* his dad. He'd been meant to meet his dad at the club. He looked down and found—*huh*—loose, lightweight material. Casual pants and a short-sleeved button-down shirt.

He looked like the asshole on the plane that had shot him up with that shit. Which had been disappointing. Like no kind of rush he'd ever tried, just a quick flip to unconsciousness. He also didn't feel that beyond-primal urge for another high, thank God. They must have roofied him or something.

Ian reached up to his forehead, expecting a bandage. But it was a compress. He dumped it on the side table next to a wide ceramic bowl. A glass and a jug, too.

Ian sat up and swung his bare feet over the side of the bed. Rust-colored ceramic tile swam below.

It'd be easy to simply black out yet again, except he'd never get out of here if he didn't get off his ass. Like his dad always said, *"You've got to work for it. No silver platters."* No matter that their formal dining room was filled with real silver.

His dad would think Ian had gone off the deep end. Run away again. Hit the skids. Nosedived. Relapsed. Failed. Whatever you wanted to call it.

Just when his father had come to trust him again. Just

when he'd come to trust himself. When they'd reached a middle ground and started to rebuild.

Aw, shit, Dad. I'm sorry, so sorry.

His stomach surged in a swift wave of disgust. Ian grabbed the bowl and lunged, splashing the water half out the window, half down the wall. He hunched, retching into the heavy bowl he clutched with shaking hands. Little came out even as he heaved.

So it had definitely been a while since he'd eaten. How long since he'd been gone?

He'd been taken from his home. The blackness had come swift and unstoppable, only moments after he realized he wasn't alone. Had anything even been disturbed? Likely not in the garage. Would his dad even suspect, or just assume…the worst?

Instinct demanded he keep his silence, but he ached to shout, *It's not my fault!* Not this time.

He crumpled to his knees as his eyes filled with tears.

No—don't give in. With a frustrated and uncoordinated movement—shit, he felt weak—he swiped them away. Then he laid his forehead against the cool tile and tried to think.

Before he'd even caught his breath, he heard a key in the lock and spun on his knees.

A monkey—

Jesus. A fucking monkey scampered into the room. A blackish-brown, furry little guy with a cream-colored face and shoulders the same—like he was wearing a baseball-style t-shirt. Didn't most monkeys live in Costa Rica or something? Ian had never been much for the zoo as a kid.

Ian stood too fast and saw black waves and bright colors rushing him.

A strong hand levered him by an armpit and propelled him toward the bed. A woman. Wearing a stern, maybe angry expression, despite the pretty face, large eyes, and swingy earrings. Sleek, dark hair with an off-center swath of white that arched from her forehead and wound into a large bun at the nape of her neck. *A la* a drunk skunk, Ian thought, and had the craziest urge to giggle, until her outfit came into focus. Traditional Mexican garb? Bright yellow, blousy shirt, and a full skirt, adorned with swirling embroidery. It did not look anything like his idea of Mexico outside his window—all he could see from the bed was green.

Where the fuck was he, anyway?

"Bienvenido a casa."

Ian looked at her like she had three heads. Had she actually said... *Welcome home?*

6

THE WOMAN PROPPED UP THE PILLOWS ON THE BED, then pushed at Ian's shoulder until he lay back. The monkey had leapt to the window, traversed it with its crazy-long tail and disturbingly humanlike hands, and then dropped to sniff at the bowl Ian had puked in. It screeched, turned up its nose, and raised its arm to strike at the offensive stuff.

"Mico, no!" The woman stamped her foot just in time. She peered at the bowl and frowned. Then she stepped to the nightstand and poured a glass of water. The monkey shifted from one foot to the other, making a repeated little *ooh* sound and staring at Ian the whole while.

The woman handed Ian the glass. He took it but didn't drink. She gestured impatiently. He raised it to his nose and sniffed.

She narrowed her eyes, grabbed the glass from him, snatched up the pitcher, and marched through a closed door at the far end of the room.

The animal crisscrossed the room, screeching and

squeaking. Again, he leapt up to the window, shimmied the bars, and jumped back down.

From the bathroom, Ian heard water splash, then she appeared in the doorway. With her eyebrows raised, she turned both vessels upside down with a hard shake. She spun again, skirt and earrings swinging. The monkey inspected the puke-filled bowl again, shoved it away with a scrape, ceramic against ceramic, and screeched his or her —better yet, Ian thought, *its*—displeasure.

All this action, the woman and the monkey in constant motion, made him feel ill all over again, and he grimaced, shutting his eyes. He heard the water run, and next thing he knew, she was poking him in the arm. She clunked the pitcher down on the table.

"Drink," she said in Spanish.

He hesitated, and her nostrils flared. She drank from the cup, then stuck it right in his hand. It was hold on or end up wet. Fine—they were done drugging him. For now, at least.

Except he still knew absolutely freaking nothing. He had no idea who these people were, why they'd chosen him, or what they intended to do with him.

She crossed her arms and waited, mouth tight. Damned if that little monkey didn't mimic her posture.

Ian sipped. Fresh and just slightly cool, and every cell in his body—okay, except his wonky stomach—ached to chug it. But he didn't want to give his captor the satisfaction. Sure, she wasn't the one that kept stabbing him in the neck with a needle, but she obviously worked for the man who did.

He handed it back, and she rolled her eyes.

"*¿Como te llamas?*" she asked.

Ian glared, feeling angry and uncooperative. Why the hell did it matter?

"What is your name?" she repeated in English. He blinked, startled. Less of an accent than ninety percent of the Hispanic kids he'd met, and most of his dad's various staff. Maybe, just maybe, he should be aiming to get on this woman's good side.

"Ian," he said, and found his voice rough and weak.

She stilled. It was almost a whisper when she asked, "Ian what?" She watched him like a hawk, like she suspected trickery from him.

"Ian Cross."

Her big eyes widened—was that alarm or anger? She raised her chin, levered her shoulders back, and pressed her lips into the flattest line he'd seen yet.

So much for that plan. Mary Poppins she wasn't. In fact, she hadn't stopped shooting daggers at him the whole time she'd been in the room. Probably, as warden, she didn't care to have one more prisoner to babysit.

He didn't care much for being locked down either. He'd had enough of that growing up on his dad's estate, with guards at the gates and too many staff constantly reporting his every move. It was why he'd come to think of the whole lot of them as the Sentinels. It was one of the reasons he'd once been so desperate to escape his father's house.

"I will bring food soon," she said. He frowned. He needed to eat, he knew, but he was still worried about what they'd put in it. She repeated the phrase in English.

Then she said, "Mico," and snapped her fingers at the monkey, who followed her out.

Weird. The monkey was a pet but didn't have a name. *El mico* meant *the monkey*. That thought distracted Ian for a moment—but all of a sudden, it hit him.

The woman had switched to English when he balked at answering her—she didn't realize he'd understood the Spanish. That might work to his advantage.

7

———

MITCH STRODE UP THE INTERIOR FLIGHT OF STAIRS to Charlie's apartment, one of four sectioned from a house, and hoped like hell the news he brought wouldn't send her further into the tailspin. He should have told her when he'd done it, but he'd been waiting for a good time. There hadn't been one, of course.

They'd had only the tersest conversations since the meeting with Gerty. Charlie hadn't come over the last two nights—and he tried to be okay with giving her space. Now, though, he couldn't wait any longer and wanted this conversation face to face.

She'd given him a key, but preferred he knock first. No answer. He tried again, listening for the shower or music or anything else that might hamper her hearing.

The apartment wasn't much, but low-maintenance Charlie didn't care about trappings. Given her history, she was just glad to be able to afford a place and live somewhere safe and clean.

He rapped a third time, but he was just stalling. After

the blowup the other day, he couldn't remotely gauge how she'd take the fact that he'd gone ahead and applied for a PI's license. Filing the application, letters of reference, passport photographs, and the surety bond with the clerk of courts had been easy. Telling Charlie was the hard part. He was afraid she'd consider it an ultimatum. Her own decision, however, changed nothing. He was doing this—with or without her. He'd passed twenty years in law enforcement, he needed this, and he was sick of waiting.

The ten days of processing time was up, and he had his official license in hand. He'd listed his apartment as his place of business until he could secure an office. And he'd given notice of retirement from the force to Marcone— who was both his chief and his mother's boyfriend. He planned to go see his mom after this, so he could explain before Marcone did.

He'd known Charlie was feeling the pressure. She had a lot of choices now—a luxury she'd never before experienced—and that big blank slate was overwhelming.

As for him, well, every time he fielded a call about another missing person—usually a teen or a child—his path just solidified. He was done with the department. The early fallout from the Macnamara case had soured things. And though he'd proven them all wrong, it didn't erase that period of time.

Furthermore, undercover work in narcotics was out. He hadn't been available or even reachable when shit first went down with Tiffany. What if he had been? What if his mom, Deirdre, had just picked up the phone and called him? If he'd been visiting both her and Tiff regularly, if he'd been paying goddamn attention—would that have changed anything?

He braced his hands on Charlie's doorframe, stretching the muscles of his back.

It was too late for Tiffany, for him, for his mom. But maybe it wasn't too late for somebody else's sister or child. He needed to be able to answer the phone and give somebody some damn hope—including himself. Just like police work, he knew he wouldn't always win, couldn't save or find them all, but at least the folks left behind would have an extra shot. Another chance. Maybe once in a while, he could give somebody a happy ending.

Mitch pushed off the doorframe and found Charlie's key on his ring. He'd stalled long enough. After gaining entry, he called out, just in case. "Charlie?"

He really wanted Charlie to work with him. Thought it'd be perfect on so many levels. She wouldn't have to incur a ton of debt or years of schooling, but could support her mom Ellen right off and stay local to get to know her again, as well as her own daughter, Mackenzie. She had the personality for PI work and, especially if they were focusing on runaways or missing kids, could add real value. She knew the streets, the dangers, and the people. She understood the fear, distrust, and desperation.

If he was being completely honest, he'd also admit a purely selfish motive. He wanted her close.

Mitch poked his head in the bedroom and bathroom, then hit the kitchen for some water. He leaned against the counter to text her.

I'm at your place. Lmk your ETA.

Charlie hadn't lost all her fear—who could blame her?

—so he liked to give her fair warning if he entered her apartment.

It only worked half the time, though. She had never owned a cell phone before coming to live here, so she often forgot to check it. Much like she forgot that other people wanted, and sometimes needed, to check in with her.

He smiled and shook his head.

Mitch slugged some water, then stilled as his eye caught a plug and its cord—to the coffee maker—lying on the counter.

He set the cup down and straightened, suddenly on full alert. The transistor radio she used was also unplugged, as was the toaster oven.

He flipped up the lid to the garbage can. A clean bag, completely empty.

A sinking feeling flooded him even as his adrenaline spiked.

Mitch strode through the short hallway to the bedroom and stalked over to Charlie's closet, wrenching open the cheap door.

Then he swore a blue streak.

Charlie's go-bag was gone.

8

Juan Lazaro Valdez Rivera sat in the high-backed leather chair in his office with a glass of iced lemon water and his supplies on the table next to him. He balanced his cane across his lap and reached for the small tub of expensive wood polish.

He uncapped it, shut his eyes, and breathed in deeply —such a clean, rich smell. Almost immediately, he felt calm wash over him.

No matter the power he wielded, he preferred to clean his cane himself. The servants used to offer, almost plead, to handle the menial task for him. Now they simply brought him soft rags and polish—and if the occasion had been gory, soap and towel, too. Likely they thought he didn't trust them.

In fact, it was simply that for Lazaro, the task was an act of reflection. Eyeing the beauty, inspecting for damage, enjoying the rich smell, polishing in a smooth, repetitive motion—it was like a meditation.

The top knob was a carving of a spider curled around a

globe—as if the fierce arachnid controlled its spin with its many legs. Lazaro loved to stare at the detailed artistry and simply let his mind explore possibilities.

He didn't consider himself a violent man. But he'd watched his father carefully over the years and learned at an early age that *violencia* had its uses.

Take Lucia, for instance. Their father had had a soft spot for his only daughter and youngest child. A soft spot was a mistake. Loss of control was a mistake. Letting the sheep out of the pen to nose other sheep and to taste other grass, that was a very serious mistake indeed. A mistake that was upsetting the applecart decades later.

His brows pulled down as he stroked the smooth length of the wood.

It was possible, in this case, that the mistake could right the applecart in the end. A thought Lazaro did not relish, yet he did not shirk from responsibility. Regrettably, blood, even tainted blood, held extreme value for a man in his position.

Over and over he had evaluated his most serious problem, the one he'd had for many years, that was now coming to a critical point. He was more than reluctant to return power to the Gomez family, and as the years marched on, he'd prayed for an unexpected solution. And here it was: the error—Ian.

With the boy's arrival, he at least had a set of choices. None were ideal, but he preferred options so that he could coordinate the best result. The determination would take time.

He didn't have much time, though—he'd have to push hard. His own fate had been sealed.

He had already been cursed well and truly in the here and now. He had no offspring, no blood to lead. Once, he had not believed the prophecy to be anything but the delusions of an old woman, but the years had proven the *adivino* true. Which meant there would be no escaping his preordained *muerte*, either.

He could hear the old seer's voice like it was yesterday. Hoarse from age and too much tobacco, it scraped him like a grindstone even in memory.

When the cruel beauty comes of age, you have only a handful of seasons more between the clouds and the dirt.

He had kept the prophecy secret, of course. It would not do to show weakness.

But now, there were possibilities that didn't exist before. Ah, not quite true. They existed, but his dear sister had withheld them.

Lucia would pay. The blow he'd given the bitch in the market last week was nothing.

He raised the cane into the wash of afternoon sunlight and smiled at its sheen and beauty.

Fear of violence inspired cooperation and loyalty, and ensured that his wishes and standards were met. All were necessary to his trade.

But it was his penchant for perceived unpredictability that set him apart, that kept him in power as the head of a powerful and growing cartel amongst so much competition.

Lazaro, however, never actually did anything unpredictable. Oh, it would appear so, but in truth he carefully considered every decision, every action, with the utmost thoroughness. He had mastered the art of possibility. The options, the infinite options, spreading out like an intricate web. He always considered carefully, so that he could afford to appear capricious and rash, seemingly without thought toward consequences, putting everyone on edge.

Everyone but him.

Would it be you, or the brother standing next to you, who suffered his wrath when he was displeased with a shipment?

Would it be your daughter or your mother or you yourself who paid the ultimate price for a transgression?

Would the punishment fit today's crime? Or be entirely out of proportion and delivered tomorrow?

Lazaro stroked the head of his cane, tracing the spider's legs with his thumb.

Not all spiders built webs—but he had an affinity for those that did. Beautiful and dangerous, the realm the arachnid created was ever so practical.

Lazaro's web had trapped something new. Now he must spin new threads to secure it and rebuild his world.

9

CHARLIE WALKED THROUGH HER SAN FRANCISCO apartment like a ghost, flitting from here to there, touching her old things, but not really feeling like she belonged any longer.

She sighed. Once, it had been her home, really her only safe haven. Now it just felt strange. Especially the bedroom. She'd tossed and turned all last night.

She hadn't realized how used to Mitch she'd gotten, just how comforting it was to have him beside her. The soft rumble of his breathing, the weight of him dipping the mattress when she rolled too close, the rough skin of his big hands when he sought her out in the dark. Even in sleep he liked to have a hand on her somewhere.

Her mouth quirked up. Made for an interesting morning when she woke to his hand in certain places.

A door slammed in the apartment above her—Henrietta Plummer, Charlie's dear friend and landlord. Charlie shook her head, listening to her friend's heavy clomping as she made her way down the stairs.

How many times had they left together, walking over to Glide to serve a meal? Working with Henry, giving back to other runaways and those who'd hit hard times, she'd had her first taste of fulfillment. Waitressing, too, for another friend, Cleo, who owned a bistro here in the Tenderloin, had given her a sense of security. She'd belonged. She'd actually grown some roots. And she'd felt content for the first—the only—time here in this apartment. All heady stuff for a runaway hiding her identity.

Of course, she'd never stopped looking over her shoulder. Still, most of her time in San Francisco had been both simple and blessedly constant.

Nowadays, her situation was anything but.

Charlie rolled her neck, trying to release the tight muscles.

She heard Henry hit the last step. Charlie snagged her messenger bag off the floor and swung around to open the door. "Ready?"

"Child, you know I gotta catch my breath." Henry fanned herself and pushed past Charlie. She always rushed around at the last minute, spritzing on perfume, freshening her makeup, double-checking the contents of her purse, and who knew what else.

Once Charlie had asked why she didn't just start getting ready a few minutes early.

"I just do it the way I do it. After all these years, I ain't gonna change."

Charlie wondered about that now. Was she, too—at the still-green age of twenty-five—too bruised and damaged to change? Stunted from all the trauma? Or could she still ripen into a nice, plump piece of fruit?

Sheesh, she thought, and shook her head. She was really a hot mess if she'd started thinking of herself as produce.

Henry raised an eyebrow. "Did you hear a word I just said?"

"Uh…"

Henry harrumphed and crossed the room. She plopped down on the couch, the only place to sit in the living room, and patted the cushion next to her.

"What about Glide?" Charlie asked.

"It'll wait," Henry said. "I'm not even on shift today, and you're just visiting, so…" She shrugged. "Sit a while."

"You just want me to yourself." Charlie propped her boots on the coffee table.

"You got that right." Henrietta laughed, her eyes twinkling. She bent forward to lift her swollen ankles up on the coffee table, one at a time. Charlie was positive that Henry had scolded her own children, and likely still scolded her grandchildren, for doing just this.

"Ah." Henry closed her eyes in relief. Then she gave Charlie a sidelong look. "So, what's the trouble? I know it can't be that hunk of a man you landed."

Charlie snorted. "I'll tell him you still approve."

"I approve of the way he looks, at least."

"You like him."

Henrietta reached over and squeezed Charlie's hand. "I do at that. I can see where you and he might have some growing pains, but the man cared for you from the very beginning. And he's been good for you."

"How would you know?" Henry had never seen them together as a couple, although Charlie and her friend had

had a few phone conversations since she moved to Blakes Ridge.

"Oh, old Henry just knows these things."

Charlie rolled her eyes.

"So?" Henry asked.

And it took some more prodding and some pointed questions, but Charlie managed to give her friend the basic idea. The decisions that were weighing on her. The pressure she felt.

Henry didn't need a lot of words. She was, Charlie knew, an expert at reading between the lines. She nodded and made "huh" sounds behind her nose. Then she crossed her arms over her generous chest.

"So you mean to tell me you ran away?" She speared Charlie with a look both accusatory and knowing. "Again?"

"I felt like I couldn't breathe," Charlie said. "I had to get out of there."

"You went and left that handsome man and that beautiful child and your poor mother without a word?"

"I didn't run away. I'm just taking a little break."

"You showed up here last night out of the blue. No hey-Henry-I'm-coming-for-a-visit phone call, no clear-your-busy-calendar-for-me warning." Henrietta tsked. "*Please* tell me you left word."

Charlie twisted her lips.

"Oh, for God's sake, girl, have some consideration. Mitch got you that phone so you could use it. Call him, right now." She waved her hands right in Charlie's face. "Go on."

"It's too early."

"There is a three-hour time difference."

"Oh. Right." Charlie dug through her bag. She hadn't thought to charge her phone last night. She never thought about it, actually. "I did try to call him from the airport," Charlie muttered.

"Tried or did?"

Charlie flushed.

"Did you at least leave him a message?"

"I couldn't make the damn thing work, okay?" She hadn't had service. Trying to sign on to the airport Wi-Fi was a labyrinth of stress, and she didn't understand all the messages that popped up about cellular data and everything else. There seemed to be sign-ins for sign-ins. And half the time when she did manage to call someone, they popped up on her screen, moving and talking. That, she hated. It freaked her out.

She'd taken hiding to heart. She didn't want people to *see* her.

Charlie woke up the phone and navigated slowly through to Mitch's number. She scowled. Hell—there were kids in that airport as young as Mackenzie all poking away on devices and having no trouble at all. It was embarrassing.

Finally, when it started ringing, she stood up and moved to the bedroom for some privacy. Not that Henry wouldn't be listening to every word, but at least Charlie wouldn't have to look her in the eye. The early February morning temperatures meant the radiator had hissed on and off all night, but a chill passed over her and she rubbed her arms.

Mitch answered, "Where are you?"

"San Francisco."

"Christ, Charlie, you couldn't have given me a heads-up?"

"I'm sorry." She winced at how whiny she sounded. "I tried to call from the airport but I couldn't figure out how to get service, and then they said I had to turn off my phone. It was late last night when I arrived, and—"

"*Before.* Before you left for the airport would have been—" She heard Mitch blow out a hard breath. "Whatever."

She didn't know what to say.

The silence stretched until he asked, "So are you coming back? Ever?"

"You think I left for good?"

"What the hell am I supposed to think? Most people don't just hop a plane and take off without mentioning it to the person they're sleeping with every night."

Ouch. She'd really messed this up. "I'm not most people."

"No shit."

Charlie cringed. That hadn't sounded positive either.

Mitch said, "I called all over, so now the Hudsons are worried, too. Not to mention your mother. *You* get to call them and tell them you're alive."

Double ouch. She rubbed her forehead and sank to the bed.

"You do know," Mitch said, his tone less scathing, "that it costs a helluva lot less money to fly if you plan ahead, right? Two weeks ahead, at least."

"Um, no," she said. She'd only ever flown twice. Once

to save Mackenzie from Thomas Weihle. And now. Both had been rash decisions born out of necessity.

"You're at your apartment? You've seen Henrietta?"

"Yes."

"All right. I guess you're fine, then. Let me know if you come back east." He laughed, but it was a harsh and ugly sound. "Actually, never mind. I won't expect to hear a damn thing."

He disconnected.

Charlie just sat there, reeling, staring at all the options the stupid phone gave her, but not seeing them. She'd been so focused on her own damn worries that she hadn't stopped to consider how her actions would affect Mitch, or the Hudsons, or even her mom. For so many years she was accountable to nobody but herself.

She blew out a long breath.

Even here in San Francisco, getting close to Henrietta…the relationship had been such a natural one. Built slowly through time and overlapping routines. Everyone in Blakes Ridge wanted—no, expected—so much from her, right off, and all at once.

She hadn't even come to terms with the things she'd done and, more importantly, hadn't done. It was…

Panic-inducing, crippling, and terrifying.

She swore. Still, there was no excuse for making people worry about her unnecessarily, making them fear for her safety—again.

"Well," Henrietta called from the living area, "that went better than expected."

10

———————

Around midday the next day, the woman—without a monkey in her wake this time—brought Ian fresh clothes. With terse Spanish, to which he played dumb, she ushered him toward the bathroom. She turned on the shower, set the neat stack of clothing on the sink, and shut the door behind her.

He thought about refusing, but what was the point? He was definitely ripe. Despite a lingering headache, the water and food yesterday had helped him feel more human. He'd been incredibly relieved to find that he wasn't craving more of whatever they'd shot him up with —just the regular urges he expected to battle forever.

The shower felt damn good. Loath to face whatever awaited him, he stayed under the water a long time. Finally, he donned the clothing: pants and a long-sleeved button-down, even boxers, all of which were lightweight and loose. He also made long-overdue use of the tooth-brush and paste. Shaking his head, he ignored the razor and shaving cream, as well as the cologne.

Dread was eating him alive, and he was pretty sure the scent would make him feel queasy all over again.

Over the past day and half, since he'd been lucid, he'd tried listening at the door, the walls, and the window. He'd heard only snatches of Spanish—nothing telling. There seemed to be plenty of people about, including children shrieking and playing, but his room was secluded. And, unfortunately, secure. He'd found nothing with which to pick the lock, no other avenue of exit, and those bars were the real thing.

He hadn't heard screaming or yelling or blows. He hadn't heard chains or whips or guns or anything freaky. Still—he'd only come up with a few reasons he could have been kidnapped that made any sense. And the scariest one by far was sexual slavery. Stories about kids being picked off had been constant fodder when he was on the streets. More than one featured snuff films. Urban legend, Ian had been sure—until now.

Ian eyed himself up in the mirror. The white shirt made his skin, always tending toward olive, look darker. He was due for the barbershop. The buzzcut he'd been sporting was growing out fast, and now his thick, dark hair stuck straight up out of his scalp.

The pants fit pretty well, and the clothing was clean, pressed, and of good quality.

He felt like a calf being fatted for a kill or tied up in a bow at auction to the highest bidder. Ian swallowed hard, tamping down the bile that threatened. He scratched the short beard that had sprung up on his face. How many days had he been gone? He normally hated to go without shaving, so he wasn't sure, but at least a few days.

Ian drew a steadying breath—it might be better to look more man than boy for whatever was to come.

When he exited, a pair of brown leather sandals sat just outside the bathroom door. Two younger women were just leaving his room. He saw that the sheets had been changed, the shutters opened, his tray from the morning removed, and his water glass and pitcher replaced.

He considered bolting through the door and taking his chances. But his keeper stood watching him and would surely sound the alarm.

She pointed to the sandals. "Come."

As much as Ian didn't want to know what awaited, he was anxious to gather some information. As they walked, he took note of the doorways they passed and the turns they'd taken. Some of the hallways were open air—but there wasn't much to see. Oak trees or something similar surrounded the place. They were tall, and Ian couldn't see well beyond, but dismay swamped him. As far as he could tell, they were marooned in the mountains in some sort of isolated compound surrounded by a high wall. No town, no neighbors. He couldn't even spot a road.

A couple of little girls ran across their path, shrieked when they saw him, and took off again.

Moments later, he'd entered a large dining room, the setup similar to a great hall in a castle, except largely open air, the walls at half height and more shutters thrown open. Two long wooden trestle tables sat parallel to the walls, and a third was situated similarly but centered in the room. The people seated around the table were dark-skinned and black-haired for the most part, varied in age from young to old, and dressed much like him and his keeper.

Well, Dorothy, you're definitely not in Kansas anymore.

When the first diner noticed him, her fork remained suspended in midair, her eyes growing wide. A ripple spread through the room, leaving stillness and silence in its wake. His keeper didn't miss a beat. She simply led him up the middle to the head table.

Two men—close to her age, Ian figured—already sat there, one at the head facing the rest of the room, the other to his right. That was the scarred one who'd stabbed him with a needle full of nasty shit. Ian drew a reflexive breath, but the man ignored Ian, seemingly focused only on shoveling food into his ugly mug.

His keeper sat opposite him and gestured Ian to sit on the bench next to her.

He hesitated, wanting to run like a wild thing, wanting to shout out questions and demand answers to find out why in the hell he was here.

But this dining situation was so far from the various scenarios he'd prepared himself for that he simply climbed over the bench.

There was a teenage girl on his left, perhaps a couple of years younger than himself, unabashedly staring. Like stair steps, the dark, glossy heads went down the table, and then climbed back up the other side. All of them females in braids or buns, who regarded him wide-eyed. Almost directly across, he met a hostile stare from a girl about his age. Her strong nose flared as if she smelled something distasteful, and her wide lips were clamped tight with anger.

Okay, then.

Between the guy who'd drugged him and the angry girl was a woman with a matching nose. No less anger in her stare than from what was probably her daughter, but a palpable look of disgust.

Ian shifted his gaze away quickly only to land on the man at the head, who regarded him steadily. Ian felt a shiver pass over his spine. It was clear Captain Injection and Head Honcho were related. But the head guy verged on classy instead of brutish. He was obviously in charge, given his position at the head of the table and of the room. Ian couldn't read him at all. He wore zero expression and hadn't moved a muscle. Ian held his eyes, let anger work its way onto his face.

"Tell him to eat, Lucia," the man said in Spanish, though he didn't shift his gaze from Ian.

"He won't, unless he knows it's not drugged."

The man inclined his head ever so slightly, and she reached for a bowl. She plopped a sizable spoonful of rice on Ian's plate and her own, then what looked like a rich stew of chicken or pork, and something fried—probably from the vegetable family. A spicy, fragrant scent reached his nose, and Ian's stomach rumbled.

Lucia stuck her fork in his dish, took a bite of each different food, then took a sip from each of the cups in front of him. She turned her attention to her own plate. Ian supposed at this point if they needed him drugged, it wouldn't be the food anyway. It'd be back to the syringe.

The man still stared, so Ian took a tentative bite of rice.

Head Honcho returned his attention to his own meal,

and the collective silence lifted. People returned to the business of eating, the clatter of utensils, the passing of dishes. Still, no one spoke.

Ian was suddenly starving, and he never thought well on an empty stomach. Despite a constant wariness—who knew what was to come?—Ian couldn't help but feel relieved for the moment. He began to eat in earnest.

When he drank and the snap of beer hit his tongue, he barely refrained from spitting the contents everywhere. He set the cup down and cautiously inspected the other. Water? He took a careful sip—and relief coursed through him. Yes, only water.

Ian was a recovering drug addict. Alcohol wasn't a good bet for him, and this was definitely no time to lose his head.

Ian appreciated the fact that he wasn't expected to understand the conversation. He was free to get the lay of the land in silence. Problem was, tonight at least, his table mates were quiet, surely uncomfortable in his presence. Other than learning his keeper's name—Lucia—and discovering that Captain Injection over there wasn't in charge, Ian gleaned zip.

Did all of these people know why he was here? Or were they just as confounded as Ian himself?

"More?" Lucia hovered a large spoonful of rice over his plate.

He nodded. She added a scoop of stew.

One thing was for sure: of all the scenarios he'd expected, it wasn't this. A civilized, communal meal. Inclusion...but for what purpose? Was it a ploy to get him to feel comfortable? To let down his guard?

The same questions he'd been asking himself for days twisted around and around. Where in the hell was he? What did these people want? When would he know? And most of all—why him?

11

———

Henrietta claimed using your hands for God's work was its own form of therapy. Luckily, at Glide, where Charlie served up trays of hot breakfast to the homeless men, women, and children of the city, there was plenty of labor to be done. Not the least of which was the dishes.

Charlie pushed her bangs off her forehead, the steam from the hot water overheating her. Despite not actively thinking about her troubles, she was feeling much more settled.

Maybe that was part of her problem. In Blakes Ridge, she'd yet to find any satisfying work. In an effort to avoid dipping into her savings any more than necessary, she served food. But the restaurant was just okay, the staff just coworkers, the hours just a shift and some cash.

The apartment there, too, was just space. The only time the place felt right was when Mitch was over, cooking in her little kitchen, commandeering the remote control, tugging her toward bed, or teasing her about her lack of stuff.

Oh, crap.

What the hell had she gone and done?

Charlie braced her rubber-glove-covered hands on the industrial-sized sink and bowed her head.

"Uh-huh," Henrietta said from behind her. "I told you."

Charlie scoffed. "Well, if you're so smart, what do I do about it?"

Henry clunked another batch of baking sheets onto the counter and slid them to Charlie, who grabbed the sprayer and got busy.

"Usually, it's best to start with an apology. And groveling is always good. Then there's make-up sex."

"Henry!"

Henry sniggered and swatted Charlie's arm. "You think I'm too old to remember the good parts?"

Charlie shook her head. "In all seriousness, all that I can manage. It's the what-comes-after I don't know what to do with. I've never even had a real friendship, let alone a full-fledged romantic relationship."

"You have, too," Henrietta said. "You have me."

"I didn't mean…" Charlie began, but Henry shushed her.

"I know you didn't." Henrietta tilted her head to the side, thinking, then said, "It's no different, girl. You spend time together, you communicate, you treat the other person with respect. Lots of times, you put them first, ahead of yourself—as long as they are doing the same, that is." She shrugged.

"What about the rest of it?" Charlie's shoulders were tense. "The prosecutor and the therapist? Should I go to school? Should I just cave and do this PI thing with Mitch?"

"Only you can answer those questions, and they aren't things you can rush. Do your research, do some soul searching, and give yourself plenty of time to roll it all around."

Charlie shut off the water, peeled off the thick rubber gloves, and exhaled big time. "You make it sound so easy."

Henry handed her a drying cloth—they'd run out of space on the counter for air drying. "Doesn't have to be near as hard as you're makin' it, child. Besides, if you just relax a little, sometimes things have a way of working themselves out."

The kitchen door swung open, and Aaron, one of the aides, popped his head in. "Ladies, you've got a visitor."

Charlie grinned at Henry. "Ian, maybe?"

She'd love to see that kid. She liked him right off when he'd been frequenting Glide, and they'd developed a friendship despite the difference in their ages. He'd been a big help when she and Mitch were combing the city looking for Tiffany, and been instrumental in helping her escape the paparazzi when she left San Fran. They'd texted some, but since she wasn't very good at that…

"No," Henrietta said. "Far as I know, he's still at home —right where he should be." She led the way through the swinging doors.

Aaron pointed out a man standing off near the side entrance. His hands were fisted inside the pockets of his tailored tan slacks. A plaid starched collar peeked out from under a fine-gauge knit sweater in a rich blue, and his chin was nearly resting on it. Charlie had a good view of a full head of dark hair, liberally threaded with gray.

The man's head snapped up when he sensed them. Angular nose, strong jaw, a decent tan, and light eyes that sized them up quickly.

He reached to shake their hands. "I'm Stephen Cross."

Concern landed, heavy as a sack of flour, across Charlie's shoulders, even as she caught Henry's eye.

"Ian's dad?" Charlie asked.

Ian had mentioned his father several times. She'd gotten the impression he was extremely wealthy, very driven, and a total hard-ass. He'd never spoken of a mother.

"Yes. Has he been here?" Stephen shook his head. "I mean, lately?"

Oh shit, Charlie thought, as Henry answered, "Not since he went home this past summer. He did make it home?"

Cross nodded. "Yes. And he's been good. But he's gone again. No warning, just…" He spread his hands, turning the palms up.

Charlie frowned. He didn't look like a tough bastard to her, simply a very concerned father, which made her worry, too.

"I've asked at the shelters in L.A.," Stephen said, "but I hoped, since he'd spoken of you by name…"

"He knew I was in Pennsylvania, though," Charlie said.

"Still, he knows me and a lot of the staff," Henrietta said. "Eventually, he'd come here. Would consider it a safe haven."

"If he was using and still high"—Stephen cleared his throat—"he wouldn't be searching out food and shelter, would he?"

"Probably not," Charlie said.

Cross looked pained, and Charlie's gut squeezed. "He spared me the details about a lot of it, so…hell, I don't even know where to look." He shook his head, his shoulders slumping. "Damn, but I'd hoped he'd be here."

"Did you know he was using?"

He blew out a breath. "There wasn't a single sign he'd slipped."

"How long has he been gone?" Charlie asked.

"A week. We had a tee time at the club, but he didn't show. He hadn't texted, and I couldn't reach him. I went home, but he wasn't there either." Stephen slid his hands back into his pockets and rocked on the balls of his feet. "At first, I really just thought he'd forgotten or slept through his alarm. He didn't leave word with the staff, and nobody saw him leave. His car is still in the garage."

Charlie could see his hands clenching and unclenching in his pockets. She said, "Ian mentioned that he had a staff of bodyguards or something." He'd actually referred to them as *the Sentinels*, but she wasn't sure if his father knew that.

"Security guards, and yes, they also watched over Ian. He said he felt doubly smothered after…having been gone. He's older and more mature now. I figured a little trust and independence would go a long way." He winced. "I let most of them go."

Henrietta's eyebrows had nearly climbed into her hairline, and Stephen's jaw clenched. "Don't judge me, Ms.

Plummer. We've still got household staff, and there's always a man on security detail, plus the grounds man a few days a week. It's not like Ian was ever really alone."

"Nuh-uh," Henrietta said. "No judgment, just never heard the like from anywhere but television."

Stephen's expression hardened, eyes fixed on Henry, and Charlie could see the intimidating man he likely was in regular life. Likely he wasn't sure what to make of her.

Charlie said, "Ian was determined to stay clean, and he wanted to be home." Disappointment and disbelief warred within her. "Are you sure he's run away?"

Stephen ran a hand over his face, and some of that stiffness disappeared. "I don't believe in absolutes, but it is the most likely scenario."

Charlie bit her lip. He had a point.

"Last time, at least occasionally, Ian would respond when I pressed him to just let me know he was alive." Stephen grimaced. "This time, not a word."

He pulled his wallet from his back pocket. He handed each of them his business card and asked them to call if Ian showed up.

Henrietta gave his arm a quick squeeze. "Don't you worry too much, Mr. Cross. Might be a long road, but your Ian's a strong one." She waddled off.

"She meant no harm earlier," Charlie said. "And she is wise about these things, so…"

He nodded once, and his hands returned to his pockets.

Charlie felt such an urge to do something. But there was nothing to do, really, but wait, was there? She crossed her arms, hugging herself. "You did report him missing?"

"Yes, although it didn't do any good the last time."

Charlie knew from Mitch just how overworked most police departments were, and, of course, Ian had a track record for this sort of thing.

"Chances are good that he won't be found until he wants to be found." That she knew from her own experiences. She tried to soften the message with a smile but only grimaced. "Have you considered a private investigator?"

"Know anyone?"

Charlie gnawed her lip again. "Maybe."

12

―――――――

BREAKFAST WAS STILL DELIVERED TO IAN'S ROOM BY Lucia, and usually Mico, too. Ian had noticed that lately, instead of guards locking the door from the outside when Lucia came, she now locked it from inside and dropped the key into a skirt pocket.

Otherwise, it seemed now that he'd recovered, Ian was required at nearly every meal. Lunch was on the late side, after which they honored siesta. Dinners were late, in turn, but less formal and very light. He tried to use the time to figure out the layout of the compound but wasn't having much luck. They always took a direct path to and from the dining hall. He fared only a little better getting a read on the inhabitants of the place.

Lucia and Jorge, a.k.a. Caption Injection, seemed to rank highly, always sitting at the head honcho's table. His name was Lazaro Valdez, but people referred to him as *el patrón*—the boss, the protector, the head. The mother/daughter pair with the strong noses and obvious resentment of Ian were Gomezes, but they also had a place of honor. Guadalupe was the mother, and Salvadora was the beautiful one closest in age to him. Too bad she seemed mean.

The Braid Contingent, as he'd come to think of the pack of younger girls always in plaits, were always in attendance and always seated as they were the first night. The girls on Ian's side of the table were Lucia's daughters, and he suspected the girls on the other side all belonged to Guadalupe.

Ian didn't have a handle on the people at the other two tables yet. Their conversations were just far enough away that he only heard snippets.

Dinners were blessedly short, since the meal was so light, and once people started to disperse, Ian looked at Lucia. She nodded, so Ian rose from the dining table and turned to head back to his room. Normally a guard or Lucia would follow. Nobody was allowing him to go anywhere alone.

He hadn't taken but two steps when he heard Lazaro's voice. "He will come."

A frisson of unease traveled up Ian's spine, but he forced himself to keep moving. He'd kept up the ruse that he didn't understand Spanish.

A guard stepped into his path, and Ian had no choice but to draw up short. The guard motioned for him to turn around. All the guards inside the house wore pistols on their belts. Those that guarded the entrance—and, Ian suspected, the whole perimeter of the compound—carried machine guns and wore ammo belts across their chests.

Unease swelled into fear as his mind tore through possibilities.

Come where? To do what? Was today the day he finally learned their purpose in bringing him here? Surely they wouldn't just march him outside and shoot him. If that was the intention, they wouldn't have bothered feeding him and sitting him at the head table. Right?

The family streamed through the veranda doors to the shaded patio and the square courtyard beyond. The servants hovered, waiting to clear the tables. Lucia motioned to follow her.

More often than not they gathered outside after the late meal, but Ian had not been included. He could not see it from his bedroom. But he had heard the chatter and children playing and the monkey's calls. Eventually an adult would clap and holler, signaling bedtime. Soon after, from one direction or another, he would hear a child crying or running feet.

Lucia followed Lazaro and Jorge to a seating area. Much like at the family dining table, outdoors they sat in a similar fashion: Lazaro at the head. Lucia and Jorge on either side. Salvadora and Guadalupe flanking them. The Braid Contingent ran off to play. There were additional chairs near the adults, but Lucia did not give Ian any indication of what to do. His steps faltered, and the guard nearly collided with him from behind.

Should he follow Lucia? Or head for those seats under a cluster of trees, or maybe the bench near the fountain?

Ian drew a deep breath. The compound's windows were always open, except at night, when the temperature dropped. And the breezeways didn't even have glass. But he hadn't actually stood outdoors in… How long had he been gone now? Over a week, surely.

A servant—a young woman he sometimes caught eyeing him up—breezed past him with a tray of drinks. She served Lazaro first. When the other adults had theirs, he raised a clear liquid in a toast.

The server approached Ian. She inclined her head, avoiding his eyes, far less bold when she was up close—or was it that they were in view of Lazaro and the others? She lifted the tray toward him. It had one more glass of what he could see now was not entirely clear but slightly golden.

Ian shook his head. "Lemonade? Soda?"

She frowned.

"Coca-Cola?"

A smile turned up the corners of her mouth. "American." She winked and spun in a swish of skirts.

How long would it take her to return? Could he wait here? He really did not want to go sit near Lazaro or even Lucia. He would never be comfortable with any of them. They had abducted him, stolen him from his home without any explanation. And, so far, with no demands, as far as he knew.

He couldn't make sense of it and had whittled his concerns down to two possibilities. One, they'd contacted his father for ransom money and were waiting for a wire transfer or something. Two, he was to be sold as a sex slave and they were waiting for some rich sickos to come and fight over him. At that point, he'd run into Jorge's needle himself. But why was it taking so long? Either scenario would have some urgency, wouldn't it?

But as his full belly turned over on itself, Ian knew it didn't make any sense. Criminals didn't treat prisoners— even those for ransom—this well. Which left him stymied.

All he knew was that he wanted to go home. He didn't know how he'd get the hell out of here or how long it would take, but he would get out. He'd play along for now —what other choice was there? But if he got a chance, he'd take it.

Ian glanced at the adults, and that prickle of unease came back. He turned away and spotted dots of yellow among the first cluster of trees. He rubbed one hand over his other arm, took a steadying breath, and then crossed from smooth patio to packed earth.

No one called out. No one stopped him. He didn't hear the guard's footfalls behind him. Ian's nostrils flared and his fists clenched. Another ten feet, and he stood in the dappled shade of a small tree.

The yellow was lemons. He reached up—

"*Señor.*"

He snatched his hand back, but it was just the server, returned with a bottle of real Coke, looking dewy and crisp like it was right out of a commercial.

"Thank you." Ian added, "*Gracias,*" as if he were trying out the word.

She grinned. "*De nada.*"

The swell of her breasts above her blouse caught his attention. Was he imagining it, or had she tugged the gathered fabric down between this conversation and the last?

He yanked his gaze upward, and she raised an eyebrow. She said, "You can do more than just look."

Ian fought not to react, pretending, as always, that he didn't understand Spanish.

She switched to halting English. "You can practice English with me anytime."

He forced a small smile. "*Gracias.*"

She pulled her tray flat against her chest and left.

He sank to the bench, slumping so that his head could rest on the back. He stared at the lemons. *Dios*, this place was complicated.

13

———

MITCH WAS PUTTING AWAY A FEW GROCERIES WHEN he heard the snippet of the *Charlie's Angels* theme song he'd set as a ringtone for Charlie. *I'll be damned.*

He'd figured Charlie would need at least a week, if not two, to get her head on straight. At which point, her action or non-action would determine the outcome. She'd return to Blakes Ridge, or she simply wouldn't. The fact that she was calling was a good sign. Maybe?

He snatched up the phone. "Hey."

There was only silence on the other end. He frowned and looked at the display to make sure it was connected. Shit, maybe she hadn't called on purpose. She wasn't exactly comfortable with technology. "Charlie?"

"Hi," she said. "I…" He heard her take a deep breath. "I really am sorry about leaving the way I did."

Mitch plunked down on his couch and propped his elbows on his knees. "I know things are overwhelming, but in the future…" Mitch shoved his fingers in his hair. "Keep me in the loop, okay?"

"Henry says a little communication goes a long way."

He smiled and straightened. *Bless you, Henrietta.* "She's not wrong."

"Um, in that vein… Are you still interested in private investigation?"

Mitch's brow lowered. "Yeah, as a matter of fact, I'm officially licensed."

"You went ahead and did it?"

"Yeah. I couldn't wait on you, Charlie. And I knew the fact that I wanted you to join me was too much pressure."

"But you didn't tell me?"

"I came to your place expressly to tell you and discovered you gone."

"You could have told me *before* that," Charlie said, "when you made the decision."

His own words, right back at him. How the hell had that happened? Because, as always, he'd been looking out for her best interests, no matter that it made him look like an asshole.

"Should I have told you when you were freaking out? Was that a good time? Should I have interrupted you running away? Should I have waited or gone ahead to give some distraught family out there the chance mine didn't get?"

He heard her suck in her breath. *Shit. Shit. Shit.*

He didn't really blame her for Tiffany's death, but she blamed herself. He'd fucked it up, too, with Tiff. So many factors had gone wrong. And in the end, there was only one person who caused it. From start to finish, the blame rested squarely with that psycho Weihle.

Mitch shook his head, disgusted at the both of them.

Neither one of them was exactly nailing this relationship thing. Nailing it into the ground, maybe.

"I'm hoping you still feel that way," Charlie said. "Because I've got a proposition for you."

Mitch stilled.

"Ian is missing," Charlie said.

Mitch's gut clenched. "As in runaway missing or…"

"Not sure," Charlie said, and drew a deep breath. "I'm willing to work with you—on a trial basis—if finding him can be our first case."

Mitch tipped his head back and clonked it repeatedly against the drywall above his couch, wishing it were brick. Of course, he wouldn't say no. He couldn't. Ian was out there somewhere at risk, and Charlie was the one doing the asking.

But this hurt, more than a little. She hadn't called for Mitch, ready to make amends. She hadn't called to salvage the relationship, to smooth things over and make things right.

She'd called with an agenda. For Ian.

Fortunately for the kid, Mitch got it. You'd do for others what you wouldn't—or couldn't—do for yourself.

14

Mitch arrived outside Charlie's apartment building in the Tenderloin area of San Francisco, with his duffel bag slung crossways, feeling grim. He'd texted his flight information and approximate arrival time to Charlie. However, they hadn't spoken since she asked for his help.

He eyed a homeless encampment down the street as he hit the buzzer. The neighborhood seemed a little rougher than the last time he'd been here.

The intercom crackled to life, and he bent to speak into it. "It's me."

He reminded himself again that it was smart to have low expectations when it came to Charlie.

"Hi," she said behind the static.

The trek up her apartment stairs was serious *déjà vu.* Here he was again: same city, same building, same woman, and expecting another reluctant welcome. The purpose was uncomfortably similar, too: find another drugged-out runaway teen, and return the kid home. *Groundhog Day* gone bad. Penance in the form of a disturbing repeat.

But that was what he'd wanted, wasn't it? Multiple chances to make things right for someone else?

It was the whole point of becoming a private investigator. To take the cases that meant the most to him. The cases that would keep another family from the tragedy his had experienced. And this kid—Ian—he actually knew.

He rounded another landing, and his footfalls creaked up the last set of stairs. He fisted his hands. Starting out with such a similar scenario couldn't be a good omen.

Mitch took a fortifying breath outside Charlie's door and knocked. He heard locks flip, and then the door swung open. Charlie—gorgeous as ever with her bleached blond hair, tight black top, and baggy pants—crossed her arms over her middle and bit her lip.

"You gonna invite me in?"

"Sorry. Yes." She stepped back. He shut the door behind him and locked it, because he knew that made her feel safer. Then he slung his bag off and dumped it on the floor.

"Want to just put that in the bedroom?" she asked. When he didn't answer, Charlie finally looked him in the eye.

He raised an eyebrow. "That what you want?"

She looked up at him. Those big eyes were too damn pretty.

"It didn't feel right without you the last few nights."

Relief dropped some of the tension from across his shoulders, and lust tingled at the base of his spine. But…

Mitch crossed his arms over his chest. "Jesus, Charlie, you don't get off that easy."

"I know. I'm sorry," she said. "I shouldn't have left without telling you."

Mitch ran a hand through his hair. "I'd just like to know where I stand. Am I a temporary screw? Until you figure out your life and learn to live in the real world?"

Her eyes widened and her jaw jutted out.

"Or do you think we have a shot for something more?"

The defensive look softened, and she shook her head. "I'm no good at so much of this, and given how easy sex is between us"—and it was; Mitch was constantly amazed at their intense attraction to each other—"I can see why you'd wonder."

Charlie drew a breath. "But you have to realize, I'm giving you more of myself than I've ever given anybody. Remember after that first night, when you told me you liked being with me?"

He did. He'd bungled it, but she got the idea: he liked spending time with her, beyond the horizontal.

"It's like that for me, too," Charlie said. "It feels right when you're with me, and even when you aren't, because I know you will be soon."

Mitch clamped down on the smile that had almost curved his lip.

"I know you'd like to be married and have kids and all that normal stuff." She rubbed her arms, obviously uncomfortable. "I used to dream of that. You know, in an abstract way. But now that I could feasibly have it, I'm completely terrified." Her eyes glistened with tears. "I want to be with you, but I also can't make you those promises. There's so much to deal with yet."

Mitch let his breath out slowly. There was nobody for him but Charlie. If that meant he'd be waiting a long-ass time for her to commit in a tangible way, then so be it. He sucked at waiting, especially when he'd already made up his mind. For her, though, he'd find a way to make peace with it.

He stepped forward and took her face in his hands. "Okay," he said, then leaned down to kiss her. She surged onto her toes and looped her arms around his neck.

Their lips fit perfectly, as always, and he slipped one hand to her neck. She dipped her tongue into his mouth, and he pulled her in tighter so he could feel her curves against his chest.

She moaned. Mitch ran both hands down her back to her rear, one cheek in each hand, tucking his fingertips into the cleft between.

She pulled away from his mouth, then arched her chest out with one hand braced against his shoulder. She reached the other down and pressed hard against his erection. Mitch sucked in air, wanting her more than ever after all the days apart.

"I missed you. A lot." She gave him a happy, naughty smile. "Let's go to the easy part."

He couldn't argue with that.

15

——————

Lucia had made it clear that Ian was expected to continue to join the family after dinner in the courtyard from now on.

Ian didn't ask where he would sit—he just returned to the bench under the lemon tree. He adopted a lazy pose as if he was resting, but kept his eyes open just enough to watch.

The same servant who'd come onto him last night crossed the veranda with a tray full of after-dinner drinks —this time there was a bottle of Coke included. She served Lazaro and the family first, then came to stand in front of him.

"Señor Ian." Her voice was husky and soft, her shirt again pulled low—lower, he thought, than when she'd served the others.

He opened his eyes. She was gorgeous, with the sun setting behind her, her pretty eyes, and all that smooth skin on display.

She plucked the bottle from her tray. He sat up to take it, but she said, "Oh, it is wet."

He frowned. Of course an ice-cold drink would sweat. The day had cooled toward evening, but it was still warm outside.

She tucked the tray under her arm and pulled the Coke to her chest, right between her breasts, rubbing it up and down as if—

Jesus. Ian felt a flare of lust—and then of panic.

But her back was to Lazaro. There was no way any of the family could tell what she was doing.

She wore a satisfied and sultry smile. In English she only said, "Enjoy." In Spanish she added, "I hope you enjoy your Coca-Cola and me."

She handed him the cold bottle.

"*Gracias*. What is your name…uh, *tu nombre?*" he asked.

She smiled brightly. "Florencia."

He tried it out.

"At your service, *señor*." Then she looked down and feigned surprise. "Oh, look, I'm wet." She trailed a finger along the top of one breast.

Ian tried to look like he was unaffected.

She tucked the tray to her chest just like last night and then glided away.

Navigating Lazaro's world was exhausting, but damn did a straight-up Coke taste good. He shut his eyes in pleasure.

He wasn't halfway through when he had another visitor: the girl that sat to his right at every meal, Dia. Mico squatted on her shoulders, one arm wrapped around her head, the tiny but strangely human fingers plastered to her forehead.

"*Hola*," she said.

"Hi."

She raised an eyebrow. "I know you speak Spanish, *pendejo*."

"Um? Eh?" Ian fought not to laugh. The word translated to "pubic hair," but it was more akin to strongly calling someone an idiot. His favorite tutor had taught him all the good insults—and convinced him to give up trying to translate literally.

"Oh, give it up already—at least with me." Her English was good; accented, sure, but she spoke confidently.

"Mico, down," she said. The monkey swung down, then scampered up the tree.

Dia flung herself on the bench beside him and switched back to Spanish. "I see you listening all the time."

"So?"

"So, newcomer, I won't tell. Just pretend like we're having a one-way conversation." She pulled her single braid over her shoulder. More hair seemed to have come loose from the plait than not.

"Why?" Ian tried not to move his mouth much.

"Because." She hopped up, and then jumped to snag a low-hanging lemon. Mico swung to another tree. In a flash, Dia was back on the bench beside him holding the fruit in front of his face. "These don't grow here naturally. Apparently my long-dead grandmother liked them." She rolled it along the arm of the bench. "Monkeys don't live here either. He was a birthday gift from my dad."

She told him a little about capuchins then said, "Don't take Florencia up on her offer."

She glanced at him, and as soon as Ian raised an eyebrow, she returned her focus to the lemon. "She's trouble. The *patrón* won't like it."

"Maybe that's a reason to do it."

"No." All the glib attitude disappeared and her tone was heavy. "You do not want to make him angry."

He wanted to ask why on both counts, but she launched into a diatribe about how much she hated her math lessons.

He realized Salvadora, who still shot daggers at him during meals, was approaching. He tried to look bored, as if he had no understanding of Dia's babble.

"What are you doing?" Salvadora glared at Dia.

"Sitting." Dia gave her a *duh* look.

"The bastard can't understand you."

Dia gave her a quick, obviously false smile. "Which makes him a perfect listener."

"You would shrivel and die if you could not run your mouth."

Ian gave Salvadora points for creativity. Dia only shrugged.

Salvadora gave a snort of disgust. Her cold look encompassed both Dia and Ian, and then she stormed off.

Ian tried to talk like a ventriloquist. "She treats you like that because she's the oldest? Not a sister, though?" He guessed Salvadora was probably close to his age, while Dia was maybe fifteen or sixteen.

"She's not my sister, she's my cousin—well, not by blood, only by oath, and she's only just turned *dieciocho*." Eighteen—Dia threw Spanish words in without missing a beat if she didn't have the right English word at the ready.

"She's always been like this," Dia said. "Always needs to be in charge." She slanted a glance at him. "She's another one to be wary of, but I doubt she'd try to bed you."

"She might try to murder me in my sleep, though."

"She might."

Ian searched Dia's face. She wasn't kidding.

16

Mitch rented a car first thing the next morning, and Charlie's eyes practically popped out of her head when they arrived at Cross's house. Ian had only given her hints about his upbringing, and no wonder. It would have been super uncomfortable to admit to people who spent all their time in a soup kitchen.

Surely very few people lived like this. She'd bet it didn't even qualify as a house. It looked more like a destination resort on a TV commercial. It was on a huge piece of private property with manicured grounds so perfect they looked fake. She saw a pool—was that a pool house *and* a guesthouse? It hardly seemed real.

Mitch had insisted on speaking with Stephen Cross before starting the investigation. He'd said, "Whenever possible, talk to people in person."

"Body language and all that?"

"Yeah. You can tell a lot from their eyes. Also from your own gut."

Now, standing in a foyer bigger than her living room

and kitchen combined, she wished she'd asked what you could glean from a person's home. A crystal chandelier big enough to crush her and Mitch both hung above them, the marble floors looked like they'd never seen a shoe, and the fancy furniture was the kind you didn't want to risk sitting in.

Mary introduced herself as Mr. Cross's longtime housekeeper. She wore her hair in a loose chignon and had pale, freckly skin—a redhead surely before going gray.

"I'm so glad you're here," she said. "You can imagine my feelings for Ian. We're all just worried sick."

She ushered them warmly but briskly into a sitting room. This room wasn't quite as intimidating as the foyer, but still lavish.

"Mr. Cross will be right in to join you. May I bring you anything to drink?"

Both Charlie and Mitch declined. They'd had breakfast sandwiches and coffee on the way here. All Charlie really wanted was a toothbrush.

"Thanks for coming," Cross told Mitch. Charlie thought he looked more haggard than when she'd seen him only two mornings ago.

"Of course," Mitch said as they shook hands. "You have a great kid, and I'm hoping we can help."

"What do you need? I do have the list of shelters I visited." Cross had resumed his search in L.A., while Charlie canvassed the shelters in San Francisco.

"Good. First, I want to go over the details again."

Charlie listened as Mitch asked a ton of questions. She gathered that some of them were repeats of what he'd asked during a prior phone conversation.

When they were mostly wrapped up, Charlie said, "We should get Ian's sponsor's number, too."

Cross nodded. "I have it. I looked him up after. He was shocked."

"We'll check with him again," Mitch said. "We'd like to take a look around, especially in Ian's room. And then interview your staff."

"I've talked with them all already."

"I know," Mitch said, "but sometimes going over it again shakes something loose—maybe something they didn't think anything of at the time or were hesitant to mention to the boss."

Cross nodded. "Of course—you can speak with everyone here, and then Mary can provide contact information for the others."

Charlie was awed again when they went upstairs. Ian practically had a whole wing to himself.

"Think like a teenager—one trying to hide stuff," Mitch told her.

They searched his room, a separate area for his desk and school stuff, his bathroom, his walk-in closet, the gaming room—*wow*.

She raised an eyebrow when Mitch tried to twist off the bottom of a shaving cream can.

"They sell all kinds of stuff that looks legit on the internet," Mitch said, "but has hidden compartments for drugs."

After that, Charlie combed through Ian's stuff a lot more carefully.

They found absolutely nothing.

"No stash," Mitch said. "No trash."

They moved on to talking with the staff, and after a few interviews, Mitch suggested they split up. "You comfortable enough?"

"Yeah. I think so."

"Go for it, then." He winked at her, and her heart did a little flip. She liked watching him work—he was good at this stuff. Plus, he was willing to teach and was willing to let her do. He would be a good partner if she decided to join him. And hey, keeping his gorgeously tight rear in view all day wasn't a bad thing either.

Charlie found she was mostly at ease talking with the staff, but she never did get comfortable in that mansion. She kept thinking of what this kind of wealth meant. Growing up under the circumstances she did, Thomas Weihle had seemed all-powerful to her—and yet he had nothing compared to this. Cross must have such a fat bank account, so many important people in his address book, so many resources. If someone like him had the inclination to do harm—maybe someone like whoever had to Ian, because it was looking more and more like he wasn't on a bender—how would they ever find him?

Rich people were terrifying, she decided. And yet, thank God, Cross seemed…maybe not down to earth, but at least like a good father and a decent man. She didn't believe he could have had anything to do with his son's disappearance. But she still wanted to know if Mitch felt the same.

On the drive back to the city, they compared notes. Every single staff member was genuinely concerned, entirely accommodating, and certainly seemed to think highly of both Ian and his dad.

The only suspicious thing Mitch found was that there was a morning when the electric gate wasn't working. Eventually the guard resorted to resetting the system, and it had worked fine. So now that was what they did when it failed.

"When I asked how often that happened, he said, 'Only twice that I know of.'"

Charlie thought about that. "Twice is enough."

Mitch nodded. "Yeah. It is."

She chewed on her lip, feeling conflicted. She was enjoying this time with Mitch—hashing over details and talking things through. If only the case wasn't Ian's.

"Anything stand out for you?" Mitch asked.

"I found it strange that the old-timers clammed up when I asked about Cross's marriage."

Interest sparked in Mitch's eyes. "He said they parted amicably."

"Maybe they did, maybe they didn't," Charlie said. "But nobody was willing to talk about Ian's mom."

17

———

MITCH AND CHARLIE SPLIT UP, SPENDING TWO whole days hitting every shelter and drug dealer's corner they could find in both L.A. and San Francisco. Cross continued to search as well, doubling back on the places he'd already been. Mitch was okay with that. Normally he'd say leave it to the police, but in this case, they'd lost valuable time. It was closing in on two weeks since Ian vanished. The extra manpower wouldn't hurt—and if Ian had passed through one of those shelters, sympathy for a worried father might get Cross information.

Unfortunately, none of them found a single person who had seen Ian recently.

Mitch and Charlie had also interviewed the rest of Cross's staff. She was a natural. She put people at ease. Maybe because she was so down to earth.

However, no one saw anything suspicious. And everyone believed Ian had been sober. In fact, Ian's sponsor swore that Ian was a regular at meetings and was one kid he thought would manage to stay clean, because he wanted it that bad.

There was a change in pattern this time. When he ran away the last time, there had been noticeable clues: erratic behavior, complete unreliability, and a belligerent attitude. And before, Ian would at least occasionally send a brief text when Cross begged him to respond.

According to Cross—and supported by Mary and the other staff—none of that was in play this time. He'd been doing great. Everything seemed fine. He'd vanished. And, so far, zero evidence. Mitch had even had a friend track Ian's cell, but the kid was completely off the grid—no activity at all.

He and Charlie agreed: it was possible, maybe even probable, that Ian hadn't run away. Mitch had to consider kidnapping for ransom or revenge. He'd started digging into Cross's business rivals, but hadn't turned up anything interesting. The only person they hadn't covered so far was his ex-wife Victoria—Ian's mother.

They called Stephen on speaker phone, and Mitch said, "We're going down to talk to Victoria."

"I told you, she's got nothing to do with it. She hasn't seen Ian in years."

"Yeah, well, we still want to talk with her."

"That's pointless," Cross said. "You should be concentrating on finding my son."

"We're covering all our bases." Charlie's voice was more calming than Mitch's would have been.

"I covered that one." Cross's words were clipped. "I spoke with her—just in case Ian got some wild hair to island-hop.

She says he didn't. And I promise you there is no way on earth Victoria would have kidnapped Ian. Going to see her is a complete waste of time. There isn't even a direct flight."

When Mitch disconnected, he looked at Charlie. "You get the feeling there's something he isn't saying?"

"You don't think he knows what's happened to Ian, do you?"

"No. I ruled that out straight off." He cocked his head. "But there's something on his mind, something eating at him."

———

CROSS WAS RIGHT ABOUT ONE THING: THERE WAS NO direct flight to Canouan, an island in the southeastern Caribbean in the Lesser Antilles, where Victoria was set up like an island queen on her own little piece of paradise.

Tan, lithe, fit, and blond, she answered the door in a skimpy bikini.

"You aren't who I was expecting. Hang on," she said, and left Mitch and Charlie in the foyer as she crossed into another room.

Most would say Victoria Cross was drop-dead gorgeous. Far as Mitch was concerned, she had nothing on Charlie. There was nothing sexier than unpainted nails, drugstore lip balm, and hip-hugging cargo pants. He slid a glance at Charlie, zeroing in on her breasts under that pack-of-three men's small sleeveless undershirt. He caught her eye.

Her lip quirked up and she mouthed, "What? Now?"

He shrugged. He couldn't help it. His Charlie was hot

as hell. He couldn't wait to get this interview over with, log two more flights, and climb into bed beside his woman.

Victoria returned in a cover-up—which was semi-sheer and therefore somewhat pointless, as far as he was concerned. What did raise his eyebrows were the earrings. Hell, the constellation of diamonds she wore neared the diameter of the button on his jeans, and he'd bet they were real.

Given that Cross called her last week to make sure Ian hadn't gotten some wild hair to suddenly get to know his mother, she hadn't been surprised to hear that Ian was missing.

"I told Stephen he wasn't here," Victoria said. "But come. Ask your questions. I could use the company."

The house was impressive: simple, spacious, and gorgeous, with huge—and probably famous—abstract paintings and what felt like half a house of glass for the ocean views. She had private access to the beach and led them to a sitting area near her private pool.

Mitch had done some digging, and Victoria seemed to have no wealth of her own. He assumed all this was due to her ex's gravy train—and their apparent desire to live far, far away from one another.

Her staff served island cocktails. Mitch stuck largely to the water and his questions, and Charlie, maybe feeling out of her element with questioning or the setting, stayed quiet. This place was way out of Mitch's element, too.

"How long were you married?"

"Three years."

"When was the last time you visited Ian or vice versa?"

"When I moved out. It was part of the agreement—though not in writing, of course."

Charlie's eyes narrowed, but Victoria was focused on Mitch, her chin jutted defiantly forward, almost daring him to mark her a bad mother.

"The divorce was amicable, or…?"

She raised an eyebrow and swept a hand out to encompass her paradise. "Stephen was extremely generous."

Victoria was pleased enough to sit and talk, until he got down to the nitty-gritty questions about her relationship with Stephen and Ian.

At that point, the gracious chitchat screeched to a halt, and she either evaded his questions or simply shook her head with a small smile, as if to say, *I'm sorry, that's private.*

Obviously not everything was kosher with this little exile to sunny town. Mitch wondered if this cushy setup was a trade for keeping mum. They had been married only a few years—not long enough for her to have received much in the way of alimony. What kind of mother slipped away to an island, never to see her son again? Had she done something so heinous that Cross banished her? Or did she have something on him—something horrid enough that she'd give up a child to get away, and he'd let her?

Stephen retained full custody, and apparently Victoria had no visiting rights. Not every woman was maternal, but still, not even the pretense of being a part of the kid's life? That was odd.

Mitch tried to pit her against Cross, aiming to get a rise out of her, get some feel for their relationship.

He put down his glass and gave her a steady look. "Could Stephen have harmed his own child?"

Out of the corner of his eye, he caught Charlie's look of surprise. He'd have to remind her that everyone was a suspect, that everyone lied sometimes, that most people held secrets, and that few people were exactly what they seemed.

Besides, sometimes when you asked a blunt question, you got an answer—or at least a crystal-clear tell.

"Fat chance." Victoria laughed, a burst of bitterness. "He put that kid above all. From the very beginning."

She looked out over the ocean, pressed her lips into a thin line, and refused to say more.

18

———

Ian was escorted to a jeep by the guards. Already wary, he became even more so when it turned out Lazaro was accompanying them. It was freaking unsettling to never know what was coming.

But he felt a measure of cautious hope bubble up when the compound gates swung open and he caught his first real look of what was beyond. It'd be good to get the lay of the land. Maybe some clues as to how to escape, or some markers to gauge the distance he'd need to be prepared to travel.

But there was nothing around, and his hopes crashed. It was like they were encased in forest—lots of oaks, some rock, a narrow dirt road. Some smaller trees were scrappy, so there were decent breaks in the foliage, but they were traveling fast, and everything he could see looked like more of the same. The air was humid, the day getting sticky.

How far did Lazaro's reach extend outside the walls? Did he own everything Ian could see?

He had asked Lucia a few questions, and she confirmed that they were in Mexico, in the state of Durango on the western side. He'd learned further from Dia that they were up in the mountains—the eastern side of the Sierra Madre Occidentals. He sure as hell wished he'd paid more attention to geography. According to Dia, there was fresh water from mountain runoff—but also mountain lions and bobcats and coyotes. No monkeys other than Mico, who came and went between the forest and the compound.

The day after Ian had been to the courtyard, Lucia brought word that his lessons would begin—and then a tutor had arrived just as he finished eating. To teach him Spanish—which was tricky. Was this excursion another lesson of some sort? He highly doubted Lazaro himself would be teaching him about flora and fauna.

The jeep veered left—another dirt road, this one climbing higher into the mountains. In a few places there were pull-offs where there seemed to be old, boarded-over holes in the rock face. Old mines, Ian thought.

The road became rougher and narrower until Ian braced himself on the frame of the jeep, sure he was going to bounce out or they'd slip right off the road and down the mountain.

They barreled straight toward a face of rock, and Ian swore. At the last second, the driver swerved left, shooting between two hills Ian hadn't distinguished separately until he was up close.

They skidded to a stop. Ian took a shaky breath as red dust billowed up. He coughed as he looked around. What now?

Everyone piled out of the jeep, including Lazaro.

Ian would have preferred to bring up the rear—the bad feeling he had was getting worse—but he was prodded between the shoulder blades by a machine gun.

They walked through a narrow canyon and came out upon a decent-sized clearing of packed dirt or rock. Trees, slabs of rock face, and more mountain loomed behind. There were a couple of shacks off to the side. In the center were a few men.

One stood with his arm stretched out to stir the contents inside a large tin pot. Two other men stood farther away, watching. Their clothes were dusty, their hands dirty, and each had a bandana over their nose and mouth.

Because it was dangerous. Deadly.

Ian stopped and planted his feet. The guard poked him hard with the muzzle of his gun. Ian held his ground—he was not going any closer.

He knew what was in that pot. Gel. The black gelatinous concoction that was later turned into fentanyl.

God almighty—how the hell had he ended up with these people, in this place?

His mind raced—but it was a jumbled mess of possibilities. Not a thing made sense. Why? Why on earth was he here? Penance?

Lazaro halted, the man nearest them approached, and they had a short conversation. Ian's head was rushing too loud for him to hear.

Then their group retreated—thank God.

As they came back through the narrow crevice, Lazaro made magic happen, opening a door from rock. Ian blinked. It was so well camouflaged that he never would have spotted it. Had Lazaro used a key fob or a code? Or something really high tech, like his eyeball? Ian wished he'd caught it.

Everyone filed inside. Ian walked between the guards, two in front of him and two behind. There were two rooms with glass doors. Again Lazaro waited. A guy in full hazmat gear came out. They spoke, and Ian caught words like "on track" and "two days."

When they moved again and Ian passed the glass himself, he could see a small room, a hood—it must vent out the mountain somehow—a work surface, and shelves…with bags and bags of pills.

Ian had been right. They were producing fentanyl. Likely some of their very shit had ended up in Ian's body when he was using.

He wanted to puke. He also really, really wanted to bust through the glass, gobble the shit down, and end this.

He fought back tears and screamed swear words in his head.

Lazaro led the way down a short warren of narrow passages with uneven ground, and now Ian was sure that the cane the man always used was a prop, not a necessity. The passages were completely rough-hewn—carved out of stone with uneven flooring or just that reddish, hard-packed dirt—but Lazaro walked at a steady, solid clip. All of it was man-made, surely a mine originally. There was electricity, somehow—bare bulbs were strung up on a line.

And then there was a metal door framed right into rock. Bizarrely, it had an electronic keypad. Lazaro blocked it with his body as he pressed buttons.

Ian's heart was beating too fast now, adrenaline surging. This had to be part of those "lessons." But to what end? Was he about to be indoctrinated—into what? Why would they choose an addict for a drug operation? To test shit out—like a human guinea pig? Maybe he'd be forced to swallow balloons. Jesus, he'd take being a drug runner if it meant he could get back across the border. Would he be sold or gang-raped or forced to perform certain acts? He'd discarded that idea over the last two weeks, but fear was ruling him now.

Ian fisted then flexed his hands, rolled his shoulders back, and tried to calm his breathing.

He couldn't, though. His nostrils flared and his chest heaved.

He could refuse whatever this was, fight back, and then what? Take on four men with machine guns? That was a sure ticket to the morgue—or more likely dinner for the vultures or coyotes.

He really didn't want to die here. Some kid far away from home, whose body would never be found, with no way for his father to know that he hadn't left willingly, hadn't let addiction win.

Survival, then. That was his only choice. Until he could escape.

And he was actually outside the compound. If there was any way to get out of this—both today's unknown and the whole shitshow—then he would find it. And he would take it.

The door scraped open. Lazaro motioned them through. Two guards accompanied Ian; two remained outside the door. Lazaro swept his hand out, and again,

Ian had to blink to be sure what he was seeing. Wrapped blocks—stacks and stacks of…cocaine, most likely. *God.*

Ian smelled it—in his mind or for real, he didn't know. Saliva pooled in his mouth and sweat beaded on his brow. Immediately shame surged, too, and his stomach rolled.

He'd had too much experience with drugs, and yet he'd never seen them in their wholesale form. Were those kilos? Like in the movies? Bulging bricks covered tightly in plastic filled the room—from floor to low ceiling, wall to wall, and twice as deep as they were high. Building blocks of despair and destruction.

Fentanyl and cocaine both, then? If Lazaro was really covering all his bases, where was the marijuana, the meth, the ecstasy, the crack?

Lazaro spoke. "Ian."

Ian jumped and choked on his saliva. He coughed hard, eyes watering.

"You see?" Lazaro said, and a guard repeated in English. "This is all my business. It is very profit." Lazaro meant lucrative, but the guard translated poorly. "It is also very dangerous. Many want what I have. Many try to steal from me. Many in my own family want power."

Ian wanted to shout, *What in the hell do you want from me, asshole? Why in God's name show me all this illegal shit?*

Lazaro backed them out into the hallway.

Again, they traveled the narrow passages in single file. Ian clenched his teeth and tried not to fist his hands too tightly.

They hadn't hurt him yet—aside from the abduction. He didn't want to give the guards a reason to now. Not deep in the earth like this, where he had no shot at escape.

His breathing calmed marginally as the distance from the drug room grew. This time they arrived at a series of doors, and Lazaro chose one of the middle ones. Ian's heart pounded like a jackhammer—maybe this was the room with crack.

But there was no keypad this time. Only a metal bar—which was not secured at the moment. Lazaro motioned, and a guard opened the door.

Ian felt his eyes bug out, and he stepped back involuntarily.

There was a man in there. He was in bad shape—bloody, beaten, sweaty, and handcuffed to the table.

Jorge lounged against a side wall, his arms crossed. His knuckles were bloody and swollen, but he looked as peaceful as if he was relaxing in the park.

This was an interrogation room.

The guard behind Ian shoved him hard—right into the room.

19

Lazaro stepped into the interrogation room behind Ian. The guard translated Lazaro's words. "This man has been stealing from me. It is something I do not tolerate."

This was the lesson? If you cross Lazaro you will be bound and beaten, probably starved and dehydrated, and likely killed later?

"I need your help with him."

Ian fought to show no reaction until the guard could translate that craziness, but inside his head he was freaking out. Because what the hell did Lazaro mean?

The man at the table was young, not much older than Ian. He'd been half out of it when they first entered, his head hanging low. Now, he looked up and mumbled through a bloody mouth that was probably twice its normal size. "Not true. I did not steal."

His eyes grew wild and latched on to Ian. "Someone must believe me. I would not." He shifted and pulled against his chains, metal clanging against metal. He was agitated, desperate, panicked—maybe high.

Lazaro nodded.

The guards seemed to know what was expected of them. Two of them went to the man in the chair and grabbed him up in a bear hug, yanking him from the table. The man cried out in pain because his wrist remained cuffed and tethered him to the table. The guard was taller than the prisoner, the chain only a few inches long.

The other guard knelt at his feet and unlocked the leg shackles. Then he moved to the wrist cuffs. First one, then the other.

The man began to struggle harder, and the tall guard leaned backward, ensuring his feet were off the floor. He flailed and kicked, but the big guard didn't even flinch.

Lazaro and the translator stepped outside the door. The guard with the shackle keys followed. He didn't look back. His expression was stony, but in a bored way. Was this nothing new, then?

When the guard lurched forward with the prisoner, Ian snapped out of his stupor. He spun to leave the room only to stop dead.

A guard aimed his weapon at Ian's chest. He shook his head. "You stay."

This time Ian's heart nearly pounded right out of his chest.

At a gesture from Lazaro, Jorge also stepped out of the room.

The tall guard heaved the prisoner at Ian. Neither was expecting it. Ian stumbled but kept to his feet. The prisoner went down. The guard stepped over the threshold and yanked the door shut behind him. Ian heard the metal bar clang.

He rushed the door, but there was no handle. He pounded, then pushed with both hands, with his shoulder, with all his weight, but it didn't give. Somehow over the roaring in his head, he heard the man scrabble to his feet, and Ian looked over his shoulder.

The man lunged for Ian with an animalistic cry. He seemed completely out of his mind. Maybe the stealing was true, and he'd sampled the goods. Ian knew what aggression looked like in a desperate druggie. Not to mention a bad fix.

Ian jumped to the side just in time.

The prisoner was fast, fueled by whatever was going on in his head. Luckily, he was clumsy and uncoordinated. Ian kept moving, his mind racing. The man dove at him again. Ian deflected by angling his body out of the way and shoving him in the chest, the prisoner's own momentum doing most of the work.

What the fuck should Ian do? Just continue to defend himself until the guy wore out? He could do it—he was a black belt. When he was younger, he'd raced through the belts as fast as the instructors would let him. He took up boxing when he got bored, but the gym was where he'd met a pack of friends—some who had introduced him to drugs. Ian had been chafing against the lonely, shallow world he lived in. One thing had led to another, until he was too deep. He'd found solace in martial arts again after returning home, and practiced at the dojo often.

Should he talk the guy down? Or maybe let him get in a few blows to see if the dude would deflate some?

What did Lazaro want to happen here? It made no sense. *Nothing* had made any sense since Ian had been taken.

This time when the man lunged, he came close, and Ian realized his hand would be forced.

He landed a blow to the man's solar plexus, doubling him over, and then an uppercut that had him rearing up and back.

Enraged, the prisoner flew at Ian. They grappled, but Ian gained the upper hand quickly.

Ian kicked off his shoes. They were ill-fitting and soft and would only trip him up.

Even as he struck and rolled and punched and kicked, he debated what to do. The only solution that seemed reasonable was to take the guy out, unconscious, not dead. A blow was dicey—he could do more damage than he meant to. Ian only knew the basics of pressure points, and he wasn't skilled in any of that, but it was worth a shot.

He tried to get a hold on the guy, pressing his fingers near his neck…but he couldn't hold him still, or maybe it wasn't the right spot. The man roared and spun.

It would have to be a blow, then. Martial arts taught you to defend yourself, to protect, to defend—not to attack.

He started aiming for the head. He didn't know what in the hell else to do. With luck, he'd take the prisoner down, but not kill him.

Another five minutes maybe, and it happened. A roundhouse kick to the temple and the man went down.

All the fight went out of him and he dropped like a bag of cement.

Ian sank to his haunches, hands on knees and head dropped between them, breathing heavily.

He couldn't believe this. It was like a bizarre fight club. Had Lazaro wanted him to fight to the death—

Ian jerked his head up. He put a hand to the dirt floor and vaulted toward the man. He pressed his fingers against his neck, praying for a pulse.

And...*yes.*

Relief tore through the adrenaline, and he shook as he stood. He kept his eyes on the man and back-pedaled all the way to the opposite wall. He slid down against it, balancing on his toes.

He hadn't had a second to regain his breath when the door swung open.

"You can fight. That is good." Lazaro clapped his hands. Deliberately. Perfectly in time. "Is he dead?"

Ian nearly answered, but managed to wait for the translation.

"No." He was still breathing hard—adrenaline, panic, confusion, exertion all playing a part.

Lazaro inclined his head. The translator went to check the man's pulse just as Ian had. The other two guards kept their guns trained on Ian. Jorge stood in the doorway and stared at Ian with his beady eyes. If he was a dog, he'd be salivating.

The guard stood. "He lives."

"Ah." Lazaro's flat gaze landed on Ian. "You will kill him." It was a command, softly spoken. The translator was speaking. But Ian barely heard.

"No," Ian said.

"He will never give up," Lazaro said. "I could leave you both here. For days until you starve and thirst and fight and become depraved. Eventually, you will kill him."

Ian shook his head hard. This was fucking unbelievable. Unreal. Insane. Fucking nuts. He didn't want to kill this guy. He hadn't even laid eyes on him before today. He wasn't going to—no matter what. Lazaro and all his cronies and machine guns couldn't make him.

"But that timeframe does not suit my purposes," Lazaro said. "You have what I requested?" Although the *patrón* didn't take his eyes from Ian, the question wasn't for him. The translator did not translate or even react.

The other guard gave a curt nod. He wore a backpack and swung it around his shoulder to his chest.

Lazaro smiled, and the guards all sprang into action, grabbing Ian by the arms, dragging him to the table.

The tall guard grabbed him from behind like he had the prisoner. The other guard flung the backpack on the table. Ian struggled, mind racing, eyes searching.

Jorge—Captain Injection—came over and rummaged through it. Shit—they were going to knock Ian out again. He stopped struggling. He'd almost welcome the blackness at this point, but then, how did Lazaro expect him to—

Jorge pulled out a small bottle with a stopper.

Fuck—no!

They were going to dope him with LSD. He'd done acid, but on little blotter squares. Could they overdose him with the liquid?

No—they didn't want him to die. They wanted him

out of his mind. They wanted him to fight with no reservations. Like a maniac.

So he did. He bucked and yelled and fought with everything he had against the guards holding him—but when Jorge pried his lips open, Ian knew he was fucked.

20

———————

Lucia hovered all afternoon and evening, waiting for the far-off grind of engines. She stuck to the front of the house where she'd have a better line of sight.

It was close to midnight when they finally came. Any later and she would have had to be in bed, because Lazaro would not have wanted her waiting up.

She had an insane urge to run out the door and meet them in the drive, but she forced herself to remain in the shadows, far from the front windows. Lazaro would not be pleased to see her watching for them, though he couldn't have thought it would be nothing to her.

When the jeeps finally stopped, Lazaro's henchmen climbed out. Lazaro, too, still perfectly pressed and in no hurry.

No Ian. Bile rose in her throat.

Wait—they leaned over a figure in the back, on the floor, and pulled. It was Ian. She crossed herself, thanked God, and swallowed the acid back. They jostled until they carried him, one under his shoulders, one under his knees.

She put her hand to her chest and stifled a sob. She should not have been so quick to thank the Almighty. She did not yet know if he was unconscious or dead.

Lucia drew a shaky breath. She had to get a hold of herself before Lazaro came in.

She heard the front door, waited, listening…shuffling steps of the men carrying dead weight and the light tread of Lazaro's fine leather loafers.

She drew herself up and crossed from the back of the living room to the *vestíbulo*.

"I thought you'd be back hours—"

She gasped, feeling the full horror of what she was seeing.

Ian was bloodied and raw—his face, his hands, his knees. His shirt was gone, his white pants torn and covered with blood, dirt, and vomit.

She could barely tear her eyes away, but she let all the anger she felt show when she stared down Lazaro. "What have you done?"

"So quick to assign blame, sister." He was so calm, so placid, that it made her crazy.

"Is he…dead?"

"Tsk now. I did not go to all the trouble of bringing him here to let him die so easily." Lazaro shifted his focus to the guards. "Take him to the bathroom in his room."

Lucia rushed to follow, but Lazaro's voice rang out against the tile. "Not you."

"He needs tending."

"He will keep. I have something to show you."

Lucia wanted to scream. She needed to assess the

damage and do what she could. Surely she would need Dia's opinion. She hesitated.

Lazaro turned, and she blinked, forcing herself to obey, forcing one leg in front of the other, forcing herself to follow her monster of a brother. It would only be worse later if she did not comply now.

Away from the stairs and down the hallway to Lazaro's office…opposite from the direction she so desperately wanted to go.

"You must be tired. Sit and wait."

Wait? Wait for what? What could be so important right now?

Nothing, most likely. He was just torturing her, purposely keeping her from where she ached to be. She clenched her back teeth so hard she heard a pop in her ears, but she sat with perfect posture in the high-backed chair facing his desk.

He unlocked a door in the wall behind his desk. She had never been allowed inside that room, but she knew enough between glimpses and talk. Lazaro watched everything to do with his business on screens and screens of video monitors, recording every move. She had never been able to decide if he monitored the family and this house with the same dedication.

What did he need her for? What did she have to do with anything in that room?

She realized she was gripping the seat of the chair, blunt nails digging into the upholstered fabric. She eased her grip and settled her hands in her lap, tucking them just between the folds of her skirt—if they clenched involuntarily, perhaps he would not see.

Finally, Lazaro returned and booted up his laptop. He put a small square—a USB drive, she thought—in one side. Two of Guadalupe's girls had had an argument about one that looked like a rocket ship, until Salvadora ripped the small piece out of their hands and smashed it. Lucia had not been allowed such things as computers herself.

Lazaro did not speak, and neither did Lucia, as he clicked and swiped. Lucia clocked every second of wasted time.

"Ah, yes. Come and see."

With a sense of dread, Lucia rose and rounded the massive desk. The screen showed an angled view—top down and from a corner—of a room. The room looked bare and cold: stone walls, a lone table and chair. Something dangled off the side of the table, but the video was not terribly clear. There were two figures, Ian—definitely—and another man who hunkered in the corner watching him.

Ian moved, fast and jerky, and he—

Dios. He threw himself at the wall. And then again and again, hurling his body forward.

Then something above him seemed to catch his attention. He ducked, raising his arms to block something, then lost his footing and fell.

"What did you do to him?"

"Nothing he didn't do to himself."

Lazaro had drugged Ian, then. With something very bad and very strong.

The last paper she had read, months and months ago, said that Stephen Cross's son had entered rehab. The Crosses were rich, very rich and very well known. It was why she had taken the chance on reading another paper at the market. Lazaro must have done thorough research.

Lazaro pressed and dragged along a bar at the bottom of the screen, and then again. The other man was circling Ian, shouting at him. Lucia thought she might recognize him. She was not supposed to notice things, but thought it was a young man who had been to the house a couple of times to meet with Lazaro.

The man lunged, striking Ian's face with a blow that knocked him off-kilter. Lucia gasped.

Ian's fist shot out, but he missed. He seemed unsteady. The man kicked, and Ian blocked. He landed a solid blow to the man's side.

She did not want to see this. "Why this fight? What is the point here?"

"Patience," Lazaro said.

Ian began to kick and punch in earnest—and finally, the man doubled over.

Lucia crossed her arms. She had to hold herself together somehow. She had lived with violence most of her life, and although little surprised her at this point, she was by no means immune.

Instinctively, she knew she did not want to see more of this. If Lazaro wanted her to watch, then it would not be good.

Ian had gained the upper hand. He was wild and frenetic, screaming something, even as he dealt blow after blow.

Finally, the other man slumped to the ground.

But Ian didn't stop. He jumped on the man, pulled at his hair, and slammed his head to the ground. Then he rolled off and to his feet. He moved through the small space, kicking at the air, punching at nothing, thrashing this way and that, his mouth open in a terrible, wide gape.

The video was silent, as was the room they stood in now, but Lucia could hear his scream in her own head as if the force of it penetrated her skin.

She sucked in a cautious breath, careful to hide her feelings from her brother.

Lazaro stopped the video. She could see from the bar at the bottom that there was more to go.

"Go on." She had to know what else. She had to know so that she could understand what Ian had been through.

Lazaro shrugged and fast-forwarded through the rest.

Ian crouched then sprang up, still fighting something only he could see. It all looked extra manic in fast motion. Fast-forward, more ducking and spinning; fast-forward and he stumbled over the man on the floor and went down. He threw the chair at something only he could see, dove under the table, and scrambled out again.

Even sped up, it went on for a long time.

Ian huddled in a corner, covering his head, rocking back and forth. He vomited on the wall.

Eventually, Ian curled in a ball, finally spent. The man on the ground never moved again.

"What do you think?"

So many things she wanted to say—to hurl all her anger and sorrow and horror at him. So many things she wanted to do—take the letter opener on his desk and plunge it into Lazaro's neck, spit hatred in his surprised eyes, flee this room, run to her son.

Instead, she steadied herself. "What do you want me to think?"

"I care not what you think. Only what you know. And you will know this—the boy is mine now."

"I knew that the second you brought him here." She wouldn't accept it, though. She had given up on herself at some point, the years under her tyrannical brother having worn her down. Ian's presence, however, lent her a strength of purpose she had not felt in years.

"A pleasant surprise. He is cunning."

She cocked her head just slightly, indicating that she did not follow.

"The boy speaks Spanish."

Her eyes widened as her mind raced. What had she said in front of him?

"You didn't know, then?"

"No." *Gracias, Dias, no.* If she had and hadn't told Lazaro, there would have been repercussions.

"He fights well. Well enough to kill."

Lucia steeled herself against reacting. She didn't want to even consider the uses Lazaro could have for him.

Lazaro said, "With the right motivation, he can—and will—kill again."

Motivation? Did he mean drugs? Maybe threats?

Lazaro steepled his hands and smiled ever so slightly at Lucia. "He'll fit in perfectly here, don't you think?"

This time, she couldn't control her shudder.

21

When Ian woke, Lucia was hovering over him, dribbling cool water between his lips. It stung. His head pounded. His stomach roiled. He didn't want to surface. He knew it as deep as he knew anything.

Ian shut his eyes and let himself sink. The next time, he woke because she was shaking one shoulder hard.

"Ian," she called. "Wake up."

She shined a penlight in his eye, and when he squeezed them shut, she pried one open. His head still pounded.

This routine happened again and again, the shaking, the light, the sips of water. He was so tired. He ached from the inside out.

At one point, he came to without being forced. The shutters were closed and the room cold, but he could see from the seams of light that it was morning.

Lucia was curled in a chair. It had hard arms and a hard back, but the seat was padded. She was small and able to tuck up her legs with her skirt wrapped around her toes. A shawl was pulled around her shoulders and over her chest. Her hair had come loose and had crimps in it where it had been in a bun. She was paler than normal, and the area under her eyes looked bruised in the half-light.

Why was she here?

Ian looked at the bars on the window, and it jogged some disjointed pieces from his memory.

The bar on the outside of the door. No handle inside. A band around his chest squeezing out his air. Big, dark shapes. The flapping of wings coming at him—but not a normal bird. Like a prehistoric vulture with a wingspan that nearly crossed the whole room. And bars and bars that seemed to close in everywhere, coming forward and then receding, like a jail cell that was also a fun house.

He shivered and his pits went clammy. Whatever Jorge had given him was strong, some really bad shit. It was by far the worst trip he had ever had.

He was sweating, shaky, and nauseated even now—but he realized it had to be from the trauma and maybe the injuries, not the drug. Acid only lasted eight or ten hours and wasn't physically addictive.

A rush of relief almost made him lightheaded. *Thank God.* He didn't have detox—the worst hell on earth—again. Those motherfuckers had only forced acid in him.

Was that purposeful on Lazaro's part? He needed Ian to hallucinate but didn't want an out-of-control addict on his hands later?

Ian shook his head—there was no making sense of Lazaro—and it throbbed immediately. He raised a hand to inspect. A bandage was taped over the left side of his forehead. There were also some big bumps and some smaller tender spots beneath his hair. Ian looked at his hand. The knuckles were bloody and scraped but scabbing over.

He attempted to curl to his side, but felt like he was splitting the skin of his knees and gave up.

That prisoner had been left in the room with him. The man had been wild, belligerent, angry, desperate. Surely he'd been even more so once he knew what Lazaro's game was.

There was only one end to that game. Ian didn't quite remember. But if he was here, beaten up but alive, then he was sure the other man was dead.

Why? Why did Lazaro do it? If he just wanted the man dead, there were a hundred other, simpler ways. He was a drug lord with his own little empire. You didn't get there without having eliminated some enemies, some problems. And his guards had probably killed for him many, many times over.

That bastard had robbed Ian of his sobriety against his will. It didn't matter if it was a drug that was non-addictive. It was so wrong, so…

Tears of frustration and disgust and horror slipped from the corners of his eyes, over his temples, and into his hair. Ian stared at the ceiling.

He didn't know what they wanted. And he couldn't see a way out.

Maybe he should just find a way to get into that stash. As soon as he thought it, his heart rate quickened and he had to fist his hands into the sheets. He wanted to leap up and go tearing from the room to find that hidden factory in an old mine, the rooms busting with illegal drugs. Dive in and just go for it. Get so freakin' high he'd never come back.

Just end this nightmare.

———

"Can you eat?" Lucia stood by his bedside. Her arms were crossed as if he was in trouble.

Ian had drifted off thinking about the only way out being dead. He didn't want to eat. He didn't want to be healed.

But she had already begun the healing, and surprisingly, the rest had pushed some of his darkest thoughts to the corners. He still didn't want to be here. But he definitely didn't want to die of an overdose, either.

He didn't know how, but he wasn't gonna let this fucker win. He wasn't going to play his sicko games. He damn sure wasn't going to kill for him. Ever again.

He had no idea how, but he *would* find a way out. A way home.

Ian nodded. "I think so."

"I'll be back," she said. Ian struggled to sit. Like the first time he'd been in this room, his head swam for a moment. But he got his feet under him and made his way to the bathroom. Every inch of him hurt. He swayed again when he relieved himself. Too long since he'd eaten.

He shifted a couple of steps and leaned his weight on the counter to look in the mirror.

Jesus. He looked like he'd been on a month-long bender *and* been hit by a train.

Weak and shuffling carefully, he made his way to the

chair that Lucia had slept in. *Enough with the bedridden thing already.*

Her shawl was draped over the back. Her scent was familiar by now, comforting even. Lavender and sage and something else. He could smell it even with his swollen nose.

She had nursed him twice now. She hadn't tried to hurt him and hadn't been the one to drug him. He had no idea if she wanted to be the one to care for him, or if she had been coerced, but she seemed warmer than she had originally.

He heard the key in the lock. No surprise, he was still a prisoner. At least he was on this side of the table, he thought, remembering the man in the interrogation room.

He grimaced. He'd killed that man. And yet he still wouldn't trade places with him.

Lucia carried a tray, Dia was on her heels, and Mico wrapped his tail around the door handle.

"Put it in my pocket," Lucia told the girl, and Dia dropped the key in her mother's skirt.

Dia stared at him. "You look better. Less disgusting."

Lucia scolded her with a *tchh* noise. She set the tray on the table beside him. Broth.

"Do I need to feed you?"

They'd been speaking Spanish, but Lucia switched now. "Lazaro knows you speak Spanish."

His eyes shot to hers.

"You responded to the man, during."

During what? The incident? The murder? The fight? The drugging?

She was right not to name it. There were no words that encompassed all the horror.

Dia said, "And here I kept your secret so well."

Dia looked as she always did as she assessed him physically with her alert eyes. Ian didn't think she knew what had happened.

Lucia's gaze, however, was heavy, sorrowful, and conflicted. She nodded at him, and he understood that he could ask her if he wanted. Find out exactly how things had gone down. Except he didn't really need to. He still saw the winged beast and the bars whenever he shut his eyes.

Lucia lifted the bowl of broth.

"I can do it," he said.

He spooned some carefully into his mouth. He had no idea how many blows he had taken to the face. His lips were still swollen, cracked, but didn't sting this time, so the splits must have begun to heal.

"How many days? Since…?" He, too, preferred to avoid naming it.

"This is the third day." She turned. "Dia, let's change the bandages."

He ate while Dia prepared supplies. The monkey explored, his bright eyes watching everything. When Ian had eaten as much as he could—not much—Lucia let Dia take the lead.

The girl perched on the arm of the chair and peeled bandages on his forehead, then his chin, then his shoulder.

She knelt and pushed his sleep pants up over his knees. One was bandaged, the other just very scraped.

She made a face and rummaged in the kit. As soon as

she opened a small bottle, he caught the strong whiff of liquid Band-Aid.

"Not that," he said. It stung like a mother.

Mico didn't like it either. He voiced his displeasure, jumped to the windowsill, and disappeared through the bars.

"Stitches won't hold over your kneecap," Dia said. "Don't be a baby."

"What are you, some kind of mini doctor?"

Lucia answered, "She's in training to be a healer." He could see the pride on her face. Her eldest daughter was smart, talented, and kind—despite her sassy mouth.

Dia pinched the skin and dabbed the stinging goo over an inch-long split in his skin. Ian hissed.

"A few more days on the stitches, but we should let the wounds dry out from here." She told Ian, "You might want to sleep with the covers off."

Lucia said. "His pants will stick to them anyway."

"Cut a pair," Dia told her.

"Let's cut the dirty ones." Lucia dug in the first-aid kit and pulled out a pair of scissors. They were blunt, like the ones he had used alongside crayons as a child.

Would they leave the kit here?

Lucia asked him to stand, so she could snip all the way around his pant legs. It took a while with such lame scissors.

"How many stitches did you give me?"

"Only twelve." Dia rolled her eyes as if it hadn't even been worth her time.

"And I have a concussion?"

"Yes," Lucia said. "You will continue to rest, and I will

monitor you." She pointed to the bed and helped him settle against the pillows. "It's a miracle you had no broken bones."

He stared at her—the question unasked but clear between them.

"Dia," she said, but didn't take her eyes from Ian. "Go and have chef prepare some rice for Ian."

Dia narrowed her eyes, but did as she was told.

"I wasn't there," Lucia said when it was just the two of them. "He has video."

"Has everyone seen it?" Ian's mind was storming through possibilities.

"Only me."

"Why show you?"

She sank to the edge of his bed. "God only knows." A shadow crossed her face. "And Lazaro."

"What will he do with it?"

She pursed her lips. "Use it to hold you here, I think." Blackmail, she meant. "He will surely take out any part he had in it."

"He drugged me. I would never have—"

"I know. He would have known it was a weakness of yours."

"It was different drugs than..." He really didn't want to explain the details to her, and yet he felt desperate that she understand that he wasn't a cold-blooded murderer. "That situation was so messed up. It was already a bad mental state to be in and a bad environment, you know, going into it, and then they gave me a lot."

"What does that mean?"

"Too much and— Never mind." Ian squeezed his head

in his hands. It didn't matter what she understood. "Whatever. It's done."

But—*shit*, maybe it wasn't done? His blood ran cold and he looked up at Lucia with horror. "Will he…will he keep drugging me?"

"I don't think so. He will want your cooperation. But he will also want you lucid and…predictable."

"I don't know who to trust."

He hadn't realize he'd spoken aloud, until she answered.

"Trust no one. Not even me."

22

———————

STANDING ONCE MORE IN CROSS'S BEHEMOTH FORMAL
foyer, Mitch wondered—not for the first time—what had
happened to implode Stephen and Victoria's marriage.
Whatever it was, it had happened early in their relationship—way back when Ian was little, or maybe even before
he was born.

Cross had known their trip to Victoria's paradise was
pointless—he'd told them not to waste the time. Did that
mean he'd ensured she'd keep his secrets? Or that there
were no secrets to keep?

As soon as Cross joined them, he said, "What now?"

"Now it's on to your business associates."

Cross put his hands on his hips and puffed out his
chest. "I told you—"

"Yeah, we know. Your partners and clients and even
your enemies wouldn't have done anything like this."
They'd already discussed in depth Cross's business, his
rivals, his enemies, anyone with a bone to pick. In fact,
Mitch had a massive list of people to check and interview.

"Mr. Cross," Charlie said, "you want your son found —and we aren't sure Ian ran away. If that's the case, then chances are good someone you know had a part in this." There was a current of compassion in her voice that Mitch hadn't been able to muster.

Cross dropped into one of the other chairs and leaned forward, elbows on knees, head bowed. "I can't decide which scenario is worse."

Mitch and Charlie had discussed this very idea. Ian deep into drugs, living on the streets, his life at risk every moment—versus abducted by God only knew who, to God only knew where, and treated God only knew how? Which was the lesser of two evils? Normally, Mitch would have said kidnapping—but the fact that there'd been no ransom demands worried him. An abduction gone wrong would mean Ian was already dead.

Mitch thought it was a good idea to change tactics, and while he was ready to move on to Cross's business associates, he still had questions. "The dates don't match up."

Cross looked up warily. "The date he…was taken?" He was clearly still wrapping his mind around it.

"The dates Ian was born and Victoria came into your life." Mitch had done some document digging: Ian's birth certificate and Victoria and Stephen's marriage certificate. Charlie had trolled the papers for gossip and announcements. The first public photo of the couple at some charity event was dated when Victoria should have been quite pregnant with Ian.

"That has nothing to do with the here and now." Cross pressed his lips together.

"We need to know everything," Charlie said. "You can't know what could matter."

If anyone understood that the past wasn't always what it seemed and that evil had a hand in things long before you were aware of it, it was Charlie.

Cross shook his head hard, then stood. "It's in the past."

"You want us to find your son or not?" Mitch was tired of the runaround.

"You know damn well I do."

And yet there was something Cross wasn't telling them.

"Then—"

Mary burst into the room. "The mail," she said, holding out a letter to Cross.

Cross said, "Put it in my office," almost annoyed.

"But…" She looked quickly at Mitch and Charlie, then back to Cross. She drew her shoulders back. "It's unusual."

Cross surged toward her outstretched hand. "From Ian?"

She shook her head, and her worry was palpable.

Mitch said, "Stop!"

But it was too late—Cross had snatched the letter. Mary's reaction told Mitch there was a good chance this was evidence, and dammit, Cross was contaminating it.

Cross told Mary, "Fetch my glasses."

"And some plastic gloves or plastic wrap and a paper bag," Mitch said.

She nodded and left in a hurry.

Mitch and Charlie looked over Cross's shoulder. The envelope was a little battered and had no return address.

"Is that a Mexican postmark?" Charlie asked.

Cross froze, then shook his head slightly, almost as if he were warding off an idea—or an evil.

Mary returned with glasses, letter opener, paper lunch sack, and blue gloves like medics would wear. At Mitch's raised eyebrow, she said, "Serena prefers them for washing dishes."

"I doubt those are necessary." Cross slid his glasses onto his nose.

Mitch said, "Humor me."

Cross pressed his lips together but set the letter on a sideboard, wriggled into the small gloves with a bit of struggle, then slit open the envelope while the rest of them hovered.

He unfolded a single sheet of paper.

Mitch had no time to read before Cross sagged hard against the sturdy furniture, rattling a tray of glasses, and Mitch had to grab the man's arm to keep him upright.

"Dear God." Cross's face was ashen as his eyes rose to Mary's. "It's from Lucia."

Mary gasped and crossed herself.

Mitch and Charlie exchanged a glance. "Who the hell is Lucia?"

23

Ian hadn't heard the usual noise of the key in the lock when Lucia and Dia left his room tonight. He crept to the door and pressed his ear there, his heart pounding with pent-up adrenaline.

He'd been in this room for, what—at least three weeks now?—and was pretty sure no guard had ever been posted outside his door. The women never greeted anyone or said goodnight. Lazaro trusted his bars and his deadbolts.

Once their voices had receded to nothing, he grasped the wrought-iron handle and pulled ever so slowly, centimeter by centimeter. Until—*yes*—the door and the frame separated into a single slice of freedom.

Carefully, he inched the door shut.

Although Lucia and Dia had checked his concussion, dabbed some salve on his wounds, and deemed him healing nicely, the mother daughter-pair had been at odds tonight. He didn't know or care about what—he only knew their distraction was his chance.

He had no clock, but it was probably around eight

p.m. He needed to wait until full dark and a quiet house before trying to make his escape. One problem, though: Lucia had still been returning to check his concussion at least once in the middle of the night. So he couldn't wait that long—surely she wouldn't forget to lock the door a second time.

Dia had been leaving the first-aid box in the bathroom, so that Lucia or even Ian had it when needed. The scissors—with a little help from him—had gotten buried in the bottom. Now they were in his pocket. He'd searched the entire room and bathroom again. But short of a toothbrush, there was literally nothing he could use as a weapon.

Usually he was a hearty eater—but since the interrogation room he'd struggled to find his appetite. Tonight, he forced himself to eat all the food they'd left. There were some dry cracker-type things that he folded into a napkin and stuffed in his pocket. God knew how long he'd be out in the wild with no food.

Water…

Ian went back to the bathroom and emptied out the bottle of shampoo into the sink. It was small, maybe twelve ounces max—but it was better than nothing. He had no idea how far Lazaro's compound was from civilization. Mountain runoff fed Lazaro's lush courtyard—if he saw it, he'd follow it. It'd be easier to travel if he got out of the mountains, surely.

Other than that, his plan was just to go north. Pretty much no matter where he was in Mexico, the U.S. border would still be north.

When Ian deemed the house had been quiet for probably an hour, he finally—*finally!*—crept out of his room. He was only familiar with the path from his room to the dining hall and back, including the courtyard that looped through, and had never seen an exit, so he went the opposite way. As soon as he hit a turn, he spotted a guard seated before a set of wide stairs.

He pressed himself back against the wall and tried to rein in his breathing. He'd gotten around the guards at his dad's house a hundred times—but he knew every inch of his home. Here, he was flying blind.

Then he heard it. Snoring. He peeked around, and sure enough the guard was slumped sideways in a chair, his legs up on a table and crossed.

Ian was in bare feet—the fabric shoes he'd been given were too floppy and therefore slapped when he walked. He'd made a sling bag of the one long-sleeved shirt in the room—in it was the still-soapy water bottle, the loose shoes, Lucia's shawl, a short-sleeved shirt, and a pair of pants. It wasn't much for cold nights, but he figured he could bury himself in leaves or a crevice in the rock or something. He'd considered the blanket, but it wouldn't stay secured, and he didn't need anything slowing him down. Maybe he'd get lucky and be able to lift a jacket.

So Ian gathered his courage and crept forward on bare feet. The moonlight streamed in the window. Ian stayed crouched and close to the wall.

A glint of light flashed near the guard, and Ian froze.

The guard still snored. The cadence hadn't changed. Ian looked harder where the glint had been, just above the narrow hall table.

Ian drew a quick breath when he realized—a knife, the metal barely showing. The man wore an ankle holster.

He also wore a hip holster with a pistol. Ian could see the belt and the bulge, but it was between the man and the back of the chair.

The knife would be incredibly useful. The scissors he carried were near to useless. He debated a moment—worth it or not?

He needed to get the fuck out of this place with no one the wiser, but he didn't relish perishing out there from starvation either. With a knife, he might actually *survive*.

The guard snuffled and stirred, and Ian tensed, ready to flee. But the guard only returned to his previous rhythm. Ian shut his eyes and crossed himself.

Now or never.

He sucked in as big a lungful of air as his pounding heart would allow and then tiptoed the eight feet to the guard.

He squatted so that he could quickly duck under the shadows of the table if the guard stirred.

Thank God the holster didn't have a snap or anything. All Ian had to do was slide the knife from its sheath.

Ever so slowly, Ian used one hand to fold the pant leg in and out of the way—it wouldn't do to get snagged—and the other hand to grasp the carved hilt of the knife. It was old school, and in some other world, Ian would have admired its beauty and imagined its history.

Right now, however, he was only focused on the move-ment—careful not to tug, not to breathe, not to shift. Slowly, ever so slowly, he slid the knife from its home.

And then it was free, and Ian was slipping down the

stairs.

He paused at the bottom to try to get his bearings and to make sure there was no guard lurking around the next corner.

Ahead, he thought, was the front of the compound—but did he dare go out the front door? Were all the floors and rooms as secure as his prison? He'd seen so little of it.

It would be what it would be. Ian crept forward.

He hadn't gotten far when a door opened. He spun to see Lucia step out. There was nowhere to hide, no way to vanish into thin air. She yelped in surprise—and he cringed—though her hands quickly flew to cover her mouth.

"Which way out?"

She seemed to be torn—opening her mouth but shaking her head ever so slightly.

Ian heard a slam—a chair? Boots?—and then a heavy footfall and shout.

"Hurry!" he said.

She pointed opposite the direction he'd been heading, and then said, "On the left—through the laundry."

He shot forward but hadn't even passed Lucia when—

"*¡Detente!*"

Fuck. He skidded to a stop. He grabbed Lucia, pulling her into his chest, and put his newly acquired knife to her neck.

She gasped and then stumbled as he walked her backward toward the laundry. "Keep up," he told her.

Pounding from the stairs too now. Guards were shouting into radios. Another guard slid to a stop by the first, and they advanced as a unit.

The one he'd taken the knife from suddenly shot past Ian, gun out.

Fuck, fuck. They had him boxed in. Ian turned sideways, hoping neither side could get a clear shot.

Could Ian just plow this guard over? They kept moving toward him. But the guard held steady. Would he shoot with Lucia plastered against Ian's front? Ian didn't know where Lucia stood with Lazaro exactly.

And then the *patrón* was there, passing through the two guards and coming to stand directly in front of Ian, who'd backed up against the wall.

Literally and figuratively.

"Let me go, or I'll kill her." In that instant, he felt desperate enough to do it. He would slit her throat right now if it got him out—but it wouldn't. He'd kill her, and then they'd kill him.

"No you won't."

"This time killing suits my purposes." Could he do it? What if he killed her and unpredictable Lazaro let him live?

Lazaro actually smiled. "I think not." He shifted his reptilian stare to Lucia. "You did not tell him?"

He'd felt the tiny tremors of fear in her body, but now she actually shook. Her voice was barely audible. "You did not give me leave to."

"Coward." Lazaro smiled, and he almost—almost— looked gleeful.

He turned his attention back to Ian. "It is past time, then, for a formal introduction." His voice was silky smooth, all the more concerning for its calmness, as it couldn't be read. "Ian Luka Cross, meet Maria Lucia Valdez Rivera de Cruz—your mother."

Nothing could have shocked Ian more. He tightened his forearm over her shoulder and collarbone, pressing the knife further into her skin. "Bullshit."

"I'm sorry," she whispered, her voice shaking as hard as her body. "It's true."

Ian stared at Lazaro, checked the guards' faces, swung back to Lazaro again.

What. The. Fuck. What the ever-loving Fuck.

Reality spun—how could that be true? What about Victoria? Did this explain why his "mom" had abandoned her only son? Was Lazaro telling the truth, or did he have it wrong?

Puzzle pieces were shifting fast in Ian's mind, giving him even more of a panicky feeling—but he couldn't focus on the past right now. Somehow, during all this talking, the guards had crept closer.

"What's your end game?" Ian asked Lazaro.

"We'll talk tomorrow when you are feeling more civilized." Lazaro nodded, almost imperceptibly.

The guards leapt into motion, and just as fast, it was over: the knife pried from his grip, his arms wrenched so far behind him he had to bend over, Lucia yanked away from Ian and thrust at her brother.

She stumbled, tripping on her skirt, and Lazaro's arm swung across his body. For a split second, Ian thought he meant to block her from falling into him, but—

Lazaro backhanded her full across the face. Already off balance, she went flying, landing hard on her left side with a cry.

Jesus.

"Return him to his room," Lazaro said, then stalked toward Lucia. He swooped down, grabbed a fistful of her hair, and started to drag her. "It seems I have need of my cane."

She fought, scraping and hitting his hands, but her feet scrabbled uselessly on the hard tile floor.

"What the fuck is wrong with you?" Ian shouted. "You mother—"

Out of nowhere, pain exploded in Ian's side—his kidney, probably. He struggled for breath through the pain.

Lazaro dropped Lucia then, her head slamming against the floor. She groaned and her head lolled to the side. *Holy mo*— Had the bastard killed her?

Lazaro straightened and brushed dirt or lint or nothing from his shirt front. "Remember, please, young Ian, that whenever you disobey, it is your mother who will pay the price."

Then, in a sudden burst of movement, Lazaro kicked Lucia in the gut—hard. She grunted and curled into a ball to protect herself.

Lazaro looked at Ian with the smallest smirk of satisfaction.

Ian was panting hard, and tears streamed down his face from pain, shock, and horror.

He didn't reply.

He couldn't think of a single thing that would matter to a monster. Not a single word that wouldn't land Lucia another blow.

24

———

Mitch let go of Stephen Cross's arm when the man braced his free hand on the sideboard.

Mary's eyes were wide and her skin had gone at least two shades paler—which was a sight, given her already light coloring. Apparently, a letter from Lucia was akin to seeing a ghost. Mary hadn't moved—and still stood with the box of gloves clutched to her chest.

Charlie reached for them and tugged some free, handing two to Mitch.

"We're all going to need a drink." Cross's voice was unsteady.

Charlie managed the gloves first—Mitch's hands were too big—and she plucked the letter from Cross's hands just as he popped off the top of a crystal decanter.

He turned over a highball glass, sloshed in some scotch —or maybe bourbon—and tipped his head back.

The glass slammed down with a clunk, rattling the others again. He blew out a hard breath and then began turning over glasses with far too much force.

"None for me," Mitch said, and moved to look over Charlie's shoulder.

"Me either." She was focused on the letter, and Mitch read over her shoulder.

STEPHEN,

Ian is here. I am so sorry. I did not know in time.

DO NOT COME. It is far too dangerous—for you and us.

If at all possible, I will see that he is returned to you.

Always yours in my heart—

Lucia

CHARLIE LOOKED UP AT MITCH. "GOOD OR BAD?" she mouthed.

Mitch shook his head. Ian was alive, or had been at the time the letter was written. But he—and anyone else who tried to find him—was in danger. This note wasn't exactly comforting.

"Where is 'here'?" Mitch asked.

Cross poured another shot and moved to a stiff-looking side chair.

Mary slid her fingers over the front edges of her cardigan repeatedly, making it even and perfect.

Cross nodded at the bar on the sideboard. "Help your-selves. You too, Mary."

The housekeeper didn't move.

"It's okay," Cross said. "No more secrets."

Mary's shoulders dropped about two inches. Relief was

her bourbon. She sank into the opposite chair like she was made of honey.

Charlie and Mitch still stood. Charlie held the letter, trying to touch it only at the edges even with her gloves.

Cross rubbed his forehead and then realized he still wore the gloves. He set the drink down, peeled them off, and tossed them to the floor. He looked at Mitch and Charlie, his expression pained. "*Here* is Mexico, somewhere."

Not good. Mitch waited for more.

"And Lucia"—Cross paused to draw a deep breath—"is Ian's mother. His real mother."

Of course she is, Mitch thought. He and Charlie had known something was off with Victoria and their wedding dates as opposed to Ian's birth date.

"I didn't think I'd ever hear from her again. I'd hoped, for a while, but then I knew—I never would." Cross was almost talking to himself. "I never thought—never once after all this time—that Ian would be in danger from Lucia's family. I thought she'd managed what she wanted."

"What did she want?"

Cross picked his glass up again. They'd have to watch he didn't get stupid. Mitch needed all the coherent information he could get before they wasted any more time, and no detail would be too minor.

"To hide Ian from her family. And me as well—our relationship, I mean."

Softly, Mary said, "It might be easier if you just start from the beginning."

Cross stared at her for a moment before nodding.

"Lucia's father, Alvaro, was at university with me. We

became friendly, but not overly so. Kept in touch here and there in the decade or so after. He contacted me about some business. I had a new complex I was turning over; he had a paving company. It worked for a while—a few projects, a few years." Cross shrugged. "He was back and forth between the States and Mexico and had some employees who were illegal. Everybody did in those days, but the authorities seemed to be focused on him."

Mitch blew through possibilities in his mind—drug smuggling? Human trafficking? Blackmail? He looked at Charlie, whose brows had knitted together.

"By then I was moving away from owning properties and into venture capitalism, so the business end of our relationship naturally fell off. A couple years later, Alvaro reached out and asked a personal favor."

Mitch nudged Charlie toward the couch. This wasn't going to be a short story.

Cross took a breath and rubbed at his forehead again. "His daughter had been lobbying for years to be allowed to go to university like he had. She refused to marry until she had a degree and had seen a little of the world. Alvaro had a soft spot for his only daughter, and he was very protective. He didn't want her staying on campus without security or living alone with someone he didn't trust. Could she stay with me or with my staff if I wasn't fully in residence?"

"Lucia." Charlie said the name almost under her breath.

Cross inclined his head. "I was in the process of selling one house and was living in another. But there was plenty of room and I wasn't home much, so I agreed.

How much trouble could a twenty-two-year-old woman be?"

"A lot, I take it," Mitch said.

Cross shut his eyes. A smile appeared and then disappeared with a pained grimace. "No. Just the opposite."

Mary crossed the room and took his glass to refill. When she set it back on the table, she patted his arm.

Cross turned up his hands. "She was a delight. A breath of fresh air. She had the enthusiasm of someone young and suddenly free, paired with the serious nature of a woman who knew she'd been granted a rare opportunity."

Charlie leaned forward. "You fell in love."

Cross nodded. "Friends first. Both of us resisted getting involved despite the amount of time we spent together. Alvaro was counting on me to be her guardian, and Lucia did not want to take advantage of her host." He lifted one shoulder. "In the end, there was no fighting it."

"So what happened?"

"I bought a ring and had intended to ask her to marry me the minute she got her degree." He stared at the glass in his hand. "But when the pregnancy happened—Ian—I proposed right away."

He took another hearty swig from his drink. "She refused."

25

───────

After the failed escape, Lucia did not come to Ian's room the next morning. No surprise—she'd taken a wicked beating before Ian was dragged off to his room. He squeezed his eyes shut every time he wondered if Lazaro had taken his cane to her—his *mother*, or at least birth mother, if it was true.

Midmorning sometime, a guard delivered a message. "You are expected at meals."

He didn't wait for a response, only turned and left—except he left the door not only unlocked but wide open.

All this time, Ian had been aching to get out. He stared, then shook his head. This wasn't freedom. He got up only long enough to shut the door and use the bathroom. Then he returned to bed, pulling the sheet over his head.

Dia came a couple of hours later to remove the last bandage.

"Is she dead?"

"She's resting."

"Is it true? That I'm her…"

"Yes." Dia was subdued, all of her usual wisecracking on hiatus.

Ian suddenly realized the full implication of what this meant. Dia was his half-sister. Hell, half the Braid Contingent must be half-siblings.

"Did you know?"

She shook her head, but it morphed into a shrug. "I suspected."

"Why didn't anyone tell me? Why am I here? It's not like some big, happy reunion—so what the hell does Lazaro want with me?"

Dia's eyes held a weight far beyond her years. "Ask your questions of my—our—mother."

Ian thought long and hard about refusing to go to the midday meal. But Lazaro's words rang in his ears and visions of violence swam behind his eyes.

When you disobey, your mother will pay the price.

———

LUCIA WAS NOT AT LUNCH OR AT DINNER.

"She'll be fine," Dia murmured at Ian's questioning look.

Afterward, Dia joined him on the lemon tree bench. "She's had worse injuries. She'll join us tomorrow. She needs a break."

Ian's blood boiled both at the treatment Lucia seemingly regularly received—and at his powerlessness.

———

THE NEXT DAY, LUCIA WOKE HIM BY SHAKING HIS shoulder.

"Will you talk with me?"

He nodded and sat up. She'd brought two cups of coffee and set them on the table. Another chair had shown up the night before while he was at dinner.

All the questions he'd wanted to fire at her lodged in his throat. Suddenly he saw all their similarities. Thick, dark hair, bold brows, golden skin. He had his father's nose and chin—but her eyes.

This wasn't some random woman. This was his flesh and blood. If not his mother, then at least his birth mother.

"I'm not sure where to start." Lucia fussed, turning the mug just so, and his too.

The white streak in her hair—he'd ceased to notice it since early on, but now he wondered as he took in her bruised and swollen cheekbone. Was it from an injury? A beating? From Lazaro's cane?

"How"—he gestured lamely to her head and then her gut—"are you?"

So many emotions crossed her face that he couldn't pick them all out. Shame, anger, embarrassment, regret?

"Fine." She tucked her hands into her skirt, drew her shoulders back, and looked him in the eye. "I'm sorry. I'm so sorry for all of this."

"Did you love my father?" This was a question he'd barely considered—they weren't together, after all—and yet somehow it was the one that flew out of his mouth.

"Yes." She smiled. "I will never be sorry for that. Or for you."

Ian wasn't feeling butterflies and rainbows.

"Then why weren't you with us? Why are you here? Why was I never even told about you?"

She took a deep breath and sat back in the chair. She started at the beginning, her expression soft and sweet as she recounted her beloved father Alvaro, going to university in California, and falling in love with Stephen despite herself. But a shadow crossed her face.

"We were careful, but you were conceived. Your father was thrilled and asked me to marry him. There was nothing more I wanted in the world—but I did not think my father would allow it. He had allowed the schooling only because it was agreed that when I returned home I would marry to link another powerful family with ours."

Her shoulders rose and fell, still tense in the telling. "I knew I couldn't let him find out I was pregnant. He would bring me home immediately, marry me off quickly—to make sure the other family could not claim a child wasn't of their blood. Stephen called my father asking for my hand in marriage, and I told my father that I'd fallen in love."

She paused, and Ian could see she was deep in memory.

"My father was furious. I thought that there was a chance—that when he got used to the idea, I might be able to convince him to let me go, let me be. But the pregnancy progressed and I grew worried. I was only able to convince him to let me finish that second year of school. You were due in April."

She blinked and smiled at Ian. "You were a beautiful baby. Even with the fear about my family, we were so happy. I still hoped my father would come around, but then he died."

Her face twisted. "Lazaro called. In one breath he told me the news, in the next that he would pick me up in three days." She held Ian's gaze. "He said that if I did not show up at the airstrip that he would slaughter my guardian and all his staff."

Tears filled her eyes. "I loved your father. I loved you even more. You have seen Lazaro in action. You know it was not an idle threat."

"My dad wouldn't have believed that." Ian's voice shook.

"No, of course not. I told Stephen it was five days, so that he could not intervene. Because he did not—could not—understand. He fought me, begged me, promised he could protect me, all of us. I tried to tell him stories, but Lazaro and the lengths he will go is unfathomable in any other world, yes?"

They just stared at each other.

"Where did his wife Victoria fit in?"

She leaned back in her chair. "Ah—I suspected that my father had not shared my wish to marry Stephen with the rest of the family. We had always known Lazaro would be head of the family. Jorge is...not quite right. I didn't want my love for your father to ever put him in danger. So in the spring, I insisted Stephen go to events— and be seen with other women. After he was photographed with Victoria, I insisted he take her to a play, to dinner, wherever. I do not know what happened after I left—perhaps he fell in love; perhaps he just wanted a mother for you."

Ian pressed his lips together. "Whatever it was, it didn't last long."

She nodded. "I saw the news of the divorce. Did you…did you have a mother to love you? Her or…" She trailed off at the look on his face.

"I had nannies and housekeepers."

"I'm sorry."

"And my dad. I had him."

Her smile was sure and yet bittersweet. "Then I succeeded."

"Until now."

She winced. "Yes. Until now."

26

———

Charlie paced circles around the couch where Henrietta sat, swollen ankles propped on the coffee table. Today was cool and rainy, but the weather didn't seem to matter to Henrietta's body. She rubbed at her knuckles as well. Charlie knew she had arthritis, but wasn't sure the cause of the swelling in her lower extremities.

The pacing made her hot, so Charlie peeled off her plain gray zippered sweatshirt. Down to her tank and reunited with her favorite cargo pants, she should be comfortable. She wasn't. She itched from inside. She'd run here to get away, and now she had the urge to run again, away from Mitch's overprotectiveness, from Henrietta's concern, from Stephen Cross's fear, and—even though she was determined—from the serious trouble she suspected Ian had landed in.

She crossed to the window and used her whole body to shove the sill up. Henrietta harrumphed and pulled her cardigan to stretch and overlap across her middle.

Mitch was in her bedroom on the phone. He'd worked narcotics undercover in Pennsylvania, and the Valdez family, Lazaro and his brother Jorge, were well known in those circles. The Valdez cartel was small potatoes compared to the Sinaloa or the Jalisco New Generation Cartel, the CJNG, but they'd found their niche in fentanyl production, and the state of Durango, Mexico was their territory. Now, however, he needed specifics. This was his fourth or fifth call to various contacts. Charlie had lost count.

In the meanwhile, Mitch had tasked Cross with contacting the Federal Agency Task Force for Missing and Exploited Children, since they should be able to coordinate response with all the other government agencies.

Mitch swore again—in fact, that seemed to be the bulk of his end of the conversation on these calls.

"Uh-uh. This is not good," Henrietta said for about the hundredth time.

"The thought of Ian in the midst of all those drugs…" Charlie couldn't seem to get past that thought. The kid had worked so hard to get clean, had been so determined to put all that behind him.

"Not good, not good," Henrietta said.

Charlie's own phone rang, and she looked at the display. Pennsylvania area code. "Hello?"

No one answered.

"Hello?"

The connection wasn't very clear, but she thought she heard a buzz in the background and then a clang. The line went dead.

She shrugged. "Wrong number, I guess."

"At least it wasn't one of those telemarketers." Henry added a harumph to show what she thought of *them*.

Charlie smiled. Maybe she didn't get solicitations because she still didn't really own anything. All she got were hang-ups or missed calls. But what did she know? They could be telemarketers that didn't expect to reach a real person and wanted to leave a message. When the calls were silent, she figured she'd hit a wrong button somehow.

Finally, Mitch came out of the bedroom. He shoved his phone in the rear pocket of his jeans and then put his hands on his hips, stretching his t-shirt against his chest. He looked stressed, and his hair was a mess—he had a habit of digging his hands in it when he was frustrated— but he still looked damn fine filling up Charlie's tiny apartment. She'd fallen for him in this very place, and she felt more strongly for him all these months later. But his nearness also calmed her jittery insides a little. He was a rock, and he'd know what to do.

"Bad as you thought, huh?"

"Yeah." He blew out a harsh breath. "They've been trying to nail the Valdez operation for years. They aren't a huge family, but Lazaro is supposed to be ruthless. His people are terrified of him. They'd rather spend life in prison or sacrifice themselves than spill. It's damn hard to bust and prosecute without an informant."

Suddenly chilled, Charlie rubbed her arms. "This is good, then. Ian can maybe give them insider information."

"This is not good." Mitch's expression was stormy. "There isn't a single good thing about this." He shoved both hands into his hair. "I don't know that we're going to be able to get him back."

Charlie halted her pacing to stare at him, with a heavy plunk in her stomach. "But we have to try."

Of course, she realized half the reason she was willing to go after Ian was to avoid the responsibility of being someone she wasn't sure she was cut out to be: state's witness, girlfriend, daughter, mother. Was running away worth running straight into trouble?

It didn't matter. Ian needed them. He might have zero chance without them.

"No, *we* don't," Mitch said.

That plunk gained about ten pounds and felt like a Glide-sized box of potatoes weighing her down. Cross wanted to come along as well, but she knew that as much as Mitch didn't want that either, he was only referring to her right now.

"Listen to me, Charlie. It's not safe. Even for me. Let alone for you—completely untrained." He looked at Henry as if to gain her as a second.

Charlie narrowed her eyes. "You wanted me in this PI thing with you. You kept saying how good I was at hiding and blending in and reading people and blah blah blah." Her voice sounded uncomfortably loud in the small space. "Now, at the first—"

"This is different."

"It's not. I can't just—"

"Charlie, listen to me. If Lucia's letter isn't bogus, Ian is inside—*inside*—a drug warlord's compound. Either willingly or held hostage in a heavily guarded compound where you might be shot upon approach just because they weren't expecting your vehicle. It's Mexico, for christ's sake. And in the illicit drug realm, there are no rules, no laws, and no protection."

"We are not leaving him there. I can't do it. I'd rather die trying." Suddenly, she realized that was true. Like saying it made it true.

"You will die." Mitch's voice was a roar. "Do you understand that? I can't let that happen."

And then there was only the sound of their breath— both of them heaving with anger, worry, and determination.

Henrietta levered one foot then the other down and scooted herself to the edge of the couch. "Help me up."

Mitch tore his eyes from Charlie and supported Henry under an elbow.

"I'm gonna let you two sort this out."

"Henry, please, stay. I want—"

"Uh-uh, child. You do not wanna know my opinion." She shuffled toward the door, pocketbook swinging. "I'm sure I'll still be able to hear you upstairs. If you need to hear my two cents, you will."

Charlie shut the door behind her and locked it before turning to face Mitch again.

"We can't just give up on him. Ian helped me escape this very apartment and get back to save Mackenzie." Okay, granted, she'd escaped a swarm of reporters because Ian had a way with fireworks that sounded like gunshots. It wasn't a friggin' drug cartel, but still. "He helped you figure out Tiffany had gone home. We owe him. He needs us. He'll die there."

Mitch's nostrils flared. "I didn't say I was giving up on him."

Charlie's shoulders fell, and that box of potatoes lost just a couple of pounds. Thank God.

"But," Mitch said, "you can't be part of it. Go home, or stay here, but it's too dangerous for you."

Charlie's blood pressure jumped. It was back to this. "You're determined to sideline me? That says a lot about what I can expect from our *partnership*."

"This is different."

"The hell it is! Every missing-person job is going to be dangerous."

"Not necessarily. Listen, this isn't getting us anywhere." Mitch spun in a tight circle. "There's basically just a few key facts here. Getting Ian back alive without us dead is next to impossible. And I can't lose you." He heaved a sigh. "I can't, Charlie."

Her heart lurched, and yet it couldn't matter. "Our wants and needs don't matter here. We can't just give up on Ian, leave him there to be killed or used or ruin himself, even."

They'd talked about all the terrible possibilities. Lucia had claimed her son for some reason—or maybe she hadn't and the family had. They might need a mule. Charlie shuddered anew at the thought of them stuffing him like a turkey. Maybe they were going to use him as leverage for something. Or they could sell him to the highest bidder for God knew what...

There were a million terrible, awful, unfathomable scenarios.

"I'm not giving up. I'm going to try. But I can't have you with me."

Again she opened her mouth and he interrupted.

"I'll be no good if I'm worrying about you."

"Mitch—"

"Please, Charlie. Think about Mackenzie and your mother. I'm not the only one who needs you safe."

That wasn't really true. Mackenzie had Pam and Ray. Her mother was connected with the couple as well as Mitch's mom. If anyone *needed* her, it was District Attorney Gertrude Kolacsko, but Charlie didn't even want to face that.

She took a deep breath. "All right. Let me help"—he opened his mouth, and she held up a hand—"at least until we decide it's too dangerous." Until *she* decided, anyway. "Otherwise, there's no way you'll ever convince me to work with you again."

And she didn't say it, but the last place she wanted to be without Mitch was Blakes Ridge. She had barely thought of Thomas Weihle since she'd found out about Ian—and if she went home…

No. No way.

Mitch ran a hand through his hair again, and now it stood on end. She knew he'd hoped this job would be the beginning of something good for them. Even something that would tether her to him. He still looked torn, but he said, "Okay, okay. Until I feel it's too risky."

She'd at least said *we*. He said *I*. Whatever. When it came down to it, the choice was probably going to be out of his hands.

She crossed her arms over her chest. "Will the contacts you called help us?"

"We don't even know if Lucia's letter is legit, if he's really there, or if he's still alive."

"Then that's the first step," Charlie said. "We see if we can confirm that he is alive and inside the Valdez camp. And then we go from there."

27

LAZARO MUST HAVE DECIDED THAT IAN WAS NOW
cowed enough to stay in line, because his door remained
unlocked and Lucia began showing him around the
compound. It wasn't as big as Ian had thought. But it was
impressive. Heavily guarded. The various suites of
bedrooms for the family. Casual gathering rooms and
more formal entertaining rooms. The guards' quarters were
separate and appeared far less nice.

One place they steered clear of was Lazaro's office and
adjoining rooms. Lucia warned Ian, however, of the
cameras watching most everything.

Ian now also had the freedom of asking her questions
during these tours.

"Which ones are your children, and what happened to
your husband?"

"Very shortly after my return, I was married," Lucia
said. "Lazaro had chosen my husband, of course. His
family was also in the drug trade. But he was closer to the
age my father would have been. He was not as strong a

leader as he once was." She knitted her brow in thought, even as she waved him on to follow, to keep up.

"It was not terrible. Because at least I was able to live at his house instead of here. Dia was born very quickly. Then it was a few years before Cat, Ana, and Tierra came along in short order."

Since it spelled "cat," Ian figured he could remember the order.

"Then Bebe, and when she was only one, Ricardo died from a heart condition. Lazaro insisted I come home with the girls. He had already been pulling the strings of Ricardo's business. He kept those loyal to him. Others, he let go. Some who wanted power, he had killed."

Always, Ian noticed, she stopped speaking as they passed other people. This time it was a pair of guards.

"It was a dark time for me. I had hoped to at least see my girls grown and married into other families before their father died."

Ian nodded. No one in their right mind would want their children raised under a roof ruled by Lazaro. He asked, "What's the deal with Guadalupe and Salvadora?"

Lucia made a *haach* sound in her throat. "Guadalupe's husband, Alejandro, essentially grew up with us. Like a cousin, but not by blood. He and Lazaro were supposed to rule together in partnership, just as their fathers had done. Both were strong leaders—smart, cunning, and not to be trifled with. But when Lazaro had the chance, he killed Alejandro."

Ian raised his eyebrows. "He's really racking them up."

"What?"

He waved her off—her English was good, but it was

formal. She'd been too many years away from slang. Dia, on the other hand, must watch a lot of movies.

Lucia continued, "Guadalupe expected to rule alongside her husband and be a very powerful woman."

As powerful as a woman could be in a drug kingpin's den—which was not very, Ian figured.

"But," he said, "aren't her children Lazaro's?"

"Salvadora is of Alejandro. And so is Guadalupe's next daughter. But yes, the next two are Lazaro's."

"But he never married her?"

"No." She waved a hand. "He took her as a mistress, but will not marry her—it would give her too much power, you see? He honors her by keeping her here. He could easily have thrown them out when he killed Alejandro."

Ian's head spun. This was like a soap opera on a bad trip.

"She's okay with it?"

The *haach* sound again. "What choice does she have?"

"Hasn't Lazaro ever married?"

"Of course, when he was younger, many times."

"Let me guess, he killed them, too."

"Accidents, but…" She inclined her head. "He needed another, and another opportunity for a male heir. A sacred direct line."

Dude probably can't get it up, Ian thought with a gleeful malice, but Lucia went on.

"There was an old seer woman. She had predicted the death of our mother with great accuracy. We believe in much of the old lore, and most of the people from this area have visited her. My father did not wish to know about his mortality, but wanted to learn the fate of his children. Lazaro has kept his silence on her prophecies. He does not know that my father told me in confidence."

She gave him a stern look. "You must never share this."

He nodded and gave her the same earnest look he used to give nannies, teachers, and guards. Bullshit or not, this he wanted to hear.

"He was told he will have no blood to lead."

"Meaning?"

She shrugged. "My father took it to mean that Lazaro would not have children that would live to adulthood. I think he perhaps cannot have children."

"You mean you think he's sterile?"

"If that's the word, yes."

Ian didn't have time to think that through before she continued.

"Also, the seer said that he will not live but a handful of seasons past the cruel and beautiful one's coming of age."

In this culture, a *quinceañera* meant a coming of age, but that didn't fit.

"The cruel and beautiful one?" But even as he asked it, he realized. "Salvadora?"

"I had hoped when she…" Lucia pressed her lips together. "Well, she turned *eighteen* only a month ago."

Ian frowned. A handful of seasons…what, like five seasons? Max? If he couldn't escape, he might be free of Lazaro in a year and a few months…

He shook his head. He couldn't put any credence in

the ramblings of some geriatric scammer. And he sure as hell didn't want to be here that long.

Lucia spoke, dragging him away from speculation. "I have seen her myself."

Okaaay. Ian tried not to look too skeptical. "What did she tell you?"

Lucia tilted her head. "That I would live to a very old age. Much of my life would be periods of great darkness and violence. That I would have great love." She smiled softly. "Your father."

"So you were very young when you saw her?"

"Most girls visit after their *quinceañera*."

"The seer also talked about a reunion." Lucia seemed emboldened with his questions and interest. She set her hand on his shoulder, light as a butterfly, but just as quickly, it was gone. Always, she was careful not to show too much interest in him. "I have connected with you finally after all these years. That part has come true."

A shadow crossed her face as she looked out past the walls of the compound. "Although I certainly wish we had met on your ground and not here. I do not wish..." She paused and looked sideways at him. "I do not wish to live a long life in the darkness—only long enough to see my girls under another's roof."

Ian got it. There would be only so much a person could take. The girls brought back thoughts of the rest of the Braid Contingent—the ones who sat across the table.

"So you think Lazaro can't have kids, but Guadalupe has two of his..."

Lucia shrugged. "It's possible he cannot make boys, only girls, but..." She shook her head. "I don't know. I have never been her confidante, but I would not put it past Guadalupe to try to provide a male heir by other means. Then Lazaro would have to marry her."

"A girl won't cut it, huh? Not good enough to warrant marriage?"

"At least not a girl he suspects is not his."

"But if he thinks she cheated on him, why wouldn't he throw her out?"

"Appearances, I suppose." She shrugged one shoulder. "He looks like more of a man breeding girl children than none."

Jesus. This family was seriously messed up.

They were quiet for a while as they walked. Then Ian asked, "Why do Guadalupe and Salvadora seem to hate me so much?"

She stopped and looked at him with consternation. "Did you hear nothing I said? They're all girls. Her children and mine. Until now. Until you."

"Me? He wants to…what? Claim me? Have me be his heir? The leader of this nightmare? A drug kingpin and psycho patriarch to all these people like him?" Ian laughed. "That's rich. I'm not even technically an adult yet, not to mention an outsider and an addict."

Lucia stopped walking to face him. Her expression was fierce. "You are stronger than that."

He shook his head. "Addiction doesn't just disappear with good intentions." Hell, just thinking about it brought an ache forth deep within him. How tempting it would be to slip into oblivion—it'd provide an escape from this bizarre reality.

"As for the rest," she said, "I don't think he means to

give up power anytime soon. Surely he plans to groom you."

Not soon? Like in five seasons? And what was he? A horse? "I don't want any part of this—ever."

"Neither do I," Lucia said. "But as you've seen, Lazaro has a way of making people do what he wants."

28

―――――

Stephen Cross made his private plane available —as well as any funds they needed. So about thirty hours after the letter arrived, Mitch, along with Charlie—much to his dismay—were in Mexico.

They'd decided to hit the Valdez penthouse in Durango first. Mitch wasn't sure how they were going to scout out a penthouse. They didn't feel they had the time to stake it out for the day, or days, it might take to figure out if the family—and Ian—was in residence. Mitch figured they'd have to get creative once they saw what they were dealing with.

Like any big city, Durango was bustling early. They couldn't idle in front of the building, but they circled the block and came at it from another direction to get a good look at the front entrance. About what he'd expect from any high-end residential unit: doorman and front desk person. Eventually they found parking only a few blocks away.

As they walked, Charlie grabbed his arm and lifted her

nose. "Oh my God. Do you smell that?"

He sure did. If he hadn't already been starving, the enticing scent of bread straight from the ovens would have jump-started his appetite.

"There." He pointed to the local *panadería*, where he could see racks and racks of breads through the window.

"I'm starving," Charlie said.

"Perfect." But Mitch wasn't thinking of their empty bellies. "You order for us, and I'll order separately."

Charlie raised her eyebrows. She had some San Fran street Spanish, but was by no means fluent. Mitch had gotten fluent fast when he was undercover.

"You'll be fine, but I want to order delivery," he said.

"We're going into the lobby?"

He shook his head. "Not us." He ordered a tray of coffees and a dozen various *pan dulce*, or sweetbreads.

A block from their destination, Mitch identified a good candidate: a kid maybe eighteen or nineteen years old unchaining a rickety bike. He wore a hoodie but no jacket and was without a backpack or lunch bag. What he did have was a bit of a swagger.

Mitch gave Charlie the pastry bags and pulled a bunch of pesos out of his pocket.

"Hey, pal, want to make an easy buck? Do a delivery for me?" Mitch lifted the tray of hot drinks and the cash, and Charlie held up the bags.

The kid's eyes swept the area then bounced between them before he checked their surroundings again. Mitch knew so many of these kids were already involved with the drug cartels—either way, it wasn't a bad thing to be wary.

"Why not do it yourself?"

"Because I don't look like I'd be making deliveries, do I?"

"Is there something bad in there? Drugs? A bomb?" He slanted his eyes at the bags.

"Nope. Just *pan dulce.*" Mitch gestured to Charlie to show him what was inside. She set everything on the sidewalk and then opened the two bigger bags for him to look.

The kid crossed his arms, and Mitch took a step closer so he didn't have to talk so loud. "Here's the deal. A thousand pesos just for going into a building on the next block and trying to deliver this food. You're just following orders, right? Your boss told you this address."

"What's the catch?"

"We need information—just to know if the family's in residence. If you can find out—either way—the other thousand is yours. If the security guy doesn't take the food for himself, that's also yours."

The kid looked back and forth between them and then shrugged. "What's the address?"

MITCH'S TWO THOUSAND PESOS—ONLY ABOUT A hundred U.S. dollars—and about a dozen pastries were well spent. The kid learned that the penthouse hadn't been used in a month. And that allowed Mitch and Charlie to head for the mountains to canvass—cautiously—the villages surrounding the biggest Valdez compound.

He'd made Charlie wear a dark wig—and ditch her blue lenses.

"Feels like old times," Charlie said.

"The wigs or going without your contacts?"

"Both."

She didn't even scratch and fuss with the wig, just settled in and made it her own.

They'd also tried to dress like backpacker-type travelers—and Charlie's boots were worn enough to make it believable. She'd traded her signature tank tops for t-shirts with SPF. And he'd bought some hiking pants and wore a stretchy neck wrap that doubled as a headband sometimes. They couldn't pass as locals—but cheesy tourists seemed far-fetched for these parts, and he sure didn't want to scream law enforcement. He might not carry the badge any longer, but he knew he radiated authority like neon. And if it got out later that two Americans were looking for Ian, the less like their usual they looked, the better.

The villages were carved out of the lower hills of the Sierra Madre Occidental mountain range. A single dirt lane ran through each, but they each had a cluster of buildings that acted as the town center.

Mitch and Charlie showed Ian's picture in cantinas, convenience stores, gas stations, and markets. They also talked to the street vendors hawking fruit, savories, blankets, carvings, cigars, and newspapers. Mitch figured, being outside the better part of every day, the vendors would have the best chance of having spotted Ian.

Since it was likely suicide to ask direct questions about a drug cartel—and he wanted her as far out of harm's way as possible—Mitch advised Charlie to be careful to speak in generalities and focus on Ian.

Have you seen this young man?

We have reason to believe he might be in this area. Someone else spotted him nearby.

Have you heard of a young American coming to the area? He probably wasn't alone.

But everyone shook their heads.

Charlie's shoulders had slumped, and he could see the stress pinching her mouth. He knew just how she felt. The buoyancy of the morning's good fortune—so quickly and easily discovering that the Valdez penthouse was unoccupied—had long dissipated. With every new village turning up zeroes, he questioned their tactics, the direction they'd chosen, and their method.

When night fell and they were forced to find lodging, they'd not found even one person who'd seen—or at least admitted to seeing—Ian.

29

———

THE NEXT MORNING, MITCH AND CHARLIE continued further into the hills to El Pase Viejo, which verged on qualifying as a town. It was clear it was more prosperous than the previous villages they'd visited: more permanent buildings, more vendors, more mouth-watering smells, more action as people went about their business. There were even some tourists. Apparently there was a hot spring a few hours away and some scenic overlooks.

Mitch was in the middle of questioning a woman selling printed t-shirts when he noticed a frisson of tension run from vendor to vendor. Nothing more than a look and a look away. A slight hush, a shifting of postures, an unnecessary tidying of wares…

He and Charlie traded glances. She'd noticed it too.

Mitch saw a plume of dust from a caravan of vehicles just coming over the hills, moving at a fast clip.

"Let's go," he told Charlie, and pulled her along the row. They tucked into a short alley between two mud and block buildings. He counted three jeeps—in good enough repair to come fast and sure. Only the government or a cartel could travel like that. Either way, they'd do well to stay out of the way and under the radar until they figured out what was what.

The vehicles stopped right in the road, blocking the main thoroughfare through town and, by default, the entrance to the market. Heavily armed men—machine guns and ammo belts plus pistols—piled out, and then a middle-aged, well-dressed man with a cane.

Holy shit. Mitch had seen pictures, and that was definitely Lazaro Valdez.

Three more people got out: a woman wrapped in a yellow fringed and embroidered headscarf, another shorter female also wearing a simpler scarf in bright blue, and a young, dark-haired man—

Charlie's fingers dug into his arm. "Ian!"

Mitch squinted. Charlie would know his body language better than he would. She'd spent far more time with him.

The group walked forward, and yes, now even Mitch could see that it was definitely Ian. No gun pointed at his back, no cuffs, and walking of his own volition and dressed well in a loose shirt and pants.

Two guards remained to protect the vehicles and watch the main entrance to the town. Four guards flanked the group. They were alert but not overly vigilant, near their charges but not creating a barrier. The group felt comfortable in this town. Mitch swore under his breath— it'd be extra hard to get anywhere if they were all in the Valdez family's pockets.

The shorter female ripped her headscarf off—a teenager, not a woman, with a scrappy braid—and handed it to the other woman, who folded it carefully and placed it in a big straw satchel. Then she unwrapped her own scarf and arranged it over her shoulders.

"Lucia," Mitch whispered. She was older than the pictures they'd seen, of course, and her dark hair now had a big stripe of white running through it, but it was clearly her.

Charlie nodded. Her grip on his arm had barely loosened.

"What do we do?" Charlie asked.

Mitch shook his head. There was nothing to do.

Lucia paused at a stall. The vendor bowed his head in deference to Lazaro, then engaged with Lucia.

The woman running the stall just before that one looked at the party. Her gaze stuttered on Ian then flicked to the alley where Mitch and Charlie hid before dropping to her table. She grabbed a cloth and dusted off some trinkets.

Lazaro said something to Lucia. She inclined her head ever so slightly—no expression on her face—and turned back to the vendor.

Lazaro, Ian, and three of the guards kept walking. The teenage girl and one guard remained with Lucia. The girl looked bored—or maybe impatient—and her gaze followed the men. Lucia said a few more words to the vendor and passed him a few bills. He wrapped something from his table in paper. She thanked him and turned to go, putting a hand on the girl's back to propel her forward.

Mitch and Charlie slipped further back into the

shadows of the alley as the men passed by speaking in Spanish.

"So you see," Lazaro said, his voice formal and almost monotone, "it is not just the family. All these good people depend on us." He swept an arm out. "If something happens to me—to us—they have little food, contaminated water, no income, no prospects, no hope."

Ian's gaze remained downcast.

Lazaro stopped short, and his cane cut the air in front of Ian, stopping an inch shy of the kid's chest. "Look."

Ian's nostrils flared ever so slightly, but he raised his chin and looked around. He turned in a slow circle, seemingly taking in everything, his eyes passing right over Mitch and Charlie in the alley.

Mitch tensed and felt more than heard Charlie suck in a breath—but Ian didn't even blink. Mitch squinted. Was there residual bruising on Ian's face, or were the sun and shadows playing tricks on his eyes?

Ian completed the circle and faced forward once more. "I see." Like Lazaro, Ian spoke in Spanish. "I see it all." His voice was oddly flat.

The group passed by, and Mitch crept forward to watch. They entered an open-air cantina just a couple of doors down.

"That was so…not Ian," Charlie said with a shudder.

"Because of Lazaro." Mitch was sure of it.

Charlie nodded. "I think so too. He's intimidating for sure, but it's still way weird. Wait—look." She poked her head out just far enough to see. "Lucia and the girl just went into that bakery." She pointed to Rosales' Panadería.

"What do we do?" Charlie grabbed his shirt near his waist and twisted.

Mitch felt the frustration too. "I doubt Ian's here of his own free will."

"He's not."

Charlie's expression was hard, but Mitch knew they couldn't assume anything right now. "It doesn't matter. Getting ourselves dead by machine-gun fire isn't an option." Mitch chanced a look around the edge of the building again. "All right. Our first goal was only to confirm Ian's alive and inside one of the Valdez compounds, right?"

"Alive, thank God," Charlie said, and he could hear both relief and excitement in her voice. "We need to somehow find out where. It seems like Ian is *with* them, not stashed somewhere on his own, so w*hich* Valdez properties are they occupying?"

Mitch nodded. They'd marked a big area on the map and some other satellite areas. He squatted and slung the backpack to the ground. They'd bought a bunch of stuff in a hurry: GPS trackers, binoculars, night-vision goggles, a camera that looked like an e-cigarette, a recording device that looked like a pack of cigarettes, and more. Some of it was in their vehicle, but some was buried in his knapsack, which had an interior section that wasn't obvious at first or even second look.

He shoved the cigarette pack at Charlie, said, "Hold this," and pulled out two kinds of trackers.

"There's no way you can get that on one of the jeeps with the guards there."

"Not me." Mitch grimaced. "You. And not the jeeps,

the women." He handed Charlie two tiny, round trackers and took the cigarette recorder back. "Go into that bakery. Buy something. Keep your face averted, but make sure one of these babies hitches a ride."

She nodded and sucked in air. His chest felt tight and his stomach did a disturbing roll.

"Try not to speak." Her halting Spanish would make her too memorable.

"What about you?"

"I'll try to get close enough to hear their convo." He tilted his head toward the cantina. If he could manage it without the men seeing him, anyway.

He didn't like splitting up, but he couldn't be in two places at once, and he'd understand the men's Spanish. Charlie would miss too much.

"Meet back here," he said. "Go."

He wanted to say so much more. *This is insanity. You shouldn't be here. I should never have let you come. I'll never forgive myself if…* And mostly, *Don't go.*

Instead, he clamped his jaw shut and watched her enter the main thoroughfare. She hovered at a table as if she was deciding whether to stop. Another table or two. A vendor tried to ply her with a thin, bright red scarf, but smart Charlie smiled shyly, ducked her head, and moved along.

Then she acted as if the sweets had caught her eye. She was good—she'd acted for years, adopting personas and hiding the real Laura. She could certainly hide Charlie to be just a hungry passerby or curious tourist.

She pushed past a purple curtain and into the catering place.

Mitch tried to draw in a breath and couldn't. The sounds of the marketplace blurred together, just a rush behind his ears. Sweat dripping down the divot of his lower spine, despite the mild temperature of the shaded alley.

He was normally cool and calm when undercover, so this was new territory. He wasn't used to having to worry about someone else. A partner who had all the same training and information as him was one thing. Someone he loved was something else entirely.

He didn't like it. Not at all. It could mean making mistakes—with serious consequences.

He closed his eyes for a moment and forced himself to push past this and shift gears.

Okay. Breathing. Hearing.

He checked the scene outside of the alley. Then he was moving too, aiming for a section of the cantina's outer wall, just beyond the last window that happened to be shaded from a fruit cart's canopy.

He steadfastly refused to allow himself to look in Charlie's direction.

30

———

Food appeared almost as soon as they sat down.
This place must know Lazaro well.

Ian stifled a groan. Always before on trips abroad with his dad, he'd savored the new foods and scarfed down everything he got a chance to try. He'd eaten frog legs and wasp rice snacks and even things he couldn't identify.

Now that he thought about it, they'd never visited Mexico—at least not since he'd been old enough to remember.

After his abduction, he lost his normally overactive appetite and had only eaten to regain his strength for escape. Now that he knew the score? Every bite of every meal tasted like jellied moose nose and made him want to hurl.

But they hadn't eaten since they left the compound this morning, torturous hours ago, and they'd been in the sun all day between the open-topped jeeps and tromping around villages. He was losing it.

Christ, he thought he'd seen Charlie's Mitch in the

alley of this town with some dark-haired woman. If he was lightheaded enough to be seeing things…

Well, Lazaro would expect him to eat regardless.

The cantina owner—all smiles and deferential nerves—had been back to the table three times in short order. He and a server brought corn stew, wild turkey stew, tamales, nogado peppers, enchiladas, fried beans—the dishes kept coming.

Lazaro's guards sat nearby, and their table was also quickly filled, though not as lavishly. Two of them dug in, but Ian realized the third one was watching for something.

"*Buen provecho,*" the owner said.

"*Buen provecho,*" Lazaro told Ian, as he raised his *agua fresca.*

Ian repeated the blessing, which was essentially the Mexican equivalent of "enjoy" or "bon appetit." His cup felt as if it weighed a thousand pounds, but the cool hibiscus flower water did feel good on his parched throat.

He glanced again at the overly alert guard then set about scooping stew into his bowl, and a little food onto his plate.

When a head peeked out the kitchen door and then disappeared, the guard nodded at Lazaro, who nodded back.

Ian held his breath. Lazaro had nodded before Ian was drugged. He'd nodded before the guards rushed Ian during his escape and yanked Lucia away. Bad things happened when Lazaro nodded.

Ian tensed from his scalp to his toenails.

The guard said something to another, who put down his sandwich. They both stood. One went out the front entrance; the other strode into the kitchen. There was a crash and thud and shout, as well as a higher-pitched yelp. A woman?

Then a body came flying out of the kitchen door and crashed into a table, a young guy, nose already bleeding. Both guards came out of the kitchen—one must have gone around to the back entrance of the kitchen to block it.

They were on him in a second flat.

With his spoon clenched in his fist, Ian half rose—but Lazaro said, "Sit."

The *patrón* didn't even look up, only scooped a bite of wild turkey stew to his mouth. He'd planned this. They weren't here for a tour or lunch.

Slowly, as if he'd splinter, Ian lowered himself to the chair.

The guards took the man's arms and legs and heaved him out of the cantina like a torpedo. People outside gasped and scattered.

The guards followed, as did a never-ending series of punches and kicks and blows with the guns. The man was on the ground, and the half-wall of the open-air venue partially blocked Ian's view. But he could see enough. He could hear the grunts and thuds clearly, because no one else save Lazaro—eating like nothing was amiss—made a sound.

Everyone else in the cantina held their breath.

The townspeople stood stock-still and watched from the safest distance they could find. They all knew better than to intervene. Just like Ian.

He shut his eyes against the violence and the powerlessness—but there was no blocking it out.

"He pays his debt," Lazaro said. "Eat."

Ian's gut clenched as hard as his fists.

He was still trapped. They all were.

31

THERE WAS LITTLE SPACE TO NAVIGATE IN THE caterer's shop, but that was to Charlie's advantage. Heart pounding, she had just crossed behind Lucia and dropped the tracker into her bag—unnoticed, she was certain—when the noise erupted outside.

Lucia and her charge finished their business quickly.

"Don't look," Lucia said, her head bent to the girl's as they left the bakery. Charlie tried to calm her heart rate and follow them with her eyes, even as she pretended to look over some goodies near the storefront. They headed away from the chaos, Lucia with her arm around the girl's shoulders to propel her forward.

Charlie slipped out too, and—*Jesus.*

Someone was getting beaten up, *bad*, by two of the armed men that had come in Lazaro's caravan. No one was doing anything, and for a second her legs stopped moving away so she could— *No.* It wasn't her fight. She'd never get Ian out of here if she got involved. Hell, she wouldn't even get herself out of here alive. Who would or could against numerous men—Lazaro's guards—armed with machine guns? Against a whole cartel like the Valdezes?

Her phone vibrated in her pocket. She checked it only in case it was Mitch telling her to meet him somewhere else. But it was another unknown call from Pennsylvania. She didn't know how to make it stop buzzing, so she just shoved it back in her pocket, bent her head, and kept moving.

Everyone's focus was centered on that horror, so she was able to pass unnoticed and slip back into the alley.

Mitch was already there. He pulled her tight into his chest, making her wig slip a little. She could feel the rapid pounding of his heart.

"They are going to kill him." His voice was strained.

"You can't save him." She squeezed his arms, shook him a bit, and looked up to see torture in his eyes. Always the cop, always the protector.

Mitch swore and sank to his haunches, head in his hands.

The afternoon sun now slanted into the alley, though against the wall they were still in shadow.

She gave him a couple of minutes—but she couldn't stand the awful noise of a man being pummeled. She squeezed his shoulder. "We can't stay right here. What now?"

Mitch sucked in air, his nostrils flaring, before he stood. "The tracker?"

"In that big straw bag Lucia was carrying." Such a riot of emotions: fear of being caught, nervous excitement, and then the thrill of success. Now, with the violence in the street, a fresh wave of fear for Ian. "Were you able to over-hear anything?"

Mitch's jaw tightened. "They weren't talking much. Lazaro told Ian the kid had a debt to pay."

"The women are at the jeeps now."

"Odd that they wouldn't join in the meal."

"They left in a hurry. She didn't want the girl to see the beating."

"We should go," Mitch said, and Charlie shook her head. She couldn't, *couldn't*, just leave Ian.

"We can't do anything for him right now. Not here. It'd be a bloodbath."

She knew he was right, but God, it went against every fiber of her being.

"I know," he said. "Believe me, I know."

32

———————

Mitch and Charlie decided to stay put in Pase Viejo until they had confirmation of Ian's location. The tracker was with Lucia—not Ian—but given the tone of the letter to Cross, they figured it was likely that Lucia would be in close proximity to her son.

Since the residents here were obviously well acquainted with the Valdezes, Mitch figured they could use this waiting time to dig a little more. *If* anybody was willing to talk about a well-known drug dealer to outsiders, that was.

"Let's eat at that cantina," Mitch said. "Maybe we'll overhear something useful. At least we can ask where to rent a room in this town."

Neither of them had much appetite, but since they'd had nothing since breakfast, they needed to eat.

The staff was unusually reticent, unwilling to engage in conversation. Mitch wasn't surprised. They'd lost one of their own today in a terrible act of violence.

In a low voice, Charlie said, "Should we talk about my…excursion?"

"Not here." Mitch watched an old man in the street. He used a broom to sweep the dirt street, covering the blood.

That kid's body had lain there for hours, until Lazaro and his posse left. Even then, it was like the town held its breath. Only one woman—likely the grandmother—staggered to the body and fell to her knees. She wept quietly, her head on the chest of the dead young man, her hands clasping one of his limp ones.

It wasn't until the caravan of jeeps disappeared over the hills and their clouds of dust had settled that the action began. The woman's keening rose to a soul-shattering wail. Others came forward. Women joined in the mourning, putting their arms around her and adding their cries to hers. Others—old and young, male and female—crossed themselves, prayed, paced.

Eventually, they bade her to stand. A few men lifted the body, and she led them out of the square. Likely the kid would be washed clean and dressed for burial right in his family's home.

Mitch and Charlie picked at their food in silence.

The cantina owner pointed them to a shop on a back road that usually had a boarding room available on the second floor.

The shop was a liquor and smoke shop, and the proprietor was an old woman with a deeply lined face and browned teeth. Despite Mitch's clear Spanish, she eyed them with suspicion and gave them a rate that Mitch suspected was far higher than normal, given their white skin. He didn't care.

"I don't wash the sheets until you leave." Her voice cracked and rasped. "How many nights?"

He looked to Charlie, who shook her head. She had information for him, but maybe nothing that would sort how long they'd be here.

"*Tres.*"

He sincerely hoped they wouldn't be here even three nights, but it'd be easier to have the buffer, yet it would seem strange if they planned to stay any longer in a nothing-much-to-offer town.

If things went terribly wrong, it wouldn't matter. If things went completely right? They'd be leaving the country in a hurry.

"You pay now," she said. "No drugs. If I find drugs, I throw you onto the street. No refund."

Mitch realized then that she was one of the women who'd comforted the distraught grandmother in the street. He held her eyes. "On my sister's grave," Mitch said, weight pressing on him for all the people, here and at home, affected by the narcotics trade.

The room wasn't bad. Sparse and clean enough, it held a full-size bed, one slim nightstand, one small table, and two chairs, one of which Charlie hooked her wig over.

There was no TV, not even a radio, but the woman promised the internet and electricity was solid. The bathroom was next door, but had a shower.

Charlie pushed her fingers through her matted hair even as she eyed a Jesus crucifix above the bed. "No way can I sleep with him looking at me."

She struggled with a God who let monsters like Thomas Weihle and Lazaro Valdez run rampant over the innocent, and this was a particularly lifelike rendering of Christ's sacrifice. Mitch peeled off his flannel shirt and hung it over the cross.

"Thanks." She took off her boots, flopped onto the bed, and pointed her toes at the ceiling. "God, I'm tired."

She'd been sleeping like a champ lately, despite her worry over Ian.

He said, "Text Henrietta to check in before you fall asleep."

They'd promised, and they both knew Henry would worry if she didn't hear from them for a while.

Mitch dug his laptop out of his bag and started setting up on the small table. He was anxious to make sure that tracker was working. Having only just gotten his license, he hadn't done his homework yet. As soon as he got home, he'd need to invest in all kinds of surveillance equipment and spend the time to learn how to use it.

Charlie watched him. "Can you see it?"

"Give me a minute."

She was too wound up and came to stand beside him. It was good for her to watch anyway, as she might need to know. After today, though, he was done pushing her to join him in Retrieval, Inc. It was okay when they were together, but it sucked when they split up. Even now, he felt his heart jitter at the thought. He couldn't handle her being in danger.

Charlie pointed. "There it is!"

Sure enough, the tracker appeared active and stationary—at least for now. Mitch pulled up the route it had traveled and tried to get his bearings on the map. He couldn't see any markers of a town or village where it had stopped.

"What a stroke of luck that Ian appeared right under our noses." She bent and looped her arms around him, squeezing hard from behind. "He's alive!"

It was great news, but it meant the really hard—maybe impossible—work was beginning. Mitch rubbed his hands over his face.

"Why aren't you more excited?" She squeezed again.

"I think you forget what we're up against."

She stood. "No. I saw it today." Her voice was more sober now.

She didn't realize the half of it, though, Mitch knew. She couldn't. Even he, with all his experience, probably couldn't.

He stood and pulled her into his arms. "I'm sorry you had to see that." Christ, he was sorry she was here at all. Why the fuck had he wanted her to partner with him? It was the worst idea ever.

She rubbed her forehead into his t-shirt, her hands fisted in the fabric at his sides. "I'm sorry Ian had to."

Mitch had to forcibly remind himself to let out his breath. People like Lazaro always preyed on the weak— innocent, young, naïve, desperate...whatever it was. Ian had street smarts. He was a tough kid and had been through a lot despite his silver spoon upbringing. But he wouldn't be a match for a twisted bastard like that.

And neither was Charlie—except she was here willingly. He'd let it happen. And now Mitch had to stop it. Somehow. Maybe on the sly.

He smoothed his hands over her back and rested his cheek on the crown of her head, only to have his scruff catch in her hair. How long had it been since he shaved?

She pulled back to look up at him. "They are having a party. That's what Lucia was there for—to talk about the catering menu with the owners of the bakery."

He raised an eyebrow, the wheels of possibility already cranking to life in his brain.

"That girl that was with Lucia? I think her name—or maybe nickname—is Dia. They are throwing her a *quinceañera.*"

Fifteen. A big deal in Latino communities—when a girl became a woman. "How soon?"

"I don't know. I didn't catch it. But I think it's going to be big."

"They usually are." He kept his voice mild and stroked his hands up and down, lower every time. Maybe he could distract her. Surely they both would benefit from blowing off a little steam.

"It's our chance." Her eyes were bright. "Our chance to go in."

Mitch could literally feel the excited tension of Charlie's body under his hands.

His own skin went cold. God help him if she was an adrenaline junkie.

33

Ian woke to a warm body and smooth strokes of a soft hand down his back and over his ass. He slept on his stomach, one leg bent, and that hand traced between his butt cheeks and slid lower, to cup his balls. He groaned and went from half-hard to full on.

It had been so long—so fucking long—since he'd been with someone. And the last times had been in a druggy haze, which wasn't the same thing at all. And getting himself off sober? Served a purpose, but it was lacking the scent, the heat, the tactile details, the...

Yes, he smelled flowers and musk. Long hair slid like silk over his arm. He felt a bite, then a wet lick on his shoulder. He braced his hand on the mattress and made to turn over, but he didn't get far. That deft hand slid around to his chest, his stomach, his cock.

He reached behind him and traced warm skin, up along the smooth skin of a thigh to a firm butt. She hooked that leg over him.

This dream was powerful, so unbelievably real. Ian

didn't want to open his eyes—and yet he did. A fantasy girl—woman—would be something to see.

It was dark, the wee hours, he thought, since moonlight filled the room. But he could clearly see her leg wrapped around his, her hand stroking him.

"God," he said, moving his hips, his breath coming faster. He smoothed his hand over all that bare skin again and then put his hand over hers. Fine bones, gripping him surely, smoothing up and down, the nails digging in hard now.

It'd been so long. He wouldn't last—

He wanted *inside*. He rolled to his back. Immediately she straddled him and rolled her hips, painting her wetness along his cock. She was curled over, her hair veiling her face, the long black tendrils tickling his chest.

He gripped her hips hard. She lowered herself onto him, then threw back her head, neck exposed, chest out. He tore his hands from her hips to test those perfectly pert breasts, smoothing up and around and then tweaking a nipple.

"Harder." A demand, full of need.

He took both nipples and twisted—hard. Her hips jerked and her head came down. "*Sí*," she hissed, and began to move.

Holy shit.

It was Salvadora—of all people. For a split second he had to run through the lineage and connections—but, thank God, no blood relation between them.

She was absolutely stunning with her mouth parted in pleasure and her eyes half-lidded. But he wanted to see her eyes, and she wouldn't look at him. She was concentrated fully on where they joined, on riding him hard.

She whimpered in frustration and put her fingers to her clit. The shift in position made something scrape his shin—she hadn't taken off her knife holster, or the knife. He'd seen her practicing all the time, for hours and hours every day. She threw like a master, hitting the bull's-eye every time.

Fucking sexy. He groaned and grabbed her ass hard, grinding her down onto him, then—

Wait—this was *Salvadora*. Who hated him. Who always looked like she wished she could use his heart for target practice. Whom Dia had said to watch out for in terms of his life. Seriously. For real. No joke.

Ian gripped her hips hard enough to stop her movement and then hoisted her off him, almost throwing her.

"What the fuck, Salvadora?" He was breathing hard from need as he shifted out from under her. "What the fuck is this?"

She blinked with surprise before her eyes changed to furious and her mouth set in a firm line. In one motion she rose to her knees, hauled off, and slapped him hard across the face before hopping off the bed.

He rubbed his cheekbone, that eye watering instantly. "That's more what I'd expect from you."

They were both panting, spoiling for a fight and reeling from the sex.

"Why would you do that—get in my bed?" Ian grabbed his sleep pants from where he'd dumped them on the floor the night before. "I'm, like, your sworn enemy. You hate me."

While he pulled on his pants, she turned and bent, dark hair falling forward, her smooth, tight ass on full display for him. He did not want to react, but his body was so starved and—*Jesus*, his body didn't care that she'd prefer to see him six feet under. She was hot.

She stepped into her pants, sans panties. She dropped her eyes to his tent.

Yeah, no way was the boner going away with her breasts heaving and those gorgeously dark areolas in full view.

She licked her lips. "We should try to get along."

"Get along? Have sex? You want to be on top so you can strangle me to death, or maybe behind so you can slit my neck? Are you nuts?"

Her eyes gleamed. She *loved* that idea. But at least she popped her shirt over her head.

"You are as violent and fucked up as my *uncle*." He spat the word.

"Where is your respect? You have his blood, *cabrón*."

My blood. Lucia's blood. Lazaro's blood. And Salvadora was *not* related by blood. He *was* an idiot. That was it.

He gaped. "You wanted to get pregnant—have my kid, my blood, under your thumb like a chess piece." *Christ.* As always, this place was effed, and so was everyone in it.

Now she shot daggers at him and her fists clenched—frustration bordering on violence.

"It's marry you or raise your seed." Her pretty features twisted with hatred. "Believe it or not, the latter is the lesser of the two evils."

"You're insane."

"That's the second time you've said that. I'm one of the only sane ones around." She raised her chin and pushed out her chest. "I'm only determined to take what's rightfully mine—stolen from my family!"

"I can't help you there."

"Are you telling me you want all this?" She swept out an arm. "That you intend to rule even though you know absolute shit?"

"Hell no."

"And yet it's yours." This time she actually spat—*spat*—on his bedroom floor!

"I don't—"

"Lazaro will never hand over his empire to me—even though I am by far the most qualified and the only one with the right personality."

She could say that again. She was a vicious cutthroat who totally got off on a power play. Ian didn't even know what to say.

"*If* I don't kill you first," Salvadora said, "you will be the next *patrón*. You'll be better off if you marry me. I will do all the hard work. You can lounge around and play with your precious lemons with your head on your mommy's lap."

"There's not a chance in hell I'd ever marry you." Besides the fact that he was pretty much still a goddamn kid himself, marriage would change nothing. He'd be more stuck here than ever, and she'd have even more reason to murder him. Although, at least until she did murder him, the sex would be—

He shook his head. The fact that he was weighing the

what-ifs of marriage? Lunacy. A complete, balls-to-the-wall mind fuck.

She rolled her eyes. "You will if Lazaro wishes it."

"Don't. Do *not* even think about asking Lazaro to arrange a marriage between us." That idea might be as terrifying as everything else he'd faced in this hellhole.

She sneered. "Haven't you learned yet? You don't *ask* Lazaro for anything."

"Then what are you going to do?"

A strange look crossed her face. And Ian realized that, probably for the first time ever, Salvadora was unsure.

34

─────

Mitch and Charlie entered Rosales' Panadería midmorning the next day in between, they hoped, the morning and lunch rush.

Just as before, there were a couple of tables piled with boxes of baked goods, some savory, some sweet, and a glass case and register between visitors and the kitchen. There were a few more small tables tucked into corners for patrons to sit.

The rich smell of coffee and baked goods filled the entire space, and Charlie hoped Mitch ordered plenty of both. She was starving.

The owner was a small, wiry man with a wide mouth. He was heavily scarred, starting along his jawbone on one side. He wore a chef's jacket this morning, but in yesterday's afternoon heat, he'd stripped to his undershirt, and Charlie knew that scarring covered his chest and left arm, too.

He was busy giving orders to a teenage girl, who slipped into the kitchen. Only a curtain separated the area.

Charlie could hear another person back there banging around. The owner turned back to a tray of pastries and started loading them into small boxes even as he greeted them with a cursory glance. If he recognized her from the day before, he didn't show it.

Mitch started the conversation saying they were visiting from the States and introducing themselves. He asked if the man was the owner.

"*Sí*, I am Enrique Rosales."

Mitch ordered two coffees and asked what Enrique recommended. "Something filling," Mitch said, "because we didn't have much appetite last night after the…you know. So, now we are very hungry."

No appetite? That was an understatement, Charlie thought. She'd nearly puked when she smelled food.

Enrique's eye twitched. The conversation was fast, but Charlie caught the gist. He avoided the incident and spoke instead of the food: tortilla, beans, eggs.

Mitch nodded and requested two, plus something with cinnamon.

"*Gracias,*" Charlie said when the man handed over her coffee and pointed at the other end of the counter for cream and sugar. Not individual packets like in takeout places in the States, but a pitcher and sugar bowl, one spoon for everyone. More like the setup they used at Glide, pre-COVID, anyway—except this pitcher was Mexican stoneware with a bright pattern.

If Charlie didn't think she'd be scrambling out of the country in the middle of the night, she'd find a pretty one and bring one home to Henrietta… But this wasn't a vacation or even a business trip. It was a rescue mission—and the only cargo that mattered was Ian.

Mitch wanted to name his new PI business Retrieval, Inc. She'd imagined runaways like herself, husbands who ran off with the other woman, kids snatched by parents who didn't get custody, maybe even a stolen piece of jewelry or some crazy family heirloom… But retrieving a friend who'd been kidnapped and transported across enemy lines by a violent drug czar, his birth mother, and a whole posse of guards with machine guns?

Yeah. The not-even-official-yet Retrieval, Inc. was out of its league. A chill ghosted over her, and she rubbed her arms.

"We hear you are catering the Valdez *quinceañera*? That is a big deal for you, yes?"

Most of the conversation was in Spanish. Luckily, Charlie had asked beforehand how in the world Mitch planned to ask this man the questions they needed, which helped her follow along.

The owner forced a smile, and his nod was terse.

"That's good, yes? A reason to celebrate? Big business."

"*Si*, it's good business."

Charlie could tell already that this guy was not exactly willing to spill beans.

"Do you have enough time to prepare?"

A halfway nod.

"It's this coming weekend? Saturday?"

No response.

"At *El Descanso de la Araña*, I guess?"

Enrique turned away and busied himself with their order.

The tracker hadn't moved all night. The Valdez family was high in the hills in the large compound the locals referred to as the Spider's Rest. Mitch's contact at the DEA had confirmed this was Lazaro's biggest holding—and, unfortunately, his most secure.

The man put their wrapped food on the counter, but held on to them. "Why so many questions?"

Mitch smiled. "We have a friend who is family to the Valdezes. I'd love to see him."

"That is not a party you want to crash, *gringo*."

Mitch pulled out his wallet and peeled off some pesos. He slid them across, then pulled the wrapped tortillas from under the man's hands. He handed one to Charlie without turning around.

"You want information."

"No one will ever know you spoke to us." Mitch had an honest face. Charlie had yearned to trust him when they first met—when he was pumping her for information about Tiffany's whereabouts.

A woman with hair half streaked with gray stepped out of a doorway behind the man. Her arms were crossed over her apron-covered chest, and she held a wooden spoon that was covered in pastry dough.

Her dark eyes took in everything. Mitch, Charlie, the food, the money, and likely the set of the man's shoulders. Given the suspicious look she gave them, she'd heard every word.

Charlie took a step forward, looking right into the woman's eyes. "He's my friend—the boy that was with the family yesterday. He was taken…"

Mitch supplied the word for "kidnapped" in Spanish when she faltered.

"From his father," Charlie said.

The woman raised her chin, even as her lips flattened further.

"Yes, we need information." Charlie looked at Enrique, then back at the woman—his wife? His sister? She didn't know. "We need a way in—to get Ian out. Please—I can't leave here without him. Even if…"

She didn't have the words and didn't want to put it in words anyway. "We have to try."

The woman looked long and steady at Enrique. He shook his head. "No good can come of this, Conchita."

"No good ever comes," she said.

They all heard voices as people approached the shop. Charlie tensed, and so did the others.

"Go now," Conchita said. "Come back tonight. To the back door. Well after dark."

35

ARMED AND ON HIGH ALERT, MITCH AND CHARLIE approached the back of Rosales' Panadería near midnight. They'd watched it for hours because Mitch was worried it was a trap.

"But *we* approached *them*," Charlie had countered.

So what? Mitch figured the town could be so far up Lazaro's ass that they'd act first and drag bodies to his doorstep after—like a cat gifting its owner with dead mice. No thanks.

But no one visited, and no one left. Not from the front or back. When most of the lights of the apartment above the shop had been out for a good long while, Mitch figured it was time.

The alley was dark and quiet as they approached the door. Mitch pointed to a spot off to the side he wanted Charlie to stay in. God forbid somebody started firing.

Just as Mitch raised his hand to knock, a dog barked.

Charlie jumped. "Jesus."

As for him, for just a sliver of a second, he thought it was a gunshot and feared Charlie had been hit. His blood still pumped too fast and his chest was too tight. Having her around was going to do him in.

Mitch moved into the shadows near a pile of discarded junk and motioned for Charlie to do the same. The dog had already quieted, and Mitch listened carefully. He heard no footsteps, nothing strange. Two minutes, five, a few more.

Mitch nodded. He stepped forward again and rapped softly on the door, not wanting to rouse the dog or the neighbors. He heard the creak of steps, a full pause, and then the turn of a lock.

Conchita Rosales opened the door only enough to peer at him with one eye. Once she was sure it was him, she opened it all the way. She poked her head out, gave a furtive glance around, then waved them in. Mitch ignored manners and went up the stairs ahead of Charlie, just in case.

In the apartment above, Enrique sat in a chair in the corner, a bottle of tequila and a glass beside him.

The same girl from the shop—the Rosaleses' daughter, Mitch assumed—stuck her head out from behind a curtain, though their entry had been quiet. Her eyes were as round as the moon. Likely it was very strange for parents who owned a bakery to be up so late at night.

"Go back to bed, Chita," Enrique said, though his focus never wavered from Charlie and Mitch.

Chita pulled the curtain shut without making a noise, and Mitch heard the soft shush of weight on a mattress.

He breathed easier. Surely the daughter—presumably also named Conchita like her mother, but nicknamed Chita, as was often custom—wouldn't be in residence if things were going to get violent.

Enrique said, "I have real reservations about helping you."

Mitch nodded. "I can understand that."

"My wife insists."

Conchita gestured for them to sit. Mitch felt his Glock at his back and the knife at his ankle—always reassuring—as he bent into a hard chair facing most of the room and in view of the door. Charlie took the soft loveseat next to Conchita.

Conchita put her palms together over her lap. "I cannot pass up this opportunity to right one wrong."

Enrique said, "Revenge is not righting a wrong." There was no fight in him, though—only years of bitterness.

"I will not deny that my heart yearns for revenge, but I will never have that. This is a chance to balance a scale. A life for a life—or two or three."

Charlie looked at Mitch, and he knew she was trying to decide if she'd understood correctly or if her limited Spanish was hampering her.

"Two or three?" Mitch asked.

"When it comes to the Valdezes, there is never just one." Enrique didn't even look at them. He stared at his drink, or maybe he saw nothing.

Conchita drew a breath, puffing out her ample chest. "The young man who was killed yesterday like a dog in the street is—was—my oldest sister's grandson."

"I'm so sorry," Charlie said.

"It was only a matter of time." The soft, plump curves of Conchita's face seemed to harden.

"What did the Valdezes accuse him of?" Mitch asked.

"Who knows?" She shrugged. "It happens to all the boys. They become part of it, or they are killed. The same for our son."

Even Charlie seemed at a loss for words this time. But Conchita didn't notice; she seemed to want to talk, to tell her son's story.

"The *Valdez* said Miguel had stolen cigarettes, so he dragged him from our shop to the square and poured lighter fluid all over him. He yelled for all to hear, 'Smoking is dangerous. Stealing even more so.' And then…"

Dear God. These people had had to watch their son…

Already tense and on edge, Mitch wanted to jump out of his skin.

"Fernando Miguel Rosales Muñoz"—Enrique emphasized each of his son's names with a pause between—"did not smoke. He had asthma."

"We begged him not to work for the Valdezes," Conchita eventually said. "To stay far away. But Miguel did not want to be with a spoon and apron his whole life. There are few prospects in this town." She waved loosely. "This country."

"Miguel's wishes didn't matter anyway," Enrique said. "*El Araña* chooses his people, and there is no saying no."

The spider. Charlie shivered. "That's how you got the…" She motioned at Enrique, not knowing the word for "scars."

His eyes were bleak—would always be. "I could not save him."

Conchita looked back and forth between Mitch and Charlie. "You will probably not be able to save your friend either. You will probably die trying."

Enrique raised his glass in a not-toast toast. "And we will probably die helping them."

Conchita said, "Dying would be easy."

Mitch imagined it would. He would never stop grieving Tiffany's death. Every time he pictured her like a broken doll, he... Well, he understood Conchita's point only too well. And as horrific as Tiffany's death and the gross failure on his part in preventing it were, what the Rosaleses had endured, and were still enduring living here... *Jesus*.

"So if we can save Ian," Charlie said, "to some degree the wrongs of your nephew and son's deaths will be offset." Mitch translated for her, and Charlie searched their faces.

"You said three," Mitch said, but he already thought he knew.

Conchita nodded. "Our daughter. We will likely die, or worse, helping you. All of us."

Conchita explained, and it was as Mitch had guessed. They wanted their daughter, Chita, to have safe passage and asylum in the States. They wanted her far out of reach of the Valdez family. Conchita's childhood friend would take the girl in—and no one would know that connection.

"As long as you can secure papers under a new name. We do not want her living on the run and hiding forever. We want her to have a chance at a real future."

Mitch's throat was tight. They wanted their daughter to have a future so badly that they would put their own lives in danger for justice and give her up forever.

No matter what happened with Ian, he'd have to do better than that.

36

———————

"The *quinceañera* for our very own Dia has been officially set for this weekend," Lazaro announced at the midday meal from the head of the table. "It will be a celebration like never before. Be ready, as I'm planning an overdue surprise."

Shouts and clapping went up from the family, the extended family, even the servants. They'd been wondering about a blood ceremony ever since they'd realized Ian was family—and Lazaro just all but confirmed it.

Normally, Lazaro wouldn't combine it with a *quinceañera*—however, the Sinaloa Cartel had been encroaching on his territory lately. They wanted more and more territory always, and a bigger piece of the fentanyl trade. Lazaro had hoped that with Joaquín "El Chapo" Guzmán out of the way, the cartel would cease to be a problem. But it had gone the other way.

The Valdezes desperately needed a show of strength and of a solid family unit. Lazaro could wait no longer.

"Dia," he said, and his niece stood. "We shall honor

you as you deserve. Please try not to have bark in your hair and salve on your hands. Flowers and jewelry this time, yes?"

Laughter from the crowd and a wink from Dia before she sat. Yes, sass. None of the other girls would dare.

Lucia hissed at her. His sister had been taught many lessons—did not want her winking daughter to suffer the same.

Lazaro shrugged mentally. No one escaped punishment if it was necessary—but so far, Dia had been lucky. She was a favorite among the family and staff. Smart, practical, and wild—though not so much as to be true trouble. They knew that one day, she would be their best bet for wellness and healing.

"Tonight, eat in good health and anticipation, for Saturday, we feast."

More hooting, clapping of hands, and clinking of glassware. He raised his glass and looked down the length of the table.

"To the Valdez family."

Guadalupe's face hardened, as always, at the toast. Lazaro longed to spit the wine right in her eyes. They could have had a promising union. She understood his role. She valued status and condoned—even embraced—violence. But no—she could not bear sons, not even whoring herself out in the trying. It might be different if she'd been loyal, but she had not.

He'd love to spit also at Lucia, the traitor. All daughters in plain sight, while she kept a healthy son—a promise for the future—hidden away in the States.

Of course, Lazaro would have greatly preferred his

own son, a full-blood heir rather than a half-blood bastard, but beggars could not be choosers. In this one thing, Lazaro was a beggar. Fury at that, as always, coursed through his veins, but outwardly, he controlled it.

Lazaro sat, setting down his glass and carefully dabbing his mouth with his napkin, then arranging it over his slacks. He took up his fork and began to eat as he surveyed the family once more.

Ah yes, there it was again—that extra spark between Salvadora and Ian. Lazaro had been watching the two since the beginning. Of late, Salvadora's hatred of Ian had a new edge to it. And whereas before the boy had largely ignored her, now his eyes seemed to spit back. Something had happened between them. Desire and distrust would make for an interesting marriage.

Lazaro might have to start taking Salvadora along on excursions again. For years she'd been the only one of this disappointing pack of girls who showed any interest. Of course, the others were too young as well.

He'd stopped for two reasons. One, Jorge. He was too...interested. Lazaro had caught him cornering the girl on more than one occasion. She was slippery and fast with her knife. But Jorge had brute strength, extreme single-mindedness, and an inability to assess consequences. He could easily accidentally kill her, as he had others. Or impregnate her—though it was possible he also could not bear sons, or even worthless daughters. None of the servants or villagers had thus far swelled with his seed.

Even now the imbecile was leaning forward, eyes locked on Salvadora's breasts. She held her head high and refused to look in his direction, although Lazaro knew she was fully aware.

Jorge's fist sat on the table, a fork sticking straight up out of it. His other hand was hidden under the table, but the elbow jutted out and moved rhythmically.

"Jorge," Lazaro said under his breath, but with a bite.

Jorge did not react, so Lazaro wrapped his fingers around his cane, angled it just so, and jabbed hard at Jorge's crotch.

Jorge grunted and pouted, but his arm returned to the table.

This family. Lazaro scowled as disgust swamped him. For all his accomplishments and successes, he had been saddled with simpletons, liars, whores, and weaklings.

Not to mention power-hungry jackals. That was the second reason he'd stopped educating Salvadora. She—along with her mother—were too power hungry.

Lazaro considered wedding the girl to Ian. He had the blood, but Lazaro was not yet sure about his character—the blood ceremony would be illuminating even for him. Salvadora, however, was ruthless enough to keep them on top.

Except Lazaro could not be sure that once he himself was gone that she wouldn't slit Ian's neck with one of her ever-present knives.

No, a marriage was likely not in the cards. Better to tether Ian to his mother and half-sisters. Already, he was growing closer to Lucia and Dia. A bit more time and he would feel bound to the little girls as well.

Blackmail was effective. Bribery, too. But bonds of the

heart—one more web spun. Yes, that was the best way to ensure Ian was caught forever.

37

After siesta, Ian and Dia were sprawled out in the shade under the lemon tree because the temperature was in the low eighties this afternoon, and even warmer in the sun. Really, though, it was because Lazaro had gone off with some of the guards to do…Ian didn't want to know what. The freak wanted Ian to learn the business—but whatever today was, Ian was left out, and that was a major relief. He wouldn't have sprawled if Lazaro was in residence, though Dia probably would.

He wondered how she managed it, how she balanced being her and living here. Far as he could tell, everybody was on edge in this place—adults and children, family and staff.

Today, with Lazaro out, the entire household was visibly more relaxed. Like an invisible cloak of doom had been lifted. Even the children—young enough to be clueless—ran and giggled with more abandon.

Lately, Ian had been feeling a strange longing to get to know the Braid Contingent. It was completely at odds with his desire to escape Lazaro and this nightmare and return to his old life. He wanted to shake his younger self—the one who'd felt so trapped and isolated and unloved, who'd turned to a bad crowd for a shallow sense of belonging and drugs as a means of escape.

It was almost unfathomable. His dad was overprotective and not the best communicator, but Ian had been loved and safe and secure his whole life. And now, perhaps, he understood a little better the reason they'd lived as they had. There'd been a reason his dad kept him so close, essentially under lock and key in private, gated properties with state-of-the-art security and a staff dedicated to the endeavor.

He'd been afraid of...this. That Ian would be stolen away and indoctrinated into a life of violence and crime. If he were younger, he'd either have not remembered a previous life, or perhaps wouldn't have cared. He imagined he would have been thrilled to have a mother and siblings.

Lucia. His *mother*. Ian still could hardly believe it.

Most days he felt pretty damn conflicted. Sometimes, he'd want to run from the yearning in Lucia's eyes. She often wore a stern expression—trying hard, he thought, to keep all the girls out of Lazaro's path, all the young women out of Jorge's, and her obvious love from inadvertently making them a sacrifice. And yet he felt her joy—and terror—at having her long-lost son near.

He could tell she tried not to push, but was desperate to get to know him, grateful for every crumb of insight and information he allowed her. Sometimes, he ached to know her, too.

It had occurred to him that either way, his time here

was probably short. He wasn't interested in playing Lazaro's long-term game. Not with Lazaro, not with Salvadora, and not solo. Not even for Lucia. So what did that leave?

Escape or death. Pretty much the only two choices. The first would surely cause serious pain—maybe ongoing —for Lucia. Lazaro certainly knew what threats worked. No way could Ian stand seeing Lucia beaten. The second, well…

So, yeah. Not a lot of time.

It made him feel weird. Maudlin and lonely.

But he'd spent his whole life feeling lonely—just him and his dad and a bunch of staff to keep him insulated from connecting with many people. Here he was, with a mother—one who'd abandoned him, of course, but at least not willingly—and a whole passel of half-sisters.

He and Dia were okay. Good, even. She was easy. They spent time together often enough, but there was never an agenda and zero emotional pressure—unlike the suppressed longing felt from Lucia.

One of the girls skipped toward them, lost in her own world, until her nose was right over his bare foot. She looked up, wide-eyed.

He smiled, but she spun and darted away.

"Why are they so scared of me?" They reminded him of sand crabs. They'd poke their heads up, come a few steps nearer, stare at him with fascination—and then skitter back to their holes to hide.

He wasn't that scary. He didn't have six legs. He wasn't that broad or tall or ugly.

Dia propped herself up on her elbows. "My sisters?"

Just then, a ball rolled to him and the girl chasing it stopped dead in her tracks rather than approach. He sat up, picked it up, and was about to throw it.

"Wait. Come here," Dia told the girl.

Cautiously, the girl did.

"Ana, right?" Ian smiled. She nodded shyly. "Here you go." He handed her the ball, and she took off like a jackrabbit.

"I don't know," Dia said. "They know my mom likes you, but I guess they've never had any experience with brothers or boys. You're the first and only."

"Might have more to do with the fact that the only men they know carry machine guns. Or canes." Because to him, Lazaro was the bigger fear.

Everybody knew what those guns did—and, at least, *poof*, it'd be over like that. But Lazaro? Who knew what new horror might come from Lazaro?

That might be beyond the children, though. For these girls, Jorge would also be terrifying. He had a habit of leering at all the younger women. He preferred his fists, but carried a handgun and wore a knife.

"How come you aren't scared of me?"

"As you say, there are bigger things to be wary of." Dia rubbed a circle in the clay dirt with the toe of her shoe. "Besides"—she flashed a grin—"scared doesn't suit me."

He chuckled. "True. And if you are going to be a doctor, you can't let them intimidate you."

A wash of protectiveness flooded him. He didn't want any of these girls to be scared. It sucked.

"Maybe we should play a game with them."

Dia raised an eyebrow. "I'm enjoying being lazy."

"Perfect timing. No Lazaro."

"Why do you want them to like you?"

He looked away. It wasn't about them liking him. It was…complicated.

Ian watched the girls for a moment. Watched one of the serving women come from a side door that led somehow to the kitchens. Watched a guard dozing in the shade of an archway that led—he didn't know where.

He had it. "Hide-and-seek."

"What? No." Dia groaned. "I'm too old."

"I'm not. I love hide-and-seek." It was a very practical game.

———

TURNED OUT THE GIRLS WERE MAD FOR HIDE-AND-seek. They also liked piggyback rides, so Tierra and Bebe decided if Ian found them, he should carry them on his back while searching for the others. Most of the time, Mico hid with one of them, and the monkey wasn't exactly quiet. All four little girls also loved building sheet forts in the nursery and had made Ian crawl under and tell them a story last night before bed.

But hide-and-seek was their jam. Ian had played more hours in the last couple of days than he had in his whole childhood. That probably wasn't saying much, given his solitary childhood, but still.

It worked out well. They took his mind off things and were no longer scared of him. Best of all, he now had a whole map of the compound in his head, from the upper floors to the tunnels below. Not all the tunnels—a couple were heavily guarded and the girls avoided them. But there were a couple that could certainly be useful. One led from under the kitchens to the outside of the house. It seemed to have been some sort of root cellar, with an outside entrance that had later been expanded to connect with another tunnel. Three converged right under the shady end of the courtyard, where Lazaro and the other elders sat after dinner.

Ian wasn't sure yet how all this would be useful, but if he was ever to get out of here, it was important knowledge.

Today he was in search of the youngest, Bebe (not her real name, but apparently the only name she went by). She got antsy if she had to wait too long, and came running.

He poked his head in the closet under the stairs, one of the entrances to the tunnels, but it was too dark. Bebe wouldn't hide there by herself.

On to the kitchens. The cook had music blasting and was chopping away, but Ian thought he heard a noise from the storeroom. He pulled open the door and stopped dead. Jorge was pounding into Florencia, his hands manacling hers to the wall. She looked right at Ian over his shoulder. She was crying, and there was a red handprint on her face and blood dribbling from her lip, but she mouthed, "Shh."

Ian stepped forward and reached for Jorge's shirt to pull him off her. Then—

He registered the patter of little feet approaching from behind him. *Oh no.* He dropped his hand and squeezed his eyes shut. The he forced himself to look at Florencia. He hoped she could read that he was sorry.

He closed the door behind him just in time.

"We can't find her! Where is she?" A chorus of girlish voices, plus tugs on his arms, his shirt.

Ian opened his mouth, but had to try twice before sound came out. "This way," he said, and led them away.

When they finally scattered, Ian doubled back to the kitchens. It had only been minutes, but he saw Florencia crossing the courtyard and heard Jorge laughing with a guard outside the kitchens. That fucker was smoking a cigarette like nothing had happened.

Ian ducked into the dining room and leaned against the wall. He felt sick—chances were good this went on all the time and everyone knew—and also relieved, because Jorge would likely have killed him if he intervened.

As he stood there, he heard Bebe's chirpy little voice. He followed it and vowed that he'd do what he could to protect his sisters from that man.

He found Bebe in a small alcove off the hall between the dining room and kitchen. He tried to forget what he'd seen and pasted on a smile.

There was no door, and he whipped back the curtain even as he said, "You're supposed to be quiet, silly."

Bebe's eyes went wide, and she giggled. Mico jumped up and down next to her, screeching in excitement.

Ian blinked. They were on a small bench, and Bebe had a phone pressed to her ear—a monstrous black receiver with a curly cord that stretched to the base on the wall.

His heart raced. Did it work?

She bounced up and down on her bum with excitement. She *loved* to be found. Had the game all backward.

"Who are you talking to?"

"Pi Pi."

Ian deflated. Pi Pi was her imaginary friend.

Bebe held the receiver out. "She wants to talk to you."

Surely she wasn't actually talking to anyone—but Ian's heart rate picked up all the same.

Mico swayed side to side beside her, also watching Ian. He cleared his throat and put the receiver to his ear. "Pi Pi?"

Silence.

"Pi Pi, are you there?"

He pressed the metal hook on the base down a couple of times.

Nothing, just dead air. His hopes sank like there was a cement block tied to his feet. *Shit.* Of course it didn't work. It was an ancient relic.

Bebe frowned up at him. "You hung up on her."

He set the receiver on the hook.

He forced a smile and poked her in the belly. "I think your Pi Pi hung up on *me!*"

She giggled. "Your turn."

"My turn what? We have to go seek your sisters."

She shook her head emphatically. "You have to call someone."

He shook his head, but she stood on the bench, lifted the receiver, and stuck a tiny finger in the dial. "*Uno…cinco…ocho.*"

"That's *tres,*" he corrected her.

She ignored him. "*Siete…ocho…nueve.* Here." She thrust the phone so hard against his ear that he thought he might end up with cauliflower ear.

"Hello?" He played along, talking to no one. "Hi, it's me. How are you?"

"Who are you talking to?" Bebe whispered in a voice barely softer than her regular volume. Mico sucked on the end of Bebe's braid.

"My dad," he told her. Because…well, just because.

She waved her little hand at him, like *go on, then*.

Ian stared at that beast of a phone with its funny round dial and all the black numbers.

"Hi, Dad." He shut his eyes against tears. "I miss you."

38

Mitch was leaning hard on his contacts in the DEA. Getting a promise of asylum, and even falsified documents, for the Rosales girl was easy. Pushing them to act? Not so much. Word in narcotics circles was that the Sinaloa Cartel was planning to take down the Valdezes by force. No one could say exactly when or where, but they believed it would be by month's end. But did that mean the end of March? Mid-March? What? The *quinceañera* was this Saturday, March fifth.

He wanted an official unit—or ten—to raid the Valdez compound. He wanted them to take over, to gather up all their evidence, finally determine it was enough for a sting, and just friggin' take Valdez down, rescuing Ian in the process. But the agency contacts he spoke with weren't about to go in unless they could nail him for good. Plus they seemed perfectly okay with letting Sinaloa handle the Valdezes. One less cartel for them to deal with.

Which sucked, because he and Charlie were not

equipped for this. Charlie was going to get killed—or worse, captured—and he'd never forgive himself.

If he was even alive to forgive himself, that was.

Mitch hung up from contact number five and swore as he smacked his cell phone down onto the table.

"Why are you trying so hard? We have a plan." She dipped her head to one side then the other, cracking her neck.

"It's not much of a plan." He didn't want to freak her out. He knew she was determined to go in no matter what before Sinaloa did, and the more confident she felt, the better. But God, he hated every single bit of it.

It was to be just the two of them along with Enrique and Conchita in their catering van. The story was that their daughter was ill, so they were short a set of hands. They'd temporarily hired the Americans, who were back-packers who'd run out of money and been asking every-where for work. They didn't want to say they were connected—friends or family—in case there was a way Enrique and Conchita could escape blame in the long run.

Fat chance.

"Lazaro won't like it. Two *gringos* out of nowhere when he's just stolen an American? It's a terrible plan."

Charlie opened her mouth.

"We're just *hoping* we see Ian at this party—*alone*—and somehow from your spot in the kitchens, since all Conchita does is bring the food and make sure it's beauti-ful, and Lazaro's staff serves it. *Hoping* we can somehow sneak him away and into the van. Meanwhile, Stephen Cross is insisting he come along in the van. Which we can't figure out a cover for and is just insane." Mitch paced their tiny flat with all the pent-up fear and frustration he felt.

"And then," he said, "because why not, we're already counting on miracles—we'll just count on one more: no one even notices Ian's gone." He threw up his hands in mock celebration. "We just load up the van and drive away into the sunset without anyone the wiser—not a single shot fired." He wanted to smash something. "Perfect, since we have hardly any firepower."

All the people he'd spoken to advised against them trying to extract Ian on their own, but had promised that their contacts would get him some firepower and some grenades. At this very moment, they had nothing but Mitch's Glock and a few knives they'd bought here in Mexico.

Charlie rubbed her arms. "A day ago, we didn't have a way in. Another day or two, and we'll have weapons."

"Even with weapons we're at a serious disadvantage. We don't know the compound—"

"That guy you just talked to said he'd send aerial photos and whatever."

Mitch shook his head. All those guards with guns, all those people loyal to—or at least dependent on—Lazaro. They had no idea if Ian was locked up like a prisoner or free to roam the place at will. Even if he was treated like family, was he willing to leave? Did he want to return to his father? Or would he prefer to stay with his mother— and all those tempting drugs—given that his father had lied to him his whole life?

Lucia's letter said she'd return him to the States if she could, but how did Ian feel?

They could be risking their lives for *nothing*.

Mitch's shoulders were so tight that he felt like he could snap the muscle.

How could Mitch let Charlie feel confident enough to pull this off and yet prepare her enough to see all the problems here?

He couldn't. This was a suicide mission. No amount of confidence or blind faith was going to make this shitshow succeed.

"Remember when we discussed you stepping back when it got too dangerous?"

"No." Charlie's hands slammed to her hips.

"We're there, Charlie."

"No," she said. "I am not backing out now. I don't care if it's not safe."

"It's so much worse than not safe!" Mitch had to adjust his volume down. The woman they rented from was downstairs. "We're going to get killed. And we're probably going to get other people killed in the process."

"I have to try. He might not recognize you. He might—"

"Ian will recognize me. But either way, we don't even know if he'll be willing to come."

"I can talk him into it. I need to be there."

That was the same reason Cross had given him, but Mitch didn't plan on letting Cross set one foot out of the van.

Mitch shook his head, returning to the problem of Ian. "I can talk with him just as easily. Or I can always knock him out." Although it'd be a helluva lot easier if he'd go willingly.

There was an idea. Mitch could knock Charlie out at the last minute—leave her here in this room.

No. If there was one thing he couldn't do, it was take away Charlie's choice. She'd been controlled for years by that sick bastard, unable to attain a single ounce of her own agency—and that might even have been worse for her than the actual sexual abuse.

So no, he couldn't. She'd never forgive him.

Charlie's body was strung tight, her gestures angry. "There is no way I'm sitting here, just waiting for you, wondering if you'll make it."

"How do you think I feel?"

"Like a know-it-all bully?"

He snorted. "I know enough to know this is a death-trap of our own making. I cannot put your life at risk here."

"Have you forgotten our partnership? We are supposed to be going into business *together*. We are *both* getting paid to get Ian back."

"We aren't going into business or getting paid if we're dead!"

"At least we'd be dead together." She spat the words—it wasn't some *Romeo and Juliet* declaration of undying love.

"How about we don't go at all?"

Her eyes bugged out.

He held up a hand. "Hear me out. Maybe we leak word about the Sinaloa attack. Valdez would pick up and move out of the mountains, out of their range, and into hiding somewhere else. Then we just wait for the DEA to take Valdez down. They could extract Ian then—when there are teams in place and all the support."

"That could take years." She was aghast.

"Not if we helped. We could stay here and gather evidence, find someone to turn."

She shook her head. "Still *years*. God only knows what could happen to Ian by then. He's a recovering drug addict sitting in the middle of his worst nightmare. And look at that poor kid in the square and Enrique and Conchita's son. Ian very well might not live years. Beyond that—if it doesn't work and the Sinaloas go in? They'll slaughter everyone, right? They aren't going to take time to figure out there's a new kid who had nothing to do with any of it!" She threw her hands up. "Or hey—maybe they'd take prisoners, and then how would we get him back from an even bigger cartel?"

She shook her head. "Any which way we look at, if we don't act now, he's as good as dead."

"But Charlie, you and I would *live*. Enrique and Conchita would *live*."

Disgust was written all over her face—but he wasn't trying to be a bastard. He was trying to save lives.

She snatched up her boots and flung herself into a chair.

"Ian might die if we *do* go in, Charlie. It's a suicide mission—for him, for us, for anyone in the crossfire." He threw up his hands. "How many lives are worth trying and failing? How many lives are you willing to sacrifice?"

Her hands stilled on the boots, and she looked at him hard. "If I say I'll stay here or go home, you'll find a way to go without me, right?"

He wasn't going to say it, but yeah. It had about killed him to watch that boy beaten to death in the street. He wouldn't abandon Ian, but he'd definitely prefer to take his chances alone.

She snorted. "I knew it. And what am I supposed to do if you die, alone? Huh, Mitch?" She stood. "Go back and face Thomas Weihle in the courtroom by myself?"

"You wouldn't be alone. You—"

"I support my mom, not the other way around, and you damn well know it. And don't even start with Mackenzie. She *has* parents. And Henrietta's just fine. She's got family." She blew out a hard breath. "You don't want me to be a part of this, and I don't want to do the rest of it alone—so where the hell does that leave me?"

Mitch opened his mouth.

"I never expected to have some long life. And even if I miraculously got one, I always knew it would never be a big life." She deflated. "These last months with you—and yes, being reunited with my mom and my daughter—have been the best of my life. Better than all my childhood years combined. It's enough. If I die because I saved Ian, or even just died in the trying, *at least* I will have tried, and I'll die far happier than I ever dreamed possible."

Mitch wanted to point out that she'd already led a big life and saved a life—she'd defeated Weihle and saved Mackenzie—but he understood. He really did. It wasn't so much the tally marks as the kind of person you were. She was a good person, through and through, with a strong sense of right and wrong. She couldn't ignore someone in need. She would have made a fine cop, first responder, or military recruit.

"I'm going in with you, and that's that. And if you bring it up one more time"—Charlie gave him a warning look—"we're still going, but we're done. You'll lose me anyway."

"That's so fucking unfair."

She shrugged as she wriggled the wig into place. Then she snatched up her backpack and walked out, slamming the door behind her.

God damn her. She wouldn't listen to reason. Who was acting like a bully now?

Mitch sank to the bed and put his head in his hands. He squeezed hard, pressing his fingers into his skull.

He knew they both needed to cool off, but he didn't even like her out in Pase Viejo without him, let alone putting herself at risk in the Valdez compound. It was called Spider's Rest for a reason, dammit.

He had only two people in the world, really. If he did this for Charlie…

Then he needed to call his mom and say goodbye, because he couldn't count on a miracle here.

39

"I NEED TO SPEAK WITH YOU IN PRIVATE," LUCIA SAID, having come up beside Ian in one of the long walkways of the compound.

She wore her usual calm expression, but Ian saw that her eyes looked almost panicky.

"What about?"

She shook her head, barely. "Not here."

Sometimes she still brought breakfast to his room, but it was past breakfast now, and he could feel her urgency. "A walk? After siesta?" he said.

"I'll meet you on the patio."

Ian continued on to the gym, which Lazaro had recently granted him access to.

Salvadora was coming the other way, from target practice, surely, as her cheeks were flushed and her hair windblown.

He waited to see what she would do. Sometimes she flipped him off. Sometimes she gave him a death stare.

Today might be different, as they were the only two in this short corridor.

She held his eyes as they neared. She licked her lips suggestively, and he tensed. Damn, he'd been trying so hard not to think about her naked body pressed against his.

Then, just as she passed him, she said, "Coward."

He shook his head and kept going. Self-preservation was not cowardice. And yet he hit the treadmill hard.

Ian hated being in there with a guard staring at him and with other guards also working out, their beady eyes always assessing, but the days were torturously long. He only allowed himself to hide in his room when he really couldn't stand it. If he ever wanted to get out of here, he had to learn the place, the people, and the routines. Just as important, they had to get used to him. Eventually, he'd become less noticed—less like a scary invasive species and more like a regular ant, one of the many, just following the colony along.

He had no job, no purpose here, nothing to fill the hours unless Lazaro decided there was something to show him—which happened, but randomly. He played hide-and-seek and gave piggyback rides to the Braid Contingent whenever Lazaro attended to business—probably counting his bricks of drugs and torturing prisoners in those adjacent rooms. Ian shuddered. He tried not to think about it.

He would like to hang more often with Dia, but she did have a purpose. If she wasn't helping someone or making some salve or some such, she was studying her medical books. Lazaro had even allowed her to take a couple of online courses; basic biology was one. She hoped the *patrón* would let her go to university—ideally in the States, though she knew that was probably a pipe dream.

At six miles and dripping sweat, he shifted to sit-ups and push-ups and a few reps with weights, then figured he was pushing the timing. He didn't want to be late for any meal, nor show up stinking of BO.

He had no idea what triggered Lazaro's anger, but he'd noticed nobody was ever late and everyone appeared groomed. He'd follow their lead—again, under the radar and biding time—and allow time for a shower.

When he finally joined Lucia on the patio, she stood among a watering can, a shovel, a small tree, and a small bag of fertilizer.

"What's that?" he asked.

"A lemon tree. Please." She gestured for him to bring it.

"Huh." It looked different that the big lemon tree he'd sat under with Dia, but of course this thing must be in its infancy.

He held the pot with one arm and carried the watering can with the other. Awkward but not heavy. Lucia took the shovel and propped the fertilizer on her hip like she still carried Bebe sometimes.

She crossed the courtyard and kept on going, passing through one of the breezeways.

Salvadora was back at the target range again—where she spent all her time, as far as he could tell—and appeared to be pacing off steps before she threw. He tore his eyes away.

"Where are we going?"

"It will not grow in this dark place," Lucia said.

Ian lifted an eyebrow. There was plenty of sun in the courtyard. The other lemon tree had grown just fine there.

On the far side of that building, she headed for a small grove of trees. "Here." She made an X in the dirt with the point of the shovel close to the others—but not close enough that it would be shadowed or a larger tree's stronger roots would leech its rare rainwater.

"My mother planted these, to represent the children they expected to leave."

His forehead furrowed.

"She expected her girls to marry and go live in their husband's family homes." Lucia sighed, seeing that he didn't understand. "I had sisters. They died very young. Lazaro and Jorge's trees are in the courtyard. They were expected to stay within the family walls."

"The tree I sit under. The biggest one?"

"Lazaro's."

Ian's skin crawled. And to think he'd found the spot peaceful.

"Jorge's is the shriveled one behind."

"Figures."

"Yes."

There were more trees than just those. Scraggly things, most of them, but there must have been other boys who died as well. Although he had no idea if this was only her mother's thing, or went back generations. Did it matter?

He picked up the shovel, stabbed it into the earth, stepped atop the blade, and put his body weight to work. The earth was hard and dry. He was sweating before long.

Lucia held her elbows, wiped her hands on her skirt,

tucked them in her deep pockets, pulled out a small rag, put it back, held her elbows… All the while she watched his progress with a look of intense concentration.

Little by little, Ian managed to dig a hole large enough to fit the base of the little lemon tree. He wiped his brow and tucked the shovel into the crook of his arm, his right hand resting atop the handle.

She knelt, her skirt puffing before settling. Around the root ball, she poured rich, dark soil—so unlike the unforgiving earth here, either rock or dense clay. She smoothed it with her bare hands, then pulled the rag from her skirt to dust them off. She stood and retrieved the watering can, looking so serious as she soaked the roots.

When it was done, she dropped the can with a thud and crossed herself.

He waited until she looked at him. "Are you pregnant?"

Her eyes went wide. "*Mon Dios.* No."

"Then who is the tree for?"

She shut her eyes for a long moment before speaking. "It is for you. I never wanted this, not any of this"—she waved a hand vaguely—"for you. I want nothing more than for you to live again beyond these walls."

He couldn't smile. "You and me both."

She looked distraught. "I do not know if it is possible. Hard as I try, I can't think of anything—anything that will work. And now…"

He couldn't decide if she was about to explode from rage or implode from hopelessness.

Ian couldn't imagine what could have possibly

changed to make him any more stuck here than he already was. He forced himself to ask, "What's happened?"

"It's what's going to happen." She took a deep breath, fortifying herself. "There will be a blood ceremony—during Dia's *quinceañera*."

"A blood ceremony?"

"It's like a swearing of an oath."

"Oh. Okay." He scratched his nose. This must have been what Lazaro alluded to—the surprise. "Isn't a *quinceañera* supposed to be about celebrating the girl's transition to womanhood, but really just a big party?" Yikes, blood ceremony? Surely it wasn't anything to do with menstrual cycles or maidenheads?

"Yes, but it's so rare to have the other associates and clients come that I believe Lazaro has decided to incorporate the blood ceremony—without telling them. Years ago, it would have been its own event. Everyone would have been prepared—anticipating—" She shook her head.

He cocked his head. "So who does this involve, then? What is it, like, some blood brothers thing where they slice their palms and press them together?" He raised the shovel and shook it like William Wallace and his Scots. "Blood brothers forever!"

"This isn't a joke!"

He shrugged. "Tell me, then. Because..." He shrugged. "No idea."

She sank to the ground, half on the wet earth, half on the dry, and for a second he thought she was going to fall right over onto the little lemon tree. Instead, she prostrated herself beside it, head bowed, and then looked up at him tears in her eyes. "It's for you…to prove your loyalty. You will have to kill someone."

Ian just stared, trying in vain to comprehend. He shook his head hard. "I already did. That prisoner."

She crushed her shirt in her hands, right over her heart, and whispered, "That was his choice. This time, there will be no drugs and he will make *you* choose."

"Make me choose…" Ian felt like his brain had sunk in quicksand.

"Who to kill." Her voice was barely more than a whisper. "It is supposed to prove what kind of leader you will be."

"No. I won't. I won't do that."

"You will have to. Or—or—"

They stared at each other, both with the knowledge that Lazaro had threatened her before—if Ian didn't comply, Lucia paid.

She jumped up and grasped his hands, pulling them to her chest. "I would willingly pay the price—with my life, even—to save you this, but he won't let us off that easy." She looked up at him with abject fear.

He simply couldn't fathom. He'd thought what Lazaro had already put him through was the worst, but…

"It could be Dia." Lucia squeezed his hands in a death grip and her eyes welled with tears. "Or the girls? I don't know. I never know what horror he will think up."

40

Charlie and Mitch spent an uneasy night together, avoiding touching in the small bed. But upon waking, Mitch knew there was no hope for it. She was coming. He simply had to do his absolute best to make sure they all survived.

"Come here," he said, and tugged her arm until she rolled to face him. Her chin was set even though he knew she'd just awoken. "You have to do every single thing I say when we're in there, you understand?"

Her eyes remained serious. "Okay, yes."

Her agreement didn't release an ounce of the heavy weight of doom he felt. He heaved out a breath and rested his forehead against hers.

They went out to get breakfast, and he had to force the food past the tightness taking up permanent residence in his throat.

They were just returning to their room when Mitch's phone rang.

"Hang on. Let us get inside." To Charlie, he mouthed, "It's Cross."

Mitch took the stairs two at a time, Charlie right behind him. As soon as they were inside, he switched to speakerphone.

"How'd you do?"

Like Mitch, Cross had been working every contact—political and financial—to see if they could put pressure on the appropriate agencies to act.

"I didn't. I got fucking nowhere."

Charlie and Mitch exchanged a glance. It was unlike Cross to swear.

"I'm not surprised," Mitch said.

"Well, I am. I can't reconcile a kid—my *son*—being kidnapped by a known criminal and no one in law enforcement remotely willing to do a thing about it." Cross's voice rose. "This is their job!"

Mitch understood the disbelief and anger. He also understood that any government agency would absolutely make trade-offs to keep the cases they'd spent years building intact. They wanted to nail Lazaro Valdez to the wall with indisputable evidence—decades of it. They weren't going to risk allowing him to operate forever to save one kid.

"And they threatened me with jail time if I acted in a way that messed up their carefully laid plans."

"Great," Charlie muttered, but Mitch almost wished they would. It would keep Cross safe in the States.

"I don't care what they say. I'm getting my son back."

Mitch said, "Ransom is not going to work. He doesn't

need money. One way or another, this is about family." They'd talked about this. More than once.

"I know. So we'll have to stick with the plan, even though it's dicey," Cross said, and Mitch's heart sank all over again.

Charlie wrapped her arms across her chest and looked at him steadily. She didn't say *I told you so* or *two against one*, but here they were.

Cross hated the plan almost as much as Mitch. Charlie had been the only one in support. The words *suicide mission* flashed through Mitch's head again so loud he almost missed Cross's next words.

"I hired a team to back you up. And you got your wish. I'm staying stateside, but ready to fly."

"You what? Who?" Relief almost made Mitch's knees wobble.

"It's a black ops team—used to be SEALs and the like but got tired of being government puppets. I don't know the whole story, and I don't care. They've convinced me that I'm needed on this end. Someone's got to be able to try again if things go haywire, and I'm the only one who might be able to pull it off."

"That's smart," Charlie said, and Mitch could see that she was relieved as well. Cross would have stuck out like a bear in a beehive down here.

"A burner phone will be delivered overnight," Cross told them.

"Delivered to where?"

"I don't know, but they'll make sure you get it. You won't see them. They'll stay under the radar."

"Good."

Charlie and Mitch had already been in place for several days. They'd booked more nights with the landlady, and Charlie had even logged a couple of shifts at the caterers so that it seemed less of a stretch for the Rosaleses to bring Charlie along to help with the party. All groundwork for the cover story. As yet, it was unclear what Mitch's role would be. Five more outsiders would definitely be out of the norm for this rinky-dink town.

Cross said. "They'll call with instructions."

Mitch felt something unfamiliar niggle at him—a tiny bit of hope. Maybe this meant they had a decent shot. Maybe this meant Charlie wouldn't be going in after all.

41

This morning, Ian was in search of Salvadora and knew just where to find her: target practice.

He'd been given a lot more freedom lately. Lazaro knew he wasn't about to risk earning Lucia a beating. The guards had given up watching him run around to entertain his little sisters and sometimes the youngest Gomez girls, too. Maybe they all thought he was on board now, embracing this family and way of life.

He wasn't. Fuck them.

The target range was set up on the east side of the south wing, as opposed to the small grove where Lucia had planted his lemon tree, which was to the west end.

Sure enough, Salvadora stood next to a wooden table, a leather case unrolled on the rough surface. There was also a box full of knives—pulled from a shallow, but open, shed to her left.

He'd assumed the structure was full of weapons; he hadn't seen inside before. *Wow.* Guns, knives, boxes of ammo...even more boxes were stacked on the floor. He couldn't see it all from where he approached, but his pulse quickened. He needed to somehow check out the lock. He needed to know exactly what was in there.

Salvadora stood in one spot and threw one after another. End over end they went. All but one hit the target. She grabbed up a few more, paced forward, and threw. The first missed. She moved half a step forward and tried again, this time hitting the target.

Knife throwing was tough, Ian knew. A weapon that rotated like that had to hit its target just so or it wouldn't embed. Salvadora's constant practice was obviously paying off.

She hadn't turned around but spoke when he was still fifteen feet from her. "What are you doing here, bastard?"

"Thought I'd see if you needed a real body for target practice."

She turned and reached for one of the knives in the leather carrier. It was beautifully carved, and she stroked it with a finger. Salvadora looked up, eyes bright and cunning. "Don't tempt me."

Different circumstances, he might have liked this chick. Certainly they'd have had fun in bed. He still got revved up thinking of that night she'd snuck in and—

She smirked and put one hand on her hip. *Shit*—she knew exactly what he was thinking.

"What do you want?"

"Teach me to throw?"

She made a face. "Why would I do that?"

He shrugged. "You know if we're to be married, it'd be nice if I could protect you."

She snorted. "I heard you can fight."

He shrugged. "I do okay." His martial arts training had, of course, included some knives, nunchucks, and bo staffs. He didn't love weapons like Salvadora did, though. His dad had also insisted he learn to shoot. He'd had decent aim, but he hadn't been to a range in a long while. He would love to get into that shed and be able to practice.

She stared hard at him, trying to figure out his end game. Neither of them wanted to marry. Both of them wanted things that seemed way out of reach. "Did you hear something?"

She meant had he heard that Lazaro intended for them to marry.

"No," he said. "It's something else."

"What?"

He couldn't answer, really. He hadn't figured out what to do, how the hell he was going to get out of this looming trap. He felt the impossibility of protecting Lucia and all her daughters like the world had cinched a garbage bag over his head. He could barely breathe—but he knew giving in to the panic would debilitate him. If he could just figure something decent out, he'd feel better. He had ideas, but there were gaps.

The biggest problem was that he couldn't do it alone.

He shifted his gaze from the targets to Salvadora and looked at her hard. "You want power, right? You want to rule this shitshow, Salvadora?"

She spun and stabbed the knife into the table—*thunk*! Then she faced him with her eyes glittering. "You know I do."

"If I found a way to open a path for you, to give you that—you'd be ready, right? You'd act without hesitation?"

She narrowed her eyes, clearly judging whether he was full of shit.

"I'm dead serious," he said.

She raised her chin and threw her shoulders back—a warrior's pose.

"I need to know. When it comes down to it, can you kill?" He almost didn't care if she did or not, but he'd need the attention on her.

She smiled, and this time her eyes shone with bloodthirsty pleasure. "Oh, yes."

42

———

NO BURNER PHONE HAD MAGICALLY SLIPPED UNDER their door overnight. Nor at the bottom of the stairs.

"Do you think they had trouble?" Charlie asked.

"Even if they did, they'll have figured something out," Mitch said.

They exited into a cool, bright morning and headed for the Rosaleses' catering shop.

Enrique saw them coming and unlocked the front door to let them in. Charlie went straight to the kitchen. She'd been skipping breakfast. Beans at breakfast turned her stomach. As had become habit already, Enrique provided Mitch a meal, and he sat at one of the tables outside, letting himself be seen.

He ate as slowly as he could—just in case someone was going to drop the burner in his lap. But the caterers kept early hours and, of course, the streets were pretty quiet. Someone heading to work. A shop owner opening a store. One drunk still stumbling around from the night before, muttering to himself.

Mitch tried to be patient. They'd get the phone to him or Charlie. Surely Cross had hired the best. Money wasn't an issue, and his son's life was at stake. Unless these guys were balls-to-the-wall crazy, Mitch fully expected to put his trust in the skilled operatives. They'd give them a far better shot at snatching Ian and getting the hell out of the Spider's Rest alive.

When he was finished eating, he balled up his wrapper and went inside to pay and say goodbye. He'd go and try to drum up some work himself at the other establishments to make it look good. Yesterday, he'd earned a free meal unloading deliveries at the same restaurant they ate in the first night.

Charlie came out from the kitchen and kissed him goodbye—taking his hands and pressing something into them.

The burner phone.

"It was in my apron pocket," she whispered.

They had already discussed and agreed not to say anything to Enrique and Conchita about the new team. Not yet, anyway, and not here.

The text that arrived a few hours later instructed them to go to Bifurcación del Diablo that afternoon. Mitch looked it up. Devil's Fork was a scenic overlook, about thirty miles southwest of El Pase Viejo.

They still had the car they arrived with—a junker that they'd been promised had a decent engine. They checked on it every day to make sure it hadn't been stolen. Today, Mitch made sure it still ran under the pretense of topping it off with gas.

The text hadn't specified a time, but man, Mitch wanted to get this meet underway already. He'd feel so much better about this whole thing once they had a decent plan.

He retrieved their cooler from the apartment and bought ice at the corner store, along with a couple of bags of chips and beverages. On the way to meet Charlie after her shift, he chose the street vendor with the shortest line and ended up with empanadas.

"Where are we going?" Charlie asked when she saw the wrapped food in his hand and the cooler slung over his arm.

"It's a surprise," he said, winking at Conchita.

"See you tomorrow?" Charlie asked.

"Yes, come," Conchita said, and went right back to sweeping the floor.

As soon as they hit the street, Mitch grabbed Charlie around the waist and kissed her.

"Ooh, a little PDA," she murmured.

"You bet. This is a date." Far as anybody watching them was concerned, anyway. And right now, Mitch wholeheartedly wished it were true, that he and Charlie were just two carefree lovebirds with a little wanderlust.

When they got in the car, Mitch squeezed Charlie's thigh to get her attention. Then he pressed a finger to his lips.

Charlie nodded and said, "Man, my feet are killing me after that shift. I don't know how those two do it all day every day. Did you find any work today?"

They conversed a bit, then fell silent when they ran out of sort-of-fake things to say. It was hard to talk anyway over the engine and the road noise, especially with the windows down.

When Mitch reached what he thought was a secluded place to pull over, they got out and he swept the undercarriage for trackers. Charlie searched inside for bugs.

All clear.

Mitch hadn't expected to find anything, but he wasn't taking any chances. They'd asked a lot of questions in the surrounding villages.

Back on the road, Charlie asked, "So where are we going?"

"Devil's Fork. From what I can tell, it's a popular pull-off with a good view. It'll be past that waterfall we saw signs for."

"And?"

"And that's it. We were told to come this afternoon." He shrugged.

She nodded, her hair whipping around her face now that they'd picked up speed.

There would likely be a lot of unknowns in the next few days. Mitch should be glad she could roll with things. Instead, he was a little annoyed that she took it in stride. She should be worried—about everything they were doing.

Neither spoke again until Charlie sat forward and pointed to the rough-hewn sign. "There it is. *Bifurcación del Diablo.*"

Mitch turned in. They were the only car, the only people. Unlike points of interest in the States, there were no placards or benches or binoculars on posts. He didn't even spot a garbage can in this flat, dusty parking area.

But there was a gap in the hills that provided a gorgeous view of the rising mountain. Three streams wound through the trees and joined together into one magnificent waterfall. It was unexpected and stunning.

"Wow," Mitch said.

"Uh-huh."

They just stood there for a few minutes taking it in, then Charlie grinned. "We're tourists, right? We need a picture."

They turned around, but Charlie had trouble managing a selfie. "You do it. Your arms are longer."

"All right. Smile."

She tilted her head to his shoulder and grinned. He wasn't sure if he smiled or not. Either way, he prayed it wouldn't be their last picture together.

"Now what?" Charlie asked as she plucked her phone from his hand.

"We eat."

Charlie grabbed the wide-brimmed hats they got in the first town they'd canvassed when they arrived in Mexico. Mitch gathered up the food and the cooler.

The hood of the car was hot between the drive and the sun, but at the edge of the parking area, the ground sloped down to a series of rock shelves. They chose a section of flat rock where they could see the view and still keep an eye on the parking lot.

Charlie unwrapped the empanadas. He ripped open a bag of chips with a little too much force. They spilled, and he ate them right off the dusty rock.

She said, "This is good." A little beef slipped out and onto the back of her other hand, which she licked off.

She looked gorgeous as always, even in the dark wig, though she was likely getting hot.

"Here," he said, and put one of the big hats on her head.

She smiled. "You could almost imagine we really are on a vacation."

"Almost." Would he ever get to take her on a honeymoon? Or would she put him off forever?

Pointless wondering. They had to get the hell out of Mexico alive first.

His eyes strayed to the parking lot.

Charlie reached over and squeezed his hand. It felt like an apology. Because they might never vacation together for real? Because she'd forced him to include her on this too-dangerous mission? Because she'd always hold a part of herself back from him?

Mitch squeezed back and just wished she'd never let go.

43

———

CHARLIE MUST HAVE DOZED OFF. SHE WOKE TO Mitch squeezing her arm. She was roasting under the hat and pulled it aside and sat up. She heard rumbling…motorcycles?

Mitch handed her some water, still relatively cool. He must have just taken it from the cooler. She glugged it down and wiped some over her hot face.

Two men pulled up on bikes and parked about a car's width from Mitch's vehicle. Big and fit, they wore jeans and t-shirts. Both had their eyes covered with reflective shades and wore bandanas around their faces—one red, one navy—which they pulled down as soon as they'd parked.

Charlie shoved her hat on her head to block the sun and get a better look.

Red Bandana was taller and leaner and sported a leather vest with tassels and rivets. Charlie couldn't see his eyes, but his coloring could pass for Mexican. Navy Bandana was nearly as tall, very broad, with a black head wrap and dirty blond hair that reached just past his shoulders.

"Come on." Mitch slung the cooler over his arm.

They both looked like rough, tough dudes—which meant they could be exactly what they appeared to be or could be their guys.

They'd have to pass right by them to get back to their car. Charlie took a deep breath and wondered how exactly they were supposed to start this conversation. *Hey, guys, are you the special ops team? Nobody gave us a password.* She clamped her mouth shut against an inappropriate nervous giggle.

The pair stretched and dug in their saddlebags.

The short walk felt like forever, but finally they were close enough, and Mitch nodded a greeting.

Navy Bandana said, "Hear you could use a little assistance this weekend."

Mitch's mouth twitched. "That's an understatement, but yeah." His shoulders dropped a fraction, and Charlie felt her own tension ease.

"I'm Ren." Navy Bandana pulled off his shades to show friendly eyes and gave them an easy smile. "We call him Chief." He nodded at the taller, vested man who stood wide-legged with his arms crossed. Charlie wondered if that was a title or a nickname or none of the above.

Nobody shook hands. They were all playing it cool, as if this was a random meeting and they were exchanging a few words with fellow travelers. Mitch put the cooler in their car as he said, "There's more of you, right?"

"Three more. Cross told us your plan. It's not bad."

Charlie saw Mitch's shoulders shoot right back up. "It sucks."

"Nah, we can work with it."

"How?" Mitch asked.

Ren brushed some dust off his bike. "You figure out a way for you to come along yet?"

Mitch grimaced. "Not a good one."

Ren looked at Chief, who finally spoke. "Tow truck it is."

Charlie detected a very slight accent but couldn't place it. "What does that mean?"

Ren said, "Catering van isn't running so well. It's gonna have some trouble tomorrow. Mitch here is handy with cars, right? So he'll get in there and fix it. Caterers are worried about the drive, so the handyman comes along. You break down on the way and can't fix it. Here we come in the tow truck."

"All of you?"

"Yeah, but it'll only be comfortable for those of us in the cab."

"Where in the world are the others going to be? Underneath?" Charlie said.

"Don't picture a real tow truck. Think of a big truck with a hitch and a trailer. We'll retrofit the vehicle to hide the guys. Down here, the less official it looks, the better."

"So we'll be arriving a little late to the party," Mitch said.

"Only enough to make them worry a little—and then feel nothing but relief when they see the tow truck. Then it'll be hustle-hustle get the food on inside."

"Conchita says in the past they've parked near the

kitchen end of the compound. So that's good—gets us all inside the gates," Mitch said. "But what then?"

"Since it'll be a scramble, you'll help get food inside but be able to come in and out to look at the truck while we tinker with it and give us updates."

"So you'll unhitch the van and we can drive both vehicles outta there."

"Exactly."

"So how do we get Ian?"

"That part, we play by ear."

Mitch's eyes bugged out. "So we're really sticking with our plan? To just escort him out in broad daylight? You guys don't have any fancy under-the-radar extraction planned. No stealth maneuvers? No explosive diversion?"

Chief raised an eyebrow.

Ren said, "Nope."

"What the hell?" Mitch asked.

"Listen," Ren said. "From what we understand, the Valdez place is riddled with guards with machine guns, and they've got explosives, too. Could we blow the entire compound? Sure. But your friend might be killed right along with how many innocents. And chances are good we wouldn't make it two miles." He crossed his arms over his chest. "Sometimes the simplest thing is the best. It's possible no one will be keeping an eye on the kid. We find out where he is and we just sneak him out, quietly taking care of anyone who gets in the way. This party should keep most everyone occupied. They don't discover what happened until we are long gone. That's the best-case scenario."

Mitch hadn't stopped shaking his head, but Charlie

liked the way Ren told a story. It sounded almost reason-able in that format.

"That doesn't work," Ren continued, "we've got a couple of options. Most of my team remains and stays hidden to attempt a middle-of-the-night extraction, but without our own wheels, that could get dicey. Or if we—or you—are discovered during the attempt, we can always bring out the big guns, grab the kid, and lay down some fire the whole way out."

"You have plenty of firepower? Enough for us as well?"

Ren nodded.

"Grenades. C4?"

"All that and more."

Mitch scrubbed his hands through his hair then pulled them down his face, making him look for a second like a scary Halloween mask.

Charlie wasn't sure what she thought. She didn't know much about special teams. This was a tough situation. She knew there was no magic, no miracle. The element of surprise was on their side. Otherwise, it was basically wit and will. Apparently they just had more wit and will now —and yeah, guns and people who know how to shoot them—along for the ride.

Hopefully a lot of luck was on their side, too.

"You want to back out of this mission?" Ren stretched his arms over his head. "Maybe wait a few weeks or a month or three? Until Lazaro and his top cronies maybe take a little trip and we can go in at night? Just us, not you. We can't stay here—we got other jobs—but we could come back if and when the intel says go."

"Hell yes," Mitch said.

"No. We can't wait," Charlie said at the same time.

Mitch looked ready to blow. "We can't think only of Ian. There are other lives at stake here."

She faced him, hands on hips and nostrils flaring. "Are you forgetting about the Sinaloa Cartel? We don't have months."

From behind her, Chief said, "Sinaloa could fail."

She glared at him and then whipped back to give Mitch the evil eye. "We're not losing this chance. Sinaloa or no Sinaloa, we don't have months. Anything could happen in that length of time. Ian could be dead by then. Besides, the longer we stay, the better chance Lazaro has of finding out about us—and then what happens to Conchita and Enrique and their daughter and even the woman who's renting us the room? The ripple effect could be devastating. Waiting is no safer. Plus, if they find out we're here for Ian, we lose the element of surprise. They lock him down and we never get him back."

Even though Mitch didn't move a muscle, Charlie could see his simmer was about to boil over.

Charlie took a breath, stepped back, and looked at all three men. "Stephen Cross hired all of us. He most definitely won't want us to wait."

Chief almost smiled.

Ren cocked his head to the side and said, "So which is it?"

Mitch swore.

44

As it turned out, Ian didn't have to sneak out to inspect the shed. Lazaro had his own preparations in the works for the blood ceremony. He and three guards roused Ian from bed and escorted him to the range.

"What's this about?" Ian asked.

Lazaro asked, "Do you know how to handle a gun?"

Ian shifted on his feet. He'd already begun to sweat. He didn't trust Lazaro for a second and feared the psycho would tie a person to the targets or some other sick shit. How to answer?

"Yes or no?"

Ian shifted on his feet. "Kind of."

Lazaro stared at him, unblinking and expressionless.

"It's been a long time," Ian said.

Lazaro inclined his head, and one of the guards nudged Ian toward the shed.

"Pick one," Lazaro called.

There were all kinds of weapons, even a couple of machine guns. Ian could barely breathe—he wanted to grab one, mow down Lazaro and his goons right this second, and flee this nightmare. He nearly salivated at all the explosives. This was the real stuff. Worlds beyond the Fourth of July stuff he'd loved so much.

He reached for a rifle, then hesitated.

The guard grunted, and Ian lifted it off the wall. It didn't look quite like the ones he'd shot before, but he was shaking a little and didn't think he could manage a handgun.

Was he supposed to be good with guns or bad? He had no idea what Lazaro wanted.

The guard grabbed a small box of ammo, and they returned to Lazaro. The guard took the gun from him, loaded it, then gestured to the targets.

There wasn't a place to lie prone, unless Ian wanted to shoot at the dirt in front of him, and the table wasn't at a good height. Ian drew in a shaky breath and tucked the rifle into his shoulder. He shifted his hands and tried to find his sight.

He was ready to pull the trigger but hesitated and looked at the guard. From behind him, Lazaro said, "I don't have all day."

Ian took a deep breath and steadied himself. Damn, he'd forgotten the force of the recoil, and the shot went wide. He looked at Lazaro, who only inclined his head again.

Ian lined up, bracing his feet differently, and this time managed to hit the wood. A handful more tries—none near the bull's-eye, but only one more wide.

"Try a handgun," Lazaro said. The guard tromped back over to the shed, and Ian followed.

Lazaro twirled his cane, his eyes tracking Ian, his face a mask that revealed nothing.

Ian used two hands, this time hitting the target on the first try. Then a couple went wide, one nicked the edge, and one—shockingly—hit damn close to center.

"Let him practice," Lazaro said to the guards.

They assented, and two stayed, while the third—nearly always with Lazaro—left with him.

The breath eased from Ian's tight lungs.

Practice, of course—the *patrón* couldn't exactly hold a blood ceremony and risk Ian being unable to hit anybody.

The guards had parked their asses on top of the far table, at the opposite end from the shed. Apparently, they didn't feel Ian was any kind of threat—and hey, Lazaro wanted him to lead the family someday, right?

They left Ian to it, choosing to sit and smoke and grunt at their phones, occasionally leaning over to show each other their screens. From the lewd chuckling and off-color comments, Ian figured they were watching porn.

He made the most of the time, aiming over and over again, trucking back and forth to the shed, trying out different handguns. He was so fucking tempted that his hands itched, but he didn't think he'd get away with sneaking a gun into his pants. Something smaller, maybe.

But there were a couple of crates covered by a tarp and an off-kilter garbage can along the side wall. Ian's mind raced. The next time he returned to the shed, he didn't put the gun back, and he—whoops—dropped a whole wooden box of knives.

"Shit."

One of the guards looked up but only shook his head before returning to their entertainment.

Ian worked fast, kneeling right between some explosives and the crates, stashing what he could behind the crates, in the crates, and in the garbage can—covering the noise with the clatter of knives he kept tossing back into their box.

He was shaking from adrenaline when he returned from the shed with the box of knives. He took a couple of breaths and then threw a few times. The attempts were dismal. The knives bounced off the dirt only fifteen or so feet in front of him.

The guards laughed. "Watch out. You'll take your pecker off."

"Even a knife can't find it."

Hardy har har. Ian wanted to tell them to shut up, but he said, "Show me, then." He held his breath, afraid they might overreact.

Instead, one laughed. "You want help finding your dick?"

Ian rolled his eyes and turned to face the target. But the other guard lumbered to his feet. He picked up a knife and said, "Look."

Ian copied how he held it.

"You let go too early," the guard said. "Release here." His knife hit the target, though it didn't stick.

Ian nodded and tried again. The first throw was marginally better. The next time, the guard nudged his elbow up a bit. It worked—he didn't hit the target, but the distance was much closer. Because Salvadora practiced constantly, she made it look easy, but knife throwing was anything but.

The guard returned to his pal and his porn. He said to the other, "Not going to be a knife guy."

Ian didn't want to be a knife guy. He threw and threw until he was sure the idiots were about to jerk each other off. Then, on the sly, he pocketed a knife, and then another.

When they showed no interest in making him leave, he returned to the handgun he liked best and practiced for a long time. If only he could practice with explosives and get out of all of this with one big bang.

45

———————

Lazaro did not wish for an audience as he drove even further into the hills. One guard only—the most trusted, in case his ears were too big. The old seer woman used to be loud. In fact, he heard her voice in his head louder than ever.

When the cruel beauty comes of age, you have only a handful of seasons more between the clouds and the dirt.

Damn, that Salvadora. She was a beauty even as a child—everyone had remarked on it. And it was clear as she aged that she had a cruel nature as well—she was her father, in female form. Alejandro had gloated with superiority—the first child, and a strong one, despite the fact that Lazaro had married first and bedded his wife daily.

Killing Alejandro allowed Lazaro some control of the child and her conniving mother, but his control would likely not matter much longer.

When Salvadora's *quinceañera* had changed nothing, Lazaro realized the *coming of age* must mean turning eighteen—which she had, recently. He had perhaps a year left. But it could be much sooner. The damn prophecy.

As they climbed deeper into the hills, pines appeared between the oaks and the temperature dropped. He pulled the edges of the blanket around him. The goat tied in the back bleated; the chickens clucked. He could barely hear them over the grinding of the engine against the hills and the rough surface of the uneven road.

Lazaro's thoughts turned to the granddaughter of the fortune-teller. He had never bothered before to visit her—because beyond your death and failed lineage, what was there to know?

Now, however, things had changed. He may well have changed them—Ian was here.

And so, on the cusp of the blood ceremony, Lazaro wondered. What if the old woman had been wrong? Or right at the time, thirty long years ago, but the decades had changed something? Perhaps a prophecy could change.

The sun was only just cresting the mountains, the air not yet warm under the tree cover. He tugged his hat down further against the wind and again adjusted the blanket. There was a fork in the road, and his guard slowed.

"Left," Lazaro said. The man had been with him a long time, but must not make a habit of seeking counsel.

There was another matter he wondered if the seer could shed light on, however. He had decided not to force Ian and Salvadora to marry. Lazaro feared the Gomez family would gain too much power if Ian was not strong enough.

But now he knew that Salvadora had visited Ian's room under cover of night, at least once. He'd seen them speaking together on the target field. He'd caught a glimpse of him grasping her arm and whispering in her ear last night. The girl had smiled—and she was the cruel, beautiful girl who never smiled.

Lazaro did not like to think of anything out of his control. Yet if these two were inclined toward each other, perhaps he should reconsider and work with that rather than against it.

The seer's place came into view, and he saw that, in the way of the indigenous people, nothing had changed. Sad rows carved out of the hill under the cabin for farming. A scrappy pen with a half roof to the side for a few animals. The ramshackle cabin itself surely was no match for the coming months of rain.

"Stop here." Lazaro did not look at his driver. "I will walk the rest of the way."

He saw the door crack open, a young woman, dark hair streaming over a black shawl and a dingy nightdress. There was a back door, and at least two young children slipped into the hill behind.

The guard sputtered as the engine quieted. "But the goat? The chickens?"

In addition to money and tequila, Lazaro had brought a crate of fruit, another of vegetables, and the animals. Perhaps he should have brought lumber and nails and farming equipment. No matter; the indigenous had lived this way for generations, and he supposed they would continue.

"Leave them here. They will retrieve them later."

A man with a sickle propped on his shoulder crossed to the pen, allowing privacy for a client, yet remaining within shouting distance. Lazaro smiled at the warning. A sickle was nothing compared to Lazaro's reach, nor his guard's firepower. But these people had nothing to fear today. He had not brought Jorge, and there was nothing the seer could tell him that would be worse than what he already knew.

By the time he neared the small shack, the woman stood in the doorway watching him with narrowed eyes. She had braided her hair in one long, thick plait and donned wide pants under the nightshirt, and the black wrap—decorated, he saw now, in her people's traditional style—was crossed in front and secured with a big belt at the waist. The hat she wore had numerous braided strings around the brim, their tails hanging like tassels from a lamp.

She looked like one of Lucia or Guadalupe's children playing dress-up—but the hat signified the power of her ancestry. Some of those tassels were human hair—of her ancestors, he believed. She might look young, but she had the ancient ones running through her blood.

She opened the door and went in, leaving him to follow. The same scarred table sat to the left of the front door. On it sat a box of stones and numerous candles. Bunches of dried herbs hung from the ceiling. Some looked dusty enough to have remained since his last visit, but others appeared fresher.

Numerous bright butterflies—thought to be the returned souls of the deceased—were tacked to the walls. Lazaro considered these carefully, wondering if she felt one represented her grandmother. Presumably, she didn't pin them up until the butterflies had died of natural causes. He didn't remember them from before.

Also unlike her grandmother, she had draped sheets to separate her visitors from their living space. Just as well. The grandmother's conditions had been squalid. He did not care for another peek.

She sat in the chair with a view of the door. The scratchy voice of her grandmother echoed again in his ears. *Ah, Juan Lazaro Valdez Rivera, you wish to know your fate. Or at least your father wishes to know. Come in.*

But this young one only said, "Sit."

Lazaro propped his cane against the wall and used the hook for his hat before sliding into the chair.

Her skin was dark, her nose wide and flat, her body stout. He drew a careful breath, hoping her powers were as strong as her non-diluted blood.

She did not make eye contact as she lit candles and some incense and chanted softly. The language was that of her people, an ancient tongue he could not decipher, and yet the tuneless litany was not unpleasant.

"Place your hands on the table, palms up."

He raised an eyebrow. The old seer woman had scattered stones.

She looked at him steadily until he complied. She said, "The generations receive their gifts in different ways. If the ancestors tell me, do you wish to know when they will call for you?"

"Yes." He laid his hands on the table, the fingers curling up slightly.

She placed her fingertips to cup his—skin to skin.

Immediately, she winced, yanking her hands back. "You are…strong."

He could have told her that.

She took in a deep breath as if fortifying herself, then repositioned her hands. She shut her eyes, then her head jerked left toward her shoulder. All the dangling pieces hanging from the old hat swayed, then she calmed, her eyeballs flickering now and then beneath her lids.

"You will not walk the earth much longer. You will not have forewarning, but I see…" She frowned. "A strange night that appears bright as day, much noise, a crackling— maybe some sort of strange storm. You are not alone. You will not suffer."

She quieted, her eyelids flickering disturbingly.

"My children?"

Even as he asked, a wave of disgust swamped him. Was he testing her or still hoping his reality—and her grandmother's prediction—was false?

"You are surrounded by the young, but…" Her expression was puzzled. She was quiet for a few beats. "Your legacy will live on beyond your natural life."

That prophecy eased him greatly, but brought more questions.

"Any weddings?"

She seemed to search, the eyes at work again. "There is pairing, but I do not see a mantilla."

She shook her head slightly, then blinked and refocused before she lifted her hands.

No, not yet. She'd given him so much to decipher and yet there was so much missing.

He should rise, and yet he did not. "What does seeing a bride's veil mean?"

"A traditional wedding, usually. Sometimes it can represent a virgin."

"Did you see my brother? He will have a place after?"

"He has no place." She spat those words.

Ah, yes. When they were here as boys, there had been two granddaughters. When Lazaro and his father visited the woman, Jorge had waited outside. His appetites were voracious even as a teen, and their father had been too soft.

Lazaro was better at controlling his brother where it mattered. Punishments did not work with a simpleton like Jorge—but bribes of a certain sort did. And there were many girls who would not be missed.

"If I bring him, you will read him."

Her eyes glinted hard as coal. "There is no need. I read him once."

It was this granddaughter, then. "And?"

The obsidian eyes did not look into the other realm. "His fate is tied to yours. These things do not change."

46

"I HATE THIS ROOM," MITCH SAID. WITH HANDS ON hips, he glared at the bed in the tiny room.

Charlie raised an eyebrow. She'd been so tired that the lumpy bed hadn't bothered her at all.

It was the night before the *quinceañera*, and Charlie knew Mitch's stress level was off the charts. He was worried about everything—especially her. The room didn't matter. It was just something he could complain about out loud.

"It's almost over," she said, peeling out of her t-shirt.

He didn't even look at her. She shimmied out of her pants and tossed them over the chair. They'd done laundry, but already her clothes felt dirty again.

The shower down the hall had sucky water pressure, too. In fact, Mitch had showered and still had a streak of grease on his jawline.

Today was the fake repair to the catering van. He'd been briefed by Ren on the burner phone. It was as simple as a loose wire, but Enrique had made a show of trying to jump it before Charlie ran to get Mitch. He tinkered around a while and added oil and wiper fluid, too.

The more people that saw them struggling to get the van working, the better. Later, Conchita made sure to talk up the whole ordeal and her concern about the drive to the *quinceañera* while there were customers in the shop. In this case, they *wanted* word to travel.

"I'm going to take a walk." Mitch sat to put his boots on.

"You've said a hundred times it's not safe for us to be out late at night around here." Charlie supposed she could go with him, safer together, but she wanted sleep and had no desire to prowl this little Mexican town.

She'd nearly forgotten, but once upon a time, she'd dreamed of maybe being a travel agent or a hotel manager in some neat place. Now, she couldn't imagine it. She'd like to go places with Mitch someday—even if it was just to the other side of the Delaware River. But traveling all over constantly? No thanks. She'd come to relish staying put.

But it made her realize she'd been racking her brain trying to think of what she'd once hoped to do. Maybe she better start figuring out what she enjoyed *now*.

Mitch said, "Unsafe out there, or out of my mind in here."

She took a boot from his hand and knelt between his legs. "Come to bed."

"There's no fucking way I'm sleeping tonight."

"Good. I don't want you to."

There—he finally really looked at her, took in her bra

and skimpy panties. But his hands were still balled into fists.

She pushed his hair off his forehead and cupped his face with one hand. He closed his eyes, but his expression was pained.

Short of sitting in this apartment while everyone else went to save Ian, she didn't know how to help him. "It's going to be all right."

He huffed out a small breath, skepticism and disagreement sans sound.

She didn't know how she knew it'd be okay, but she did. She wasn't naïve or stupid. She knew the risks. She was smart enough to be scared. All Mitch's concerns were valid. Even the ones he hadn't spoken aloud. She knew too well the worst that people had to offer—she bet she'd even imagined some possibilities he hadn't.

She'd survived worse, years and years of worse. Not that she'd ever make light of this thing they were undertaking, but it was a drop in the pan. Over and done. One way or another.

Charlie stood. She slid her hands along his forearms, intending to grasp his hands and pull him up and to bed. But Mitch curled, resting his forehead against her belly. She caught a faint whiff of car oil. He grabbed her hips and squeezed.

She stroked his hair, ran her hands down his shoulders, circled his shoulder blades and up his spine. His body was hard as a rock. He kept in shape always—even here—but this was all stress. She repeated the sequence over and over. Emotion welled, and she had to squeeze her eyes shut to ward off tears.

She wasn't used to giving comfort. Sex was her go-to with him. So this was something new in the relationship. Something good and…wow, emotional.

Huh, look at that. Here in some real shitty circumstances, she was handling a relationship. And pretty well, too.

Finally, he let out a long breath.

Mitch pulled back, his thumbs caressing where he held her hips. His gaze traveled from the skin of her middle, up to her breasts, then back down to the triangle of material that dipped low.

Always, she felt his gaze like he'd touched her. Her nipples tightened with small pricks of pain, her skin tingled, and heat gathered.

She peeled off his t-shirt. The lamplight was dim and the shadows made him look even more cut, even more fierce.

She straddled him and fit her mouth to his. His hands came up to dive into her hair, his hips thrusting upward.

His jeans were rough, his chest warm. He arched, one arm supporting her lower back, the other sliding down her front to push aside the cups of her bra. He buried his head in her chest and feasted—God, she was extra sensitive tonight from all this emotion—and she moaned.

He pulled back and slipped his thumb under her panties to rub her where it mattered. She grasped his shoulders, hips rocking with the rhythm he set. He watched her eyes, and his glittered.

"Inside, too," she said.

"No."

She growled—pure frustration. He increased the pace.

"Just like this, baby. For me."

And she understood—he needed her willingness, her compliance.

She'd refused him everything on this trip, butted heads with him at every turn. He'd given in to her—on all of it —against his better judgment.

He wanted this one tiny thing. This one little capitulation. This one ounce of control over her.

Charlie bit her lip, dug her nails into his shoulders— and let him have it. Because maybe she was just as scared to lose him as he was her. For all her running and despite her threat of walking away, she needed him alive and well.

47

———

Enrique and Conchita said goodbye to their daughter in the wee hours of the morning. Poor Chita looked terrified and clung to her father, until Conchita dug her nails into the girl's arm and told her, "No more. It is time."

Charlie bit the inside of her cheek hard to keep from crying. She'd left her own mother under duress. Completely different circumstances, of course, but the emotions of leaving your parents before you were remotely ready were the same: fear, terror, loss, heartbreak.

Mitch spirited the girl away to meet a contact they'd been promised they could trust on the edges of Durango proper. She'd be given a new identity, passed to another vetted contact, and booked on a flight out of Zacatecas International Airport. Those same contacts had confirmed with Conchita's childhood friend, who was ready to receive her.

The grieving but stoic Rosales couple, along with Charlie, went straight to work in the kitchen. Everything that couldn't be made ahead had to be made or baked or finalized this morning. They'd need every minute.

When Mitch returned, he helped them in the kitchen, until it was time to load the van. Enrique had shelves that attached to the sides of the van when trays of food needed to be transported, and the men worked to get everything attached and then loaded.

Enrique drove, Conchita rode shotgun, and Mitch and Charlie sat behind them in the van's jump seats.

The unpaved and curvy roads through the hills were slow going. They passed a few clusters of buildings, but mostly there was a lot of nothing.

Charlie saw a tear roll down Conchita's full cheek and had to swallow the growing lump in her own throat.

Mitch's face looked like granite—but his eyes never stopped roaming across the largely barren landscape. Just looking at him made her hurt. He'd been so sure that everything was okay, but now…what if? What if something happened to him? What if he got into trouble trying to protect her? The lump in her throat got unbearable, and she felt the pressure of tears climb. What if…what if Mitch died?

Enrique crossed himself, and Charlie squeezed her eyes shut to pray. She called on all the deities she'd never believed in.

She wasn't done when a wave of nausea crashed over her. Carsickness or fear? Either way, she better keep her eyes open. She tried to look out the windows, but invariably, her gaze sought out Mitch's solid frame.

Finally, they reached the agreed-upon breakdown spot. Here it was wide enough to pull aside into the shade, and unlike much of the way, here they could see a fair distance in either direction.

Mitch jumped out to raise the hood and do some easy-to-undo damage, even putting a little smoke bomb in there somewhere. Enrique called for a tow truck—a call that the black op teams would intercept.

"What now?" Conchita asked.

"We wait."

An hour later, they'd all asked *how much longer* and *what if they don't come* too many times. Charlie's apprehension grew and grew, making her feel like she couldn't stand to be in her own skin.

Charlie's phone rang, and they all jumped. She dug it out of her pocket and her face flushed. "Stupid wrong number." Mitch had showed her the other day that she could just hit a button to make the ringing stop.

"Put it on silent now," he told her, and did the same to his phone.

Anxiety boiled just under the surface as everyone listened for approaching vehicles.

Finally, Mitch pointed. "Someone's coming."

Charlie squinted. *Please, please let it be the team.*

All she could see was that it was a vehicle that seemed to be powered by a cloud of dust.

"It's not them," Mitch said. "Keep cool."

Charlie was already strung tight with the waiting and worry about later—now this? *Shit.*

"What?" Enrique asked. Mitch shook his head and repeated what he'd said in Spanish.

Two cars pulled up, and inside were a few nicely dressed couples between them. Partygoers, probably some

Valdez associates, given the high-end vehicles with the air conditioning blasting.

The men got out, and Charlie saw their eyes take in the van marked *Rosales' Panadería,* Enrique and Conchita, and then Mitch and Charlie, whom they regarded suspiciously. She fought not to fidget, not to rub her arms or gnaw on her lip.

"What's wrong?" one asked Enrique. "Are you going to the Valdez compound?"

"Yes, yes, but it's terrible, now we will be late." Conchita wrung her hands. It was easy to look anxious right now—they were all overflowing with it.

One man insisted on going over to look at the engine, and Mitch and Enrique accompanied him. Charlie couldn't follow the Spanish, but eventually there were shrugs.

"You can't fix it either?" Conchita asked the man.

Enrique interrupted. "Calm down, the tow truck should be here soon."

One of the women called from the car, "Should we take any food for you? Does that help?"

"Thank you, *señorita*," Conchita said. "Thank you so much, but the trays are way too big to fit."

Enrique said, "Please tell the family the trouble we had but that the tow is nearly here. The Rosaleses will be there soon, and the food will be perfect."

When the group had pulled away, Charlie said, "Maybe that was for the best—they won't be too angry when we do get there."

Thankfully, the next cloud of dust brought the tow truck, and it was just as Ren said. A truck with big side wells, a huge winch welded on the back, and a metal ramp on wheels behind. It was a good-sized truck, but nowhere near the size of a U.S. towing company's, nor did it have the flair of all the decals and shiny advertisements. This looked like two guys started a business out of scrap metal and a huge chain. Both Ren and Chief now looked the part in tan mechanics coveralls and grease-stained hands. They still sported their bandanas, but Ren had his hanging out his back pocket.

When Conchita saw the angle of the ramp, she said, "*Dios*, the food will slide off the trays."

Charlie was busy eyeballing the truck. She asked Ren, "Your guys are really in there somewhere?"

"Yep."

Okay, she thought. Okay, they'd doubled their numbers, plus one. And somewhere in that truck was hidden a whole bunch of weapons, too. Maybe this doubled their chances of success.

Quick introductions were made, and then Ren spoke with Mitch in private for a couple of minutes near the hood, as Chief maneuvered the truck and ramp to line up with the van.

Charlie couldn't decide if she were relieved they'd really arrived or more scared now that they had to move forward. She tried to gauge Mitch's expression, but it was pointless. He was as stone-faced as he'd been all day.

Not much more time and they were on their way again. Closer to danger, but closer to being done with all this, too.

Every time they hit a rut, there was a soft thud—food hitting the floor. Conchita muttered and crossed herself.

Charlie got it: there was so much more at stake here today than a few lost pastries. But the Rosaleses had worked hard their whole lives, and this was their reputation on the line.

Charlie fervently hoped that still mattered after today.

When it finally came into view, the Valdez compound looked more imposing in person than in the pictures Charlie had seen, and she drew a shaky breath. She knew it was a big, misshapen rectangle with a green courtyard in the middle and some surrounding land with small outbuildings, but from the approach nearly all she could see were thick walls of concrete and an iron gate. If they got stuck inside…

What had she done? She'd plowed on, dead ahead, knowing she couldn't stay back, couldn't abandon Ian—and yet she'd dragged Mitch in too. She knew he was worried about her. But she'd been an imbecile not to think harder about the fact that she'd be friggin' terrified for him, too—for everyone involved. Far more than for herself.

What if something happened to Mitch? What if he was hurt—or killed—because of her? Good Lord, just thinking of telling Deirdre made her physically ill. Then there was Conchita and Enrique's daughter. It was one thing to go away, knowing you might not see your parents again. It was entirely another knowing they were dead—gone forever.

Charlie shouldn't have dismissed her own mother and daughter—Ellen and Mackenzie—so readily either. She should have written them each a letter. Something like *I know I just found you—or at least you just found me—but I can't live with myself if I don't try.*

The imposing wall surrounding El Descanso de la Araña—was it too much to ask that the spider rest today? —seemed to grow as they approached. Her stomach clenched hard

And then she saw the machine guns and forgot to breathe.

48

———

At the main gate to the Descanso de la Araña, the guards waved around machine guns like they were flags, directing cars to park to either side of the front gate, which faced north. Charlie found herself clenching the seat in a death grip, just waiting for the sound of gunfire, accidental or not.

Enrique called out the window to the spec ops team in the cab of the tow truck. "Tell them we need the back gate —the kitchens!"

The back gate must not be manned, because two of the guards jumped into a jeep and met them there.

As soon as they all got out of their vehicles, the guards zeroed in on Mitch and Ren, giving them dirty looks. Chief somehow looked more Mexican today, and when he opened his mouth—to her untrained ear, at least—he sounded native, too. Charlie got a sideways glance, but they didn't seem to think she was much threat, and they completely ignored Enrique and Conchita, likely because they were known from town. The rest of them were frisked, Mitch and Ren more roughly and thoroughly than everyone else.

The guards used mirrors to look under the van and the tow truck. Probably for bombs, but Charlie held her breath and every muscle still, as if that would keep the special ops team from being spotted from underneath.

Conchita fretted and complained just a little. "This cursed van." And "Hurry, they are waiting on the food."

Charlie made herself snap out of it. She had to play this cool and collected. She put a hand on Conchita's shoulder and rubbed. "It's okay, we made it here. It will be fine."

But really her nerves collected into an electrified mass of fear.

They could see the other gate, where a caravan of three cars approached. She hoped by the time they had to sneak out of here—with Ian, please God—there'd be a steady stream of cars leaving the party to keep these gates open. Surely the guards wouldn't inspect cars leaving, right?

Finally, the guards grunted their okay and spoke into a walkie-talkie, and the metal bars finally began to open. They all climbed back in the vehicles and lurched forward. One guard pointed with his gun at the kitchen's outside entrance.

"Yes, yes, we are going straight to the kitchens," Enrique told him from the towed van.

And then it was a lot of hustle, just as Ren had predicted.

Lucia, wearing a gown and her hair up in a looser style than when she'd been in town, rushed out to talk with Conchita, who apologized profusely for the delay. A uniformed woman, maybe a cook or housekeeper, accompanied her.

Lucia didn't look twice at the tow truck or the men in the front. So far, she hadn't paid any attention to Charlie either—a good thing, because Charlie desperately wanted to grab the woman's hand and beg her to tell them where Ian was, how he was, what the situation was.

Charlie tore her gaze away from the prominent white streak that shot backward from Lucia's forehead and climbed in back to quickly rearrange any food that looked too jostled. Better to be hidden and not draw attention to herself. She was breathing fast, anxiety from the search mingling with excitement of being this close to their goal.

Enrique and Mitch began pulling trays out of the back of the van.

Lucia enlisted the kitchen staff to help, and the ant parade went very quickly.

In no time at all, Conchita and Charlie were ushered inside. Charlie sucked in a big breath. She was standing in the place Ian had been living. They were *so close.*

The Valdezes' fine serving pieces were laid out waiting for them, and they began plating from the trays. Conchita directed in a no-nonsense manner. Her specialties would partner with the hot dishes the Valdez staff had made.

Charlie had a moment of comfort—this felt so much like being at Glide's soup kitchen, feeding a crowd with bossy Henrietta at her side. But this wasn't the time for nostalgia, and she pushed the memories away. She needed to remain totally alert.

Mitch leaned in near her ear and said, "All the food is in. You okay?"

He looked worried, but she could see the same electrified tension she felt in him. She went to squeeze his arm, but she had powder and crumbs all over her hands. His hand closed over her shoulder instead, the pressure both a comfort and a warning.

She nodded. As agreed, she'd remain in the kitchen with Conchita, both in their Rosales aprons, and come out when she had something to report. Charlie was sure Mitch would find an excuse to come in at some point as well, but in general the men were expected to stay with the vehicles, not hang about in the kitchens with the women.

Louder, to Enrique, Mitch said, "Let's go see what can be done about your van."

Charlie watched as Mitch left. She didn't like him being outside—not only away from her, but in view of all those machine-gun-toting guards. What if they got suspicious and decided to take another look? What if something happened and she didn't even know it because she was stuck in the kitchen playing this role?

Conchita hissed at her.

"Sorry," Charlie whispered. Then she continued the plating. The task helped—it was a small action, but action was better than too much thinking. She chewed her lip and tried to recall how she'd done it when she was on the run. A lot of it was just giving yourself over to instinct. But it was different then, because she'd only had to worry about herself.

She had to remember that Mitch could do this. The team certainly could do this. And Conchita seemed to be holding up just fine.

As soon as a plate was ready, she carried it to the

doorway herself, brushing off the Valdez kitchen staff. She had a job to do. She needed to be able to get the lay of the land and look for Ian.

There were multiple doors. One led to the courtyard and another to a sort of butler's pantry, and then to a huge dining area with multiple tables. At the rear was the one they'd used to go back and forth to the van, and another that appeared to be a storeroom.

The party was ramping up. Music had begun and the swell of voices from the courtyard grew louder. People passed in and out of the large dining room.

If Ian was a part of this event, whoever saw him would figure out a way to pass by him and tell him to come to the kitchens, maybe to the storeroom, or wherever they decided was the best place for a few minutes of privacy.

If he didn't show, they'd wait until the guests were focused on Dia—perhaps during speeches or the father-daughter dance—and somehow sneak through the large house in search of him.

Charlie waited until the servants' bathroom off the kitchen was occupied and then asked to use the bathroom—making it seem dire—and was directed out into the main hallway. On the other side of the living room was a large powder room. Beyond that seemed to be a small receiving room off the foyer.

She stared at herself in the mirror. Beyond the wig, she looked so normal. How was it that the panic that hovered inside wasn't showing in her eyes?

On her way back, no one else was in the hallway, and she took a second to peek behind a curtain. She expected a coat closet, but no, it was a relic—a phone closet from decades ago.

As soon as she reentered the kitchen, Conchita waved her over.

"Take this to the dining room, and see what needs replenishing." Then, barely moving her mouth, Conchita said, "I saw him."

Charlie's chest filled like someone pumped helium in.

"In the courtyard," Conchita said. "He was talking with some little girls."

Charlie told her about the phone booth.

"Good," Conchita said. "I'll give one of the little girls a treat and tell them to come get more and bring the boy."

It worked, and before Charlie knew it, she could see a passel of little girls with flowers in their braids orbiting Ian like little planets, the littlest one pulling him by the hand.

Dear God—she had eyes on Ian. He was here. He was walking around freely. And he appeared okay. Physically, at least, he looked perfectly fine.

One of her biggest fears was that she'd find him completely strung out on drugs. A close second was that he would be constrained and beaten and bloody. Third— and okay, these weren't in order—was that they wouldn't even be able to find him, that he'd be hidden away so deeply that she couldn't get to him.

Her heart soared with hope. The fact that he was out and about and seemingly healthy would make it so much easier to get him out.

But as he got closer, she could see that his features looked carefully controlled. Hiding what? Distress? Worry?

Fear? Homesickness? All of the above, maybe. *Don't worry, Ian. We're here.*

She ached to run out back and tell Mitch and the team, but there wasn't time. She simply nodded at Conchita and slipped out. They couldn't let Ian spot her when other people could witness his reaction. Somehow, Conchita would get Ian to meet Charlie in the phone closet while distracting the children. Charlie ducked behind the curtain and hugged herself tight so she wouldn't burst. *Please,* she prayed. *Please, let Ian—and only Ian—come soon.*

49

Being outside—separated from Charlie and from the action—was killing Mitch. He had to force his fingers to unclench from fists when Ren asked him for a wrench. He tried to pretend that he was focused on what was under the van's hood, but really, his peripheral vision and his head were squarely inside that kitchen. He could hear music from the courtyard. The party was definitely in swing, but nowhere near over. Waiting wasn't his strong suit. His legs ached to run, and his arms needed to pump, or pummel, or strangle—and it was all he could do to just stand here.

Being relegated to the sidelines was one hundred times worse with Charlie doing the work inside.

He should have stopped this. He should have found another way. He was so friggin' angry at himself. They shouldn't be here. It should be just the spec ops team. He had a lot of training, but it was nothing compared to the men Cross had hired. Charlie, Conchita, and Enrique had none. Zero, zilch, nada. This was an absolute disaster in the making.

Finally, Ren shook his head. "Go check, then."

Mitch didn't need to be told twice—but when he walked into the kitchen, he stopped short. His stomach clenched and he felt like he couldn't breathe.

No Charlie and no Conchita. No staff, either.

Jesus.

If it was just Charlie missing, he'd suspect she'd wandered off to do some sleuthing, but Conchita, too, and all the staff? Had they been discovered? Had—

Conchita bustled back into the room with an empty platter in her hand. Her eyes widened with panic.

"Go!" She shooed at him. A server was on her heels, so she mouthed, "He's coming!"

Ian? Or Valdez? Instead he said, "Where's Charlie?"

"She's fine! Go!"

Mitch's head actually swam—relief that she was okay for the moment coupled with fear that Lazaro Valdez was bearing down on Conchita for some reason. Just then, through the far doors that led to the patio and central courtyard, he spotted a gaggle of children dragging a dark-haired young man along.

Ian! Not Valdez. *Thank God.*

Mitch spun and strode out the door. He had to trust that Charlie and Conchita had a plan. And just in case the timetable needed to be sped up, he had to let the team know they needed that van drivable, pronto.

Ian was being dragged by Bebe and the other little girls—Lucia's and Guadalupe's both—toward the kitchens. Something about a "sweet before dinner," but he hadn't paid much attention.

His insides were a riot of dread and fear. A sweet before dinner might make him throw up the nothing he had in his stomach.

The guests had all heard by now there was some prodigal nephew from America, and he felt all those eyes on him. Jorge and a few of the top guards kept shooting him glances. They knew about the blood ceremony and were dying to know what he'd do.

Lazaro himself, of course, barely acknowledged him—but one always felt the *araña*'s eyes. Ian shuddered.

Lucia kept her distance, but he felt her gaze as surely as he'd felt her hand on his brow when he was so ill. Forget the pride and excitement she should be feeling about Dia's *quinceañera*—she was as tortured as he was about this blood ceremony.

He hadn't been able to ease her mind at all, because although he had a loose plan—a lot of which counted on Salvadora—it had a lot of question marks. Worst of all, he still hadn't decided who the hell he was going to kill if he couldn't get out of this nightmare. He didn't know where anyone would be standing when it came time, and that meant the whole thing was a total contingency plan. Off the cuff, play it by ear, see how it went—total nightmare.

He was completely in his head by the time Bebe tugged on his hand and pointed at a tray of desserts.

A woman with gray streaks in her dark hair, a lined face, and an apron—must be the catering staff—spoke to him. "I promised the girls a sneak peek at dessert. Okay if they taste something?"

He didn't know. Christ, the smallest things here had to be weighed. But the girls were all bouncing up and down, and it was a special occasion, so he shrugged. "Just one," he told the girls.

They squealed, and the woman pointed out what was what.

"Go outside to eat it, so you don't miss your sister's speech," she said, then put a hand on Ian's arm. The girls ran off in excitement, dresses bouncing. The woman nodded at the desserts, as if to ask him which he wanted to try, but she said softly, "There's someone here to see you."

He blinked. *What?* What had she said?

She nodded again. "Do you know the old phone booth?"

"Who?" *Who* in the world could possibly be here?

She set the tray down and pressed a small pastry into

his hand, closing his fingers over it. Her skin was warm and dry like Lucia's. "You know where it is?"

He nodded.

"Go now."

Despite the whispering, she sounded urgent. He turned, mind spinning. This could be good—or this could be some kind of trap. He didn't think so looking at the woman's eyes, but always in this place there were very few to trust. He glanced around, but no one, not even the woman, was paying him any attention.

Then he walked out the door, down the hall. Plenty of people making plates of food in the dining hall, no one in the living room. Two steps more and he was at the curtain. He drew a careful breath and slipped inside.

Immediately he halted, crushing the small, powdery sweet in his fist. Charlie? With dark hair? Had they slipped him drugs? Was he hallucinating from stress?

"Ian." Charlie wrapped her arms around him and squeezed hard.

And as soon as he heard that flat American voice saying his name and felt how solid and real she was, relief rushed over him and he hugged her back, probably too hard.

He wasn't alone.

Immediately on the heels of that thought, his mind was awash with terror. He didn't want anyone he cared for to be here, caught up in this shit. "Jesus—what are you doing here?"

"Trying to get you the hell out."

"Like now?" Fuck, that would be great. Could he

disappear? Vanish like a magician's assistant from behind this curtain?

"Later tonight. After dark—with the catering van and the tow truck."

The hope that had flared up as big as a hot balloon deflated like the material had torn in two.

"It will be too late. How about now?"

Charlie cocked her head, considering.

He shook his head. "No. Not now." Still light, and they'd be looking for him too soon.

"Listen." Ian grabbed Charlie's arm. "There isn't time to tell you about it and have it make any sense, but this party is going to go sideways. Seriously sideways. Violent and terrible. Be ready. I don't care about me. I need you to…"

His mind spun, wildly ping-ponging between scenarios he could barely envision. "Just get the girls out. The little girls—my sisters. I told them to hide in the sheet fort after the *quinceañera* dances. That's in the nursery. To keep them out of the way when the bad shit starts." He was rambling, barely able to think straight.

Charlie was shaking her head, but he wasn't done. "And Dia," he said, "she's the girl in the sparkly blue dress that this party is for. Lucia"—he gulped—"my mother— she's the one with the big white streak." He pointed to his forehead. "You have to get them out of here."

He'd made Salvadora promise that if she ended up in power, she'd let them all leave—or not, as Lucia chose for her and her girls. But that was before. This was better. This was *now*. *Tonight.*

"We came for you."

"We?"

"Me and Mitch, the Rosales couple who brought the food, and a small special ops team."

"Then you can do it."

"There isn't room." Her eyes were big, and she sounded almost panicked.

He didn't care. "Make room. You have to—"

There was a thump on the wall, and Ian clamped his mouth shut.

Charlie put her eye to the edge of the curtain. "Mitch says we've got to get out of here. Ian—"

She was going to argue with him. He gave her a hard look. "There's no hope for me. Take Lucia and my sisters with you. Promise."

"I—"

"Say it!"

"I'll try."

It was as good as he was going to get. This hellhole wasn't a place where anyone could promise anything, and he knew it. He blew out a hard breath, tried to smile, and slipped out of the tiny space.

51

Dia stood on the small dais, surrounded by imported greenery and twinkling lights strung through the trees of the courtyard. She looked so unlike herself, dainty and feminine in sparkling tiara, fancy blue dress, and high heels.

Ian preferred when her hair was falling out of her low bun and her face was buried in a book. She should wear a stethoscope or something. She should be saying something irreverent.

He only heard half of her careful speech into the microphone—a big thank you to her mom and plenty of praise for her uncle's graciousness in throwing this lavish party. The guests clapped like mad. Everyone adored Dia.

Lucia stood next to him and squeezed his hand. What should be a wonderful moment for her—her eldest daughter's *quinceañera*—was overshadowed by the impending blood ceremony. Neither of them knew when it would be announced. Both dreaded the event and feared what the rest of the night would become.

Dia must have said something in closing, because Lucia's hand slipped from his, and both she and Lazaro approached the stage. Dia fumbled the microphone into its stand, making it thump and crackle. Then she hugged her mother tight, and Lucia managed to smile though tears fell.

Lazaro bent for a kiss to his cheek. He took Dia's hand and raised it. "And now, we dance!"

He swept Dia forward into some sort of traditional dance.

Ian had been to only one *quinceañera* in the States, and the girl and her friends had all rehearsed a choreographed dance with partners of their own ages well ahead. This was entirely different.

The Braid Contingent—both his sisters and Guadalupe's girls—ran forward, squealing, the youngest partnering with each other. A couple of older boys and girls from other families were pushed onto the floor to dance with the older girls. But there were very few kids from other families. Thank God.

Woodenly, Ian walked forward and extended his hand to Salvadora. He'd been told it was expected of him. She looked stunning, wearing makeup and a gold dress. The tight bodice came up over only one shoulder, exposing plenty of skin. Her full skirt reached the floor. Gold dress, bronze skin, and dark hair in a fancier ponytail than usual —she looked like a goddess. As always, the thought crossed his mind: if this was another world, he'd be all over this.

As it was, her eyes glittered. Determination? Excitement? Obsession?

He put his hand to her waist and pulled her in for a slow dance. He didn't know the traditional one. Dia had tried to teach him, but it was a last-minute thought and he'd been too distracted to learn it properly.

"How many weapons are you wearing under that skirt?" He looked down and saw the toe of her boot poke out from under her dress. Very Salvadora—and he was glad for it. She might need to run or fight.

"Enough."

Lazaro and Dia swung by, and Lazaro gave a smile and nod. Not for their benefit, but for the crowd, Ian thought. Dia's lips curved in a smile, but it didn't reach her eyes. No one could be comfortable in the spider's arms.

And Dia, too, surely felt the weight of the impending violence. Like Ian and Lucia, she knew very little. Unbelievably, here he was again, most likely forced to hurt someone. Other than Lazaro—and that would be suicide —he had no real hatred for anyone. Most of these people he barely knew. So yeah, he'd asked Dia to have her bag of surgical tools and medicines at the ready. Maybe she could save them.

She'd wanted to know *who*.

So did he.

So many *who* questions there were no answers to. Who would he target? Who would retaliate? Whom could he trust?

Even Lucia had once told him to trust no one, not even her.

But there was Charlie and Mitch.

He still couldn't believe it. He'd gotten another

glimpse of them passing by the kitchen, and his heart both swelled with joy and shriveled with fear.

Salvadora hissed at him. "You aren't dancing."

He forced his feet to move. "Sorry."

"Get your head straight," she said. Her dark eyes were hard. "You have my promise on all counts. It's for the best."

Easy for her to say. If this worked, she was going to get her fondest wish and not die. She didn't care about anyone but herself—and maybe her mother.

If he lived, she'd gladly kick him out of this compound. If he died, Salvadora's promise meant Lucia would have options. Because she could not be separated from her daughters. She'd been through that once, with him. He didn't know if rule would be kinder under Salvadora, given that she and her mother would always hold a deep hatred for the Valdez family. What Lucia's options were otherwise, he didn't know. But at least she'd have choices—something she'd never had under Lazaro's iron fist and gold-topped cane.

Salvadora's fingernails dug into his shoulder. Shit— he'd gone off in his head again. She was right. He had to find a way to steel himself for whatever happened.

"Do I need to lead, starting now?" Her smile was belittling.

"You might as well," he said. "You know I don't want to."

She raised an eyebrow and tucked her lithe body tighter into his. It wasn't quite a grind, but it was close, her thigh between his, pressing hard as her hips moved.

"Feel free to grab my ass," she said. "This is the last chance you'll ever have with me."

"Tsk, tsk, Salvadora," he said. "This is a family party."

The song ended. She looked up at him—smile cold, eyes hot—and said, "Soon to be a bloodbath."

She might be a goddess, but she was a lusty, pushy, bloodthirsty bitch, too.

She shoved his chest hard enough to make him step back. Then she spun away, her long skirt flaring out. There were knives strapped above each boot.

He hoped the knives and her bloodthirsty determination were enough.

52

———

THE MUSIC PICKED UP TEMPO AND THE YOUNG GIRLS all danced and spun and hopped around. The adults mostly gathered in clusters to talk. Laughter, toasts, shrieks —a festive atmosphere for everyone blessed with ignorance.

Ian wanted to run. Dark was descending everywhere but the lighted courtyard. The cakes had been cut and the pastries set out. After dinner, drinks had been served. He wanted to find Charlie and Mitch and beg them to just take him now. What had Charlie said? A catering van and a tow truck?

If only he didn't care. If only he hated Lucia. If only he hadn't warmed to his sisters. If only he was a cold bastard like Salvadora was a cold bitch.

But he couldn't, just couldn't leave Lucia to suffer the repercussions of him disappearing. He couldn't leave Lazaro in power now that he had the chance to stop it. Not even if it meant he didn't live past tonight.

Crazy that for a long time on the streets, he hadn't

cared one bit whether he lived or died. Now, when he was most likely staring at the hour of his death, he wanted nothing more than to live.

Lucia was gathering the girls, corralling them away from the dancing and toward the house.

She held his gaze for a long moment as she passed. *Soon.*

"Find us in the sheet fort for a story," Tierra told him.

He smiled. "Just as soon as I can," he said, wishing it were true, wanting her to know he'd always be there if he could.

As it was, he was just glad they'd be tucked away. Safe —and unable to see him shoot anyone.

He didn't know how much time had passed, but all of a sudden, it was happening. Lazaro was standing on the small stage, tapping the microphone with the head of his cane, waiting patiently for people to quiet.

All the key players—Lucia, Dia, Salvadora, Guadalupe, Jorge—stood on the fringes. All the visitors turned, their attention caught by the sweeping hush.

"Thank you for coming tonight," Lazaro said. "The Valdez family is honored to have such important friends recognize our incredible Dia. She studies hard, honors her family, and is a gifted healer. No." He pointed at a couple of the visiting associates or clients. "Don't get any ideas. She does not yet seek a husband."

The crowd laughed. Ian wanted to be sick. He'd never heard Lazaro joke before, and in reference to Dia, it was doubly unsettling.

Two guards appeared at Ian's elbows. It was like feeling the walls closing in.

Then Lazaro called out some other men by name. Ian did not know if any of these men were heads of other drug cartels or partners in the Valdez business or people he sold to. "Please, come join me. With us gathered, it's the perfect time to celebrate another tradition."

A murmur ran through the crowd. Eyes narrowed. The men passed their drinks to their wives or a server as they approached the small stage. They all gave Ian a look of warning. They knew without being told exactly what this was. The old ones among them had been here when Lazaro took power. The younger ones had heard the stories over and over. Not just the Valdez/Gomez story, but those from generations before.

Lazaro gestured to Jorge to join him up there on the right. Then to Lucia, to flank the dais below and right, and to Guadalupe to flank below and left. The same arrangement as when they dined, essentially—and exactly what Lucia had led Ian to expect. Salvadora moved to stand alongside her mother. Ian would be on a raised platform somewhere central.

There—yes, behind him, there had been a bush trimmed into the number 15 there earlier, but now the base was empty. A small, horrible stage, waiting for its reluctant star.

Quickly, Ian scanned the crowd. Guadalupe's other daughters, the younger ones, had also disappeared. The visiting families, however, had no idea that they should stash their children away, and he saw a few of the mothers tuck their offspring behind them.

Lazaro spoke again. "You all have heard rumor by now that I have been blessed with a male heir."

Even Ian—tortured as he was—felt the air swell with anticipation. They'd heard the rumors that Lazaro was sterile and that this miracle nephew—legitimately a Valdez —had appeared.

"I'd like to introduce you to Ian Luka Valdez, my nephew."

Nice touch, fucker, Ian thought, replacing his father's name.

The guards wrapped their hands around his upper arms, and as they moved, the crowd parted. They lifted him up onto the platform, and it was either stand or fall. Woodenly, he turned to face the front.

Lazaro clapped, his ring clanking against the lacquer of his cane and echoing via the speakers.

"Ah, but I almost forgot." Lazaro held Ian's gaze. "Dia, my love." He waved her forward. "Now that you have crossed into womanhood, you are an *integral* part of this family."

Ian's blood turned to ice. It was a warning. It would not be Lucia who paid this time if Ian didn't comply. It would be Dia. Lucia had been right.

Lazaro's dead stare never shifted from Ian—and Ian couldn't look away.

Dia moved forward and stood next to Lucia below the stage. Lazaro shook his head slightly. "Come, come," he told her, and held out his hand.

She had no choice but to climb the steps and stand next to him. He grasped her hand and finally broke his gaze from Ian's to smile down at his niece.

The bastard. It wasn't just a warning—it was insurance.

He knew Ian couldn't risk shooting him when Dia might possibly be hurt.

Then Lazaro lifted his chin and spoke into the microphone. "And now, it's time for our traditional blood ceremony."

A small gasp went up. They'd known, but here was confirmation.

A third guard approached Ian with a shiny wood box and flipped open the lid. Lying in red velvet was one of the handguns from the range—the one he'd had the best aim with.

"You have been informed of the purpose of the blood ceremony?"

Ian's eyes shot to Lazaro's. Ian nodded like a marionette, and Lazaro smiled. Ian fucking hated that evil little smirk.

Lazaro looked at the crowd. "My friends, don't worry. I am nowhere near retirement."

He chuckled, forcing the guests to do the same. All fun and games for psychos.

"But as young Ian is new to our world," Lazaro continued, "it's important to ensure his loyalty to the family and our enterprise. As for me, when I see his choice, I'll know how best to steer his…education."

Four men—no, five—now stood on the stage to the left of Lazaro, spaced out because, of course, one wouldn't want to be accidentally hit by a bullet meant for someone else. All of them narrowed their eyes, their faces hard and menacing, their bodies tight with warning.

"Ian, the gun." Lazaro sounded like he was telling Ian

what fork to use. This was fucking insane. Panic rose in Ian's throat.

Jesus. He had no idea who all these men were. Lazaro hadn't taught him this. He'd told him some about the other leaders—who dealt in what, where their properties were—but he didn't know who was who. Was "the Butcher" the one that looked like a bull or the one with the toupee?

Lucia and Dia both had been too busy with the preparations to have time to coach him. He should have asked Salvadora, but he probably wouldn't have trusted her guidance anyway. And now he was out of time to ask.

Ian reached for the gun, feeling like he was underwater. His breath came fast and choppy, but time slowed, drawing out torturous seconds.

The old guy from that one family—was he sick? The other one—he'd rubbed his dick while eyeing up his own daughter. Would Ian save her if he chose that sicko? Or was there something worse in line for her?

All he could think of was that butterfly movie he'd once seen, how the smallest action could have such a devastating ripple effect for years and years. And he didn't *know.* He couldn't even make an educated guess. He hadn't been here that long.

He had pressed Lucia on the purpose of the blood ceremony. You might take out a rival and claim his wife and his men, thereby increasing your empire or ensuring an alliance of a rival family. In Lazaro's case, he'd taken out his childhood friend and the man he'd been meant to rule with. Lucia said that it'd been shocking. Unexpected, horrifying, and unscrupulous. She'd been just called back from the States and was glad her own father had not lived to see it. But no one rose up, no feud broke out. Guadalupe—who might have—had literally had a child tucked to her side, Salvadora.

It was unusual to choose someone from your own circle. But it had, Lucia said, definitely set the stage for how Lazaro ruled.

Ian's pits were soaked with sweat. Rivulets ran down his back into his pants. And his palms—*shit*.

He wiped one palm on his pants, transferred the gun, and wiped the other. Then he took a breath and raised it again—pointing it squarely at Lazaro.

He could do it. He could manage to hit Lazaro and not Dia—if they stood still. On the gun range, for the guards' sakes, he'd aimed off bull's-eye so they thought he had shit aim. Ian saw now that that was a mistake, leading Lazaro to keep Dia too close.

Tempting—so goddamn tempting—to go for Lazaro, but what if he missed? Lucia had warned him that if he shot at nothing, he'd be forced to shoot again and again.

What if he didn't miss? Would Jorge turn and take out Ian? What would Jorge's leadership look like? Worse even than Lazaro's, with his pure propensity for violence and rape? Would he set his sights on Lucia or Dia? He seemed to have no boundaries and no conscious.

It didn't matter, though. Ian couldn't risk Lazaro pulling Dia in front of him like a human shield.

Also, for Salvadora to be recognized going forward, she had to be the one to take Lazaro out. And if Ian had no choice but to fucking do this, he wanted a goddamn change in management.

Second on his list was Jorge—but if Salvadora missed Lazaro and he still ruled? Ian's life would be pure hell. Lucia and Dia would surely pay along with him.

If he chose Guadalupe, Salvadora would slaughter him, and not only would she refuse to let Lucia and the girls leave, she'd—

Don't think about it.

He wiped his forearm over his forehead. It was the gun arm, and the crowd gasped and dipped.

Lazaro chuckled. "I did not personally teach him to shoot. So watch out. It could be anybody." Then to Ian, he said, "If you miss, you'll simply keep trying."

Good God, the sicko was running a nightmare fun house. Half these people would die of heart attacks before this was over.

He wanted to tell them all he was sorry, to beg forgiveness already, but he couldn't speak.

His mind was on overdrive as he surveyed them.

What about that old woman always in the courtyard that suffered so much from—well, he didn't know from what, and he didn't know how she was related, but she sure had a high level of pain and a shit quality of life. He could maybe wrap his mind around a mercy kill, but he didn't even know the woman's name.

Jesus.

He'd been over and over this—and then his eyes caught Lucia's. Her shoulders were nudged back, her mouth in a tight line. But her gaze was steady—comforting, even. She dipped her chin just a bit.

And suddenly he knew. He knew exactly what he had to do.

53

———

ALL THE STAFF HAD LEFT THE KITCHEN, ABANDONING the food and alerting Charlie and Conchita that something was wrong, very, very wrong. A man's voice said something on the loudspeaker, and Charlie realized the music had quieted and so had the guests.

They'd poked their heads into the hall, the butler's pantry, then the dining room—all empty. They could see through the open doors to the courtyard lit up with fairy lights. Men lined up on the stage. The Valdez family was placed around them like chess pieces. Opposite, there was a platform on which Ian stood alone.

With a gun.

Charlie couldn't believe what she was seeing.

Ian aimed forward, toward the stage, but he swayed slightly, and she feared he might pass out. Or maybe she should be afraid that he wouldn't.

All the kitchen help was hovering at the edges, tucked into the shadows of the patio by the house. Conchita slipped out, wrapped her hand around one of the girl's forearms, and bent her head close.

The girl spoke fast but quietly. Charlie could hear nothing, but when Conchita crossed herself, the sense of doom grew. Enrique appeared at her shoulder, concern etched heavily in his features.

"What is it?" Charlie asked the second Conchita returned.

"They call it a blood ceremony. The boy must prove his loyalty, and she says…" She shook her head, eyes wide. "He has no choice in the matter. The only choice he has is who he kills."

"I'm going outside." Enrique was already in motion. "The men need to know."

This was what Ian meant when he said things would go *seriously sideways*, Charlie realized. What a friggin' understatement.

But this seemed sanctioned—insane, yes, but sanctioned by the head of the family—so why did Ian think there was no hope for him? Why did he want Charlie to save Lucia and her daughters? He feared retaliation?

That meant… Dear God, he was going to kill his uncle—the head of the family and the boss of the Valdez cartel.

Lazaro's voice boomed out from the speakers. "Ian, who will it be?"

Ian braced his feet, raised the gun, pointed it forward, and then braced it with his other hand.

This time, Ian looked steady as a rock.

54

Ian pointed the gun forward. Dead center of Lazaro's chest. He shifted his gaze to Salvadora.

She looked furious and shook her head ever so slightly in warning, her eyes wide.

He wouldn't ruin this for her. He only needed to be sure she was ready. She'd prepared—he'd seen her standing in the same spot once they built the stage, eyes closed. Counting paces and imprinting the distances of multiple scenarios, he suspected.

He lifted the corner of his mouth just barely—all he could manage of a reassuring smile—and then shifted.

He swung left, passing over Dia and Jorge. Then lower, off the stage.

And lower still, fearful his aim wasn't good enough to avoid any major organs, he aimed for the legs, steadied, and...

Pulled the trigger.

The shot was deafening, searing his soul.

Lucia went down, hit in the thigh, as a gasp of horror from the crowd rose.

Yes—he'd shot his own mother. *God forgive me.*

Ian looked away just in time to see the knife plant itself in Lazaro's neck. The patriarch hadn't seen Salvadora throw—he, too, was still facing Lucia, momentarily stunned at Ian's choice. He'd gone stiff and reached up to grasp the handle.

Dia yanked her hand from Lazaro's, jumped off the dais, and ran for Lucia.

Salvadora had appeared next to Lazaro and wrapped her hand around his. With a yank, the knife came free and blood sprayed as if shot from a hose.

The cane hit the stage with a bang, then Lazaro pitched forward, taking the microphone down with him. It crackled and thudded.

Jorge roared and rushed forward, arms out like a zombie, intent on reaching Salvadora. But Guadalupe fired at him. He looked down, blood blooming over the belly of his shirt and through his hands. He fell to his knees, then canted over onto his side.

The guards raised their guns, but Salvadora and Guadalupe had split, and the guns waved as the guards tried to track them. A few bursts of gunfire went off, and some people fell to the ground, screaming and clutching wounds. Not Salvadora or Guadalupe, though. Guests panicked, creating total pandemonium.

None of the guards aimed at Ian. He'd been rooted in place. For days, he'd tried to come to terms with dying tonight, but instead he was watching it all unfold.

He wasn't dead. *Holy shit.* And he couldn't just stand here.

Ian jumped off the low platform. He kept an eye on the action as he darted around people, trying to reach Lucia and Dia.

He saw Guadalupe as she rolled and rose, holding her gun to a surprised guard's neck. She used the man's large body as a shield.

Salvadora, still on stage, stood tall and bellowed the scream of a warrior demanding attention. Everyone stopped to stare, even Ian.

Lazaro's blood covered much of her face and her gold dress. She slammed her boot down and raised her bloody knife high. In a clear, booming voice, she said, "I have rightfully killed Juan Lazaro Rivera Valdez—vengeance long overdue for the death of my father Alejandro and the stripping of our family's given place, per their father and grandfathers' oath."

The guards glanced at one another. They'd been reacting, but now realized their *patrón* was dead, his brother was dead, and, most of all the girl spoke the truth. All was fair in drug wars and blood ceremonies.

Guadalupe dragged the guard with her up the steps to the stage. Taller than her, she kept him canted backward, off balance, his legs scrambling to keep up. If she accidentally shot him in the neck, he'd still die.

Salvadora's chest heaved and her eyes gleamed. She pointed the knife at the shitting-himself gift her mother had brought to her.

The place was now nearly dead silent, and a drip of Lazaro's blood fell from the knife. The microphone was still on, and the small plop sounded throughout the courtyard.

"Kneel or die," Salvadora said to the wide-eyed guard.

Guadalupe raised the gun with a flourish and shoved him forward.

He knelt. He even bowed his head in deference.

"Guards," Salvadora yelled. "Drop your weapons. You answer now only to me."

Ian reached Lucia and Dia just as all those machine guns were placed on the ground.

Oh, God. Oh, God. Lucia looked bad. Like a rag doll, splayed out and unresponsive.

Dia pressed her whole weight hard against Lucia's thigh, deep red blood welling up around her hands. Too much blood.

"Idiot," Dia said. "I think you hit an artery."

55

———

MITCH, THANKS TO ENRIQUE, HAD SEEN THE WHOLE thing go down.

Ian—*Christ*, he still could barely believe it—had shot his own mother. The woman didn't raise him, of course, but still. Mitch wondered just what in the hell had occurred in this place since Ian arrived to make him do that. It must have been some pretty fucked-up shit.

Then, lightning fast, their biggest obstacle—Lazaro— was no longer a threat. His brother was eliminated, too, as all hell broke out.

Mitch heard Conchita's hiss from behind him. "Burn in hell, Valdez bastards."

The crazed girl in the blood-spattered dress yelled like a banshee, declared victory, and had the guards lay down their weapons.

This rescue mission was suddenly looking up.

Mitch spotted Ian and the *quinceañera* girl, Dia, lumbering toward the house with an unconscious Lucia slung between them.

"Incoming," Mitch shouted. He didn't know how serious it was, but he shoved all the dishes and platters on the center countertop to one end. Others had been hit, too. The nearest hospital had to be miles and miles away.

Conchita produced a tablecloth. She laid it over the surface just as Mitch and Ian hoisted Lucia up.

Mitch had grabbed a dishcloth—hopefully clean—and Dia said, "Yes. Pressure." Mitch pressed down with both hands—but Jesus, there was already blood *everywhere.*

Dia darted into the other room and returned with a leather bag. Her hands were covered in blood, and she ran to the sink to wash.

Ian looked like he was going to pass out. "I didn't mean to, I didn't mean to. I mean, I meant to, but I—"

"Shh," Charlie said, grabbing his shoulders. "It's all right. She'll be all right."

"We need to go," Mitch said. No one reacted. Everyone was focused on Lucia. He said it louder.

Charlie looked at him. "Ian, he's right. We've got to go now. The team in the van, they have more medical training than us."

"Dia is trained. Like a doctor. Dia can fix her now. Right? Dia?"

Dia was digging in her bag. "Who the hell are you people? What van? What team?"

"There's no time to explain." Sweat rolled from Mitch's forehead down his nose and hovered there. He kept the pressure heavy but couldn't tell if it was working. Ren had told Mitch in no uncertain terms that he wanted Ian in the van the minute the bullets stopped flying.

Mitch realized that Dia had understood Charlie's

English, so he spoke in English to keep curious ears from following. "Listen—if we get her to the van, we can get the hell out of here and get her real medical help. There's a chopper that's supposed to meet us."

The rest of them might be stranded, but…

"She can't be moved." Dia's hands worked like quicksilver, cinching a length of rubber tubing tight above the wound.

Ian said, "Can you promise she'll live if she stays?"

Dia didn't answer—she'd motioned for Mitch to lift his hands and was already pouring something over the wound.

"Dia," Ian said.

Dia dropped her head to her chest. "No."

She swore and packed the torn flesh with gauze. She grabbed another cloth from where someone—Conchita or the kitchen help, maybe—had stacked them.

"We need more," she yelled. She tied another cloth around the whole thing. "Where's this van?" She slung her bag over her and nodded when she saw Conchita with an armful of clean dishrags.

Enrique, Mitch, Ian, and Dia all grabbed fistfuls of the sheet and started to move toward the kitchen's outdoor exit.

"The girls!" Dia said. "Ian—she won't want to leave the girls."

"I'll get them. I promised," Charlie said—giving Mitch a small heart attack.

"No," Ian said. "I'll go. Take my place."

"But you have to—" Charlie said.

"No!" No way in hell Mitch was letting Charlie go traipsing about this place now.

"It's faster for me," Ian said. "I know the place. No one will stop me. And the girls don't know you." He stepped back a little, making room. "Take my place."

"Can we come back for them?" Charlie asked, even as she grasped the tablecloth supporting Lucia.

Ian and Dia exchanged a glance. Dia shook her head. Ian looked toward the courtyard, then shook his head. "We all go."

Charlie looked at Mitch. He nodded tightly. He didn't like it, but what the heck was there to do? It was clear they weren't getting Ian, Dia, or Lucia in that van if they didn't get the children, too. Whatever the situation here, they didn't think the girls were safe.

People were streaming through the dining room, and Ian took off like a shot, right through the crowd.

Those carrying Lucia paused at the kitchen door. Mitch thought it would be faster to just carry her himself —she weighed almost nothing with her weight distributed on the sheet—but Dia and Enrique were in the lead, and they just shifted and squeezed through. Mitch and Charlie tucked together on the other end.

Mitch swore when he saw the backup at the main gate. Every guest who'd come had a car and was trying to fit through the gate at the same time. It appeared that two of the cars had collided and were almost wedged now, blocking everyone. Horns honked, guards yelled, and men jumped in and out of their cars waving and shouting. He could see a dusty cloud where a couple of cars had sped through first, but everyone else was stuck.

Thankfully, the tow truck and van blocked them from even seeing the back gate. And the guards, for whatever reason, hadn't opened it.

Ren swore when he saw them bearing Lucia, but he yanked open the rear door of the van. Chief climbed in first, and they passed Lucia to him. Dia hopped up and curled over her mother, already opening her bag.

Chief knelt and spoke with Dia. Then he stepped over the prone body and hopped out. "We need to get to the helo fast. And we need Davy."

They all had medical training, but Mitch knew their team member Davy had served as a medic.

Ren nodded. Chief said, "Davy, you're on." The spec ops teams were all wired.

A few seconds only and Mitch saw a camo-covered body hit the ground under the truck and roll. He was a couple inches shorter than Mitch, and his brown hair was closely cropped. Oddly, Mitch saw a bit of fur sticking out of his pocket that looked like the tip of a raccoon tail. Chief met him there.

"Damn glad to be out of that box," Davy said.

His gaze took in everything during the ten-second walk to the van. Dressed as Davy was, Mitch was relieved that he was getting *in* the van and would be out of sight. The green camo worked for covert ops in this mountainous landscape, but party duds they weren't.

"Alternate way out?" Mitch asked.

"We blow the back gate," Ren said. "If it wasn't for that"—he inclined his head toward Lucia—"I'd join the pack in the slow slog out and keep up the cover." He looked at Mitch. "Where the hell is our mark?"

Mitch grimaced. "He went to get his sisters."

"Fuck me."

"We couldn't get him to agree to fly solo. One big, happy family, apparently." But he thought of that cluster of little girls who'd swarmed around Ian and couldn't blame him.

"How many sisters are we talking about?"

Ren wasn't the only one who wanted to know. The numbers would matter when it came to the bird lifting them out of the country.

56

Ian tore through the hall, up the stairs, and toward the nursery. No guards were stationed at any of the usual points. Surely they'd snuck away to witness the blood ceremony and now were caught up.

He threw open the door so hard it banged the wall behind. Cat stared wide-eyed. Mico screeched and hopped up and down from mattress to mattress, waking the younger girls. They were all in pajamas.

"Guess what?" Ian tried to catch his breath. "We're going on an adventure."

Sleepy smiles. "Is the party over?"

"Everyone's leaving. Us too. Come on." He waved them forward and picked up Bebe. Mico sounded like an eagle—it was the monkey's alarm call.

"Shut up, Mico. *Jesus*." And Ian had a moment of giddiness thinking they'd be leaving the beast behind.

"You swore. Mama says don't swear."

He ushered the girls out the door into the hall, shifting Bebe from his hip to his back. "I know, sorry—"

A shot rang out and something whizzed by. *Holy fuck.*

Guadalupe had just crested the stairs at the end of the hall and fired at them. It was only because he'd shifted the child that she missed them.

"Back inside now!" He swept out an arm and pushed them all at once.

He slammed the door shut and reached up high—a lock meant for adults, not children—to throw the bolt.

"What's wrong?" a little voice asked.

Ian spun, looking around wildly.

Mico had started screeching again. He swung from the bars on the window to the bedframe and back again repeatedly.

The bars—*shit.* Just like Ian's room, there was no way out. They were trapped.

Ian set Bebe down.

Mere moments and he heard Guadalupe tug on the door. She banged with her fist. "Come out and face me, American bastard."

"Fuck off!" he shouted, then told the girls, "I'm allowed to swear in this situation."

"You won't get out of there alive." Guadalupe screeched like the monkey. "And it will be my pleasure to take Lucia's rats with you."

The girls may not understand entirely, but they knew enough to be scared, and scampered onto the beds behind the sheet fort, hugging pillows and stuffed animals to their chests. Tierra crawled under the covers to hide.

Last night, he'd snuck back to the locked weapons shed and found the items he'd hidden just as he left them. He had the handgun from the ceremony in his waistband, a knife in his pocket, and another strapped to his ankle. The other ankle had another gun. But it'd be insane to start a gunfight with the girls underfoot. And he didn't want to let this crazed woman in to use the knives or his fists.

The explosives he'd left hidden in his own room in case of future need. He'd itched to use them, but there was no way to know how the party would be set up.

"I gave Salvadora what she wanted," Ian shouted, even as he yanked open a closet to search it. "What you both wanted. She promised I—*we*—could walk away."

He didn't know what he was looking for, but there was *nothing* useful in this room. Furniture and toys. Bunk beds, pillows, clothing.

"A stupid promise. Her place will always be in jeopardy if you live."

Cat whispered, "She's a witch. A real one."

Ian couldn't agree more. He told Guadalupe, "A promise all the same."

"It wasn't my promise," she hissed. "I am not bound to it."

She slammed her body against the door. The lock should hold—she wasn't that big.

He put his shoulder to a dresser and pushed it in front of the door. This was fucked. They needed a way out—fast, for Lucia's sake—and here he was barricading them in. He longed for the damn C4 so he could blow those bars off the window.

A shot rang out, and a few shards of wood splintered. The girls started to cry and wail.

The monkey screeched louder than ever, then swung

himself up on the window ledge, scampered through the bars, and disappeared.

The bars. *The bars!* Too narrow for Ian, and that monkey was small, but so were the girls. They could fit.

He ran over and looked down. It was full dark now, so he couldn't quite see the ground, but this was the same floor as his, not that far from the ground. He could see the corner of the house where the kitchen was and just a glimpse of the van Charlie had mentioned. The tow truck must be there too, out of his line of sight.

He started ripping sheets from the fort. He tied two together, then three, as fast as he could, praying the knots would hold.

"We're going to play a game. Escape the wicked witch!"

Four sets of wide, dark eyes stared at him.

He tied the sheet rope to a bar and tugged hard, testing it. He pulled with his whole weight. If it held him, it would hold the girls. He shoved it through the bars and let it drop.

"Cat, come here." He lifted her under the armpits to look out between the bars. She was the biggest, but *yes,* she could definitely squeeze through. "See by the kitchen— that van?"

She nodded.

"That's our goal. That's our new hiding place." He turned her around and looked right into her eyes. "You're in charge. You have to wait for all your sisters at the bottom and then run—all together—to that van. My friends are there, and they'll keep you safe. Got it?"

Her little chin jutted out and she bobbed her head in a firm nod.

"Good girl."

Another shot rang out. He ducked instinctively—more splintered wood.

"Bebe, you get to ride on Cat's back. But you can't get on until you get outside these bars. Understand? Just like climbing trees!"

Thank God they'd climbed trees together. Not one was scared of heights. Hell, they were almost as much monkey as Mico. At the time, Ian had worried. Now, he was just grateful.

He hoisted them one after another to the wide base of the open window, and they wriggled through the bars—no problem.

Ana and Tierra had climbed up to the top bunk. He said, "You listen too, okay?"

He turned back to Cat and Bebe standing outside the bars two stories up. God help him.

"Face me and hold tight to the bars. Okay, now, Cat with one hand, reach down for the sheet. Keep your feet braced against the wall. You are going to walk down the wall, holding on to the sheet. Do not let go!" She did as instructed. "Go down just a little and stop. Yes. Okay, Bebe. On to your sister you go. It's the most important piggyback ride ever. Do not let go for anything."

Ian prayed and pasted on a confident smile.

They went down slow and steady. As soon as they passed the halfway mark, he turned to lift Tierra.

They were ready when the first two hit the ground.

"Go now, little by—"

Tierra slid fast all the way to the first knot, and Ian's heart hit the dirt below. *Jesus!*

She looked up, and he saw she was grinning.

"Okay," he said. "Okay, that works too." She was the best climber of them all. Completely fearless.

Bang! He cringed at another shot at the door—then *bang*, another.

Guadalupe shoved, and the lock popped free, the wood around it finally giving. She shoved again, and the door banged against the dresser. Another heave and the dresser slid a good foot.

He grabbed for Ana, the last one. "Up you go!"

57

CHARLIE HEARD THE GUNSHOTS SAME AS THEM ALL. But she had to follow the men's body language to see where it had come from. There were still cars bottlenecked at the main gate. Two irate guests had hit each other. Guards were trying to back the cars in the rear up, so they could un-wedge the ones blocking the whole pack. The gunshots only increased the yelling and honking.

They all shifted to see around the corner of the building, and—

"Oh my God," Charlie said. It was dark on that back side of the house. "Is that…?"

"Shit," said Mitch, while Ren and Chief's swears were more choice.

Two little girls—one on the other's back—were sliding down tied-together sheets. Another was slipping through the bars on a second-story window.

Ren said, "You guard." He and Mitch took off running.

Charlie looked at Chief. "Go," he said, "I got this."

She ran. The girl underneath was wriggling. Trying, Charlie thought, to get past the fat knot under her bum. Or maybe because the little one on her back was choking her. At the top, she saw Ian as he lifted another girl to stand at the bars. At the top now, it was one inside, one outside waiting their turn.

Dia had told them she had four younger sisters—so that was everybody.

What the hell was going on up there that Ian had no choice but to send these children out a window?

The gunshots.

Her mind continued to race as the next little girl sank to her knees, one hand on the bars.

The first two had gotten past the knot and slid—whoosh—another six or so feet. She did better with the next knot, and then the girl at the top was sliding fast.

Mitch skidded to a stop and plucked the little one from the back of the older girl. Ren grabbed the other. They met Charlie halfway. Mitch handed her the little one, and Ren set down the oldest—probably no more than Mackenzie's age.

Ren told Charlie, "Get them to the van."

There was shouting and banging from above. Ian disappeared for a minute, and then he was directing the last girl.

Charlie grabbed her charge's hand and, with the other child held tight to her side, said *"Vámonos."*

They ran, but awkwardly. As she bounced on Charlie's hip, the little one said, "Are you Ian's friend?"

"I sure am."

As they neared, Chief opened the front door of the van. "Put them here."

Good plan. They did *not* need to see their mother unconscious and bloody.

She piled them in and slammed the door. "Stay here. Your sisters will be here soon."

The older one asked, "Where's Mama and Dia?"

Charlie smiled. "Already here."

She turned and ran back. Wow—Ren was rappelling from his own line with the last girl in his arms. She must have gotten stuck, because she was crying.

Ren yelled up, "Do we need to yank these bars so you can jump?"

Ian flinched and ducked, and a knife actually whizzed through the bars. "No time!"

Charlie spun. "I'm going up there."

Mitch grabbed her arm. "No. Get the girls safe." He took off running back to the kitchen.

Ren said, "Chief, follow Mitch." He kept running with the one girl and pointed at the other who was running after him.

Charlie yelled after Mitch, "Good luck." But her heart seized. They'd gotten this far, everyone unharmed except Lucia, and that had nothing to do with them. What if this was it? What if Mitch didn't come out?

She looked over her shoulder just as Mitch and then Chief disappeared into the big kitchen.

She shouldn't have said good luck. She should have shouted, *I love you! Come back to me!* Or better yet—*Don't go; let Chief handle it.*

It was too late now. She prayed her insistence on this rescue mission wasn't a gross, unforgivable error on her part.

Ren yelled her name. They'd gotten way ahead of her, even the girl on foot. *Crap.* Charlie ran.

When she caught up, Ren said, "Chief has his back."

"Mitch will have his." But that was part of the problem. She knew damn well Mitch would put himself in danger if it meant he saved Ian or Chief.

They'd reached the van, and Charlie lifted the girl right into the front. "Everybody up. Climb around behind the front seats." They'd have to put them on their laps or on the floor when they all piled in.

"We won the game," the smallest girl said.

"What?" Charlie asked. Did she not understand the child's Spanish, or was there a break in logic?

"Ian's new game. Escape the wicked witch."

Charlie frowned, but Ren translated for her. "Oh," Charlie said, "you definitely won."

Another asked, "Where is Ian?"

Charlie wished she knew.

The girl who'd already been crying now whimpered. "I want my mama."

Charlie pointed to the back of the van. "She's sleeping just back there, but we have to let her rest." Thank God they'd tacked the canvas between the front and back of the van.

Ren said, "ETA?" Then, "Good."

His earpiece, Charlie realized. "What?"

"Gotta get our exit ready." He tore forward and practically vaulted into the back of the tow truck. He was talking in his mike, and another man rolled out from below.

This one was about Ren's size, Caucasian and bald. He stretched, surveyed the scene, and said, "Looks better out here than it sounds."

Another appeared out of nowhere—dark skin and thick, dark hair and eyebrows, maybe of Middle Eastern descent—and asked Ren, "Van or truck?"

"Truck. Unhitch the ramp, then be ready for my go."

The man nodded and got to work.

Baldy grinned. "Time to make some music." He took something from Ren. They both ran for the gate that was around the other side of the kitchens.

Enrique and Conchita had been hovering. Conchita asked, "Should we go get some trays—make it look good?"

Charlie debated. The whole spec ops team was out and about; the jig was up. "No—safer to stay here. We'll need to go in a hurry. You should get in the van, too."

Thankfully—so far—no one was paying them any attention.

Then machine-gun fire rang out from the direction Ren and the bald guy had gone. She couldn't see them in the dark.

Already on edge, she crunched down. She had to fight herself to stay put.

She looked up—just in time to see a guard near the main gate, where it was lighted, looking their direction. He was pointing and gesturing animatedly to another guard.

Shit. They must have spotted the spec ops guys.

She jumped into the driver's seat and started the engine, hoping like hell everyone would return, with Ian —*now*—before she had to do something drastic.

58

———

Iᴀɴ ʜᴀᴅ ᴏɴʟʏ ᴇɴᴏᴜɢʜ ᴛɪᴍᴇ ᴛᴏ ᴛᴜʀɴ ᴀʀᴏᴜɴᴅ. Guadalupe had climbed up onto the dresser. She knelt and aimed, the gun pointed at his chest.

No movie monologue—she just pulled the trigger.

Ian leapt to the side, but—*thank God*—the gun didn't fire. The magazine was either empty or the gun had jammed.

She looked at it in disgust and threw it to the floor, then pulled a knife from her hip and leapt down from the dresser.

He'd regained his legs and moved toward her. This room was big—the bunks near the window, comfortable chairs in the corner for tucking up with a child on your lap, big closets that were still open. And plenty of open play space.

He circled her, and she lunged.

He reached for the gun in his waistband, but—oh crap, it must have fallen when he leapt to the side.

She swiped at his gut, and he spun out of the way. She

wasted no time, cutting her arm through the air in the opposite direction. He punched her in the side, and she grunted. He was taught never to hit a woman. But he had to get to that van.

He thought too long, and she slashed again. That fucking hurt. She'd gotten him—a slice from his ribs and back down his side.

She smiled—the evil bitch—and slashed again. He grabbed her arm—damn, moving hurt—and twisted until she was forced to drop the knife. Then, hoping to knock her out, he punched her in the face.

This time he didn't even think about remorse. She was trying her damndest to actually kill him. He didn't have a choice here. He bent for the gun on his ankle, and she jumped on him. He threw her off.

She stumbled but recovered, and they began circling again. He pulled the knife from his pocket.

Then Mitch was in the room, gun drawn. "Stand down, *señorita*."

She roared and lunged at Ian—

Midway, her head exploded out one side and her body collapsed.

Jesus. That was…

Ian's chest heaved.

A huge guy in tan coveralls had popped her with a long gun…no—a gun with a suppressor. The guy said, "We don't have time for that shit."

Mitch said, "You're okay, right?"

Ian looked down. *Uh-oh.* He was bleeding pretty good.

The big guy shoved the dresser completely clear of the door. "Let's go."

Ian looked at Mitch.

"That's Chief," Mitch said.

Ian circled wide to get around Guadalupe's pulpy head and most of the spatter. He did his best not to look at her directly.

They went left but hadn't reached the turn or the stairs when a shout came from the other end of the hall.

"*Bastardo!* What the fuck's going on?"

Salvadora—shit.

She had two guards with her, and they all broke into a run.

Chief already had his weapon raised. "Go, go, go."

"Not her," Ian said—why, he didn't even know—as Mitch grabbed his arm and tugged him back into a run.

Chief fired, and the guard in the lead didn't have a chance.

The other guard pulled the trigger. Bullets flew for only a few seconds and, luckily, somehow missed them.

Ian looked awkwardly over his shoulder to watch as he ran. The guard's eyes went wide as he went down.

Chief aimed at Salvadora next, but she saw the open door of the nursery and veered off.

Not good.

Mitch had his gun drawn as he ran ahead.

"Faster," Chief demanded, and practically shoved Ian down the stairwell.

A long, bloodcurdling scream rent the air. Salvadora had found Guadalupe.

Chief spoke again, but not to them. "Got some heat. Coming out. Blow 'er."

Ian could hear Salvadora shouting orders and more guards running. Walkie-talkies crackled as messages were shouted back and forth.

They hit the bottom of the stairs and headed for the kitchens, only to see a posse of guards running toward them from the courtyard.

"This way!" Ian doubled back and wrenched open a door under the stairs. It looked like a closet.

"No," Chief said.

But Ian pushed aside a stack of crates to reveal rough stairs going down.

"That wasn't on the map," Chief said, and pulled the door shut.

The tunnel wasn't long and opened up to what Ian believed was a root cellar under the kitchens. This portion had a single dim bulb hanging from the ceiling.

Out of nowhere, Florencia stepped into his path. Ian pulled up short.

Both Mitch and Chief had their guns pointed in the corners, and Ian realized some of the other serving girls were in the shadows along the walls. They were all hiding from the chaos above.

"Take me with you," Florencia said.

"No can do. Let's go," Chief said.

Florencia grabbed Ian's arm. "*Please.*"

Ian said, "Jorge's dead. You'll be all right." He pulled away and ran for the gap in the far wall—that one led to the outside. The other led under the courtyard. Mitch and Chief followed. The girls, thankfully, did not.

The climb out of the tunnel taxed Ian even though there were handles. He couldn't lift his one arm—his whole right side was searing pain. Chief had moved a slab of rock, revealing dark night and then lay down to haul Ian quickly up the rest of the way.

They were outside the house but inside the compound's outer walls. Ian knew some tunnels led under the wall, but only because those had been locked tight underground. He'd stashed some C4 at two of them, just in case.

As soon as Mitch crested, a huge boom blasted their ears. Chief and Mitch who'd both gotten their bearings, instantly took off. Ian stumbled, then followed, trying to make sense of the noise. Had someone found and set off the explosives he'd hidden?

Then he saw it—they'd blasted out the back gate. That was what Chief had meant.

As they neared the vans, Ian could see the insanity at the front gate. He didn't have time to sort it out because Charlie jumped out of the van and rushed him.

She caught him up in a fierce hug. He hadn't cried since Lazaro had tricked him into killing that prisoner— but the tears in her eyes made his well up.

He still couldn't believe they'd come—*how?*—and were still here. They hadn't left him.

"What's with you and explosive exits?" she asked.

He laughed. "I could say the same about you."

She had blood on her shirt now—his. His head swam a little, but oddly, it didn't hurt as much now.

"Come on." Chief practically dragged him away from the van. "You too," he told Mitch.

"Lucia? The girls?" Ian asked.

"They're in there, but you guys are with Ari."

He shoved Ian in the cab of a makeshift tow truck from the passenger side. Another camo-clad dude, dark-haired and darker-skinned—maybe Greek?—was already in the driver's seat. He revved the engine. Mitch reached up to climb in behind Ian.

Shots rang out—right at them, metal hitting metal.

The door was still open, and he heard Charlie gasp, then swear. Her head disappeared from view.

Mitch dropped to the ground and lunged toward the van yelling, "Charlie!" But Chief grabbed him and pretty much launched him up and into the truck, even as he barked out orders to his team.

"She's hit, she's hit," Mitch kept saying.

But the driver, whom Ian already thought of as the Greek, took off with a spin of tires, the door swinging shut. Bullets pinged against their sides—now coming from two directions, Ian realized. They didn't seem to do damage. Ian craned around to see the van follow suit, but their driver's-side window shattered.

His heart pounded hard with adrenaline and fear. It looked like Chief had made Charlie move to the passenger seat and was driving. She was upright, at least. Were the girls on the floor? Surely Lucia was in back? Ian couldn't do anything for them or Charlie up here, and it was killing him.

They swung to angle toward the gate. *Uh-oh*. The gates hadn't blown clear—they were hanging half attached, half not, in a giant cloud of dust that hadn't yet settled. There was little rubble, though.

Their driver hit the gas, and the engine roared as they plowed through. Ian held on to the dash even as he instinctively ducked—but they made it, the gates flying free.

The Greek said, "Yeah, baby," and laughed.

As soon as they were through, they slowed. Ian craned around, trying to see what the hell was going on now.

The van sped through—the truck had cleared the space for it—and kept going.

Two men Ian hadn't even noticed—one bald dude wearing camo, the other guy with a dirty blond man bun and mechanic's coveralls, both with damn big guns—ran from the wall and leapt into the back of their truck. Their driver hit the gas again.

The men took up positions in the back, covering them. They were still being shot at, but only from one direction now, because Ian was pretty sure they'd killed the guards that had been running toward them from the main gate.

Mitch asked, "Who's back there with Ren?"

"JonBon," their driver said, but he seemed to be concentrating on the road.

Finally, Ian realized they were out of range of machine-gun fire. *Thank God.* He didn't want anyone else hurt on his account and prayed that Mitch was wrong and that Charlie had not taken a bullet.

Ian looked back to the compound and saw sparks flying from a machine gun and a flash of gold dress.

Salvadora.

She must also have realized she was no longer in range,

because she slammed the gun down between the bars. It tumbled out the window, then end over end, to land in the dirt below.

Ian couldn't even hear it from this distance—and he took his first easy breath in days.

59

Mitch doubled down on himself until he was sure he wasn't going to hit someone or throw himself out of the truck.

Charlie was hit—he'd nearly had a heart attack when she doubled over. And he'd tried to get to her, but Chief, that hulking bastard, tossed him in the truck like a bag of gravel. And Mitch wasn't a small guy.

He kept an eye on the rearview mirror. They'd killed the lights inside the vehicles, but he could see Charlie just barely, and she was sitting up. If she was in a bad way, she wouldn't be, right?

He would give anything to be back there with her right now, but he had no choice but to trust that Ren and Chief and the guys knew what they were doing. If they thought it was time to make serious tracks, then even a few seconds wasted could mean—

No. Don't go there.

He forced himself to breathe and to focus on their

forward progress. He squinted through the dark at the dusty road—more of a path—and wooded hills. They were taking a different route out than they'd come in on. He'd studied the maps. This had a spot clear enough for the helicopter to land, though it would eventually loop and allow them to fork off toward El Pase Viejo. The mash-up at the gate meant they shouldn't get stuck behind anyone else, plus, not everyone would head in the same direction.

He checked the rearview mirror again for Charlie's upright shape. For now, he decided he'd just be damn glad to be on the other side of that wall. They'd done it—holy hell, they had done it.

No celebrating yet, of course. He wouldn't rest easy until he could get Charlie in his arms and check her wound himself, they were all flown over the border, Lucia was somewhere suitable for surgery, and—well, he'd still worry about Enrique and Conchita.

He shook that off. One thing at a time.

He glanced at Ian, who was sandwiched between him and the driver, Ari. Kid still had one hand braced against the dash like he'd frozen there. But the way they bounced along, it was just as well.

Ari told Ian, "Take off your shirt and use it to stanch the bleeding."

Ian swiveled his head to him and then looked down. Mitch twisted to help, ending up popping the buttons off. He folded the shirt up tight, put it against Ian's side, and pressed Ian's own hand over it. Ian grunted in pain, then grunted again when they took a rut hard.

"Not too bad," Mitch said. It was a long gash and still

bleeding freely, but the wound appeared deep only at the top.

"I'll live?"

"You'll live."

Ian shook his head. "Wild."

Mitch said, "We thought it was the Valdez brothers we had to worry about. They're dead—and now there's two women out to kill you?"

"One. 'Cause the other one's now…" Ian made a *poof* gesture and winced. "And Salvadora would have been fine if Guadalupe hadn't…" He started to make that gesture again but closed his hand in a fist instead.

Mitch raised an eyebrow.

Their gate-busting driver said, "He might be in shock." To Ian, he said, "I'm Ari, by the way."

Ian said, "I'm not in shock, I don't think. It's complicated."

Ari's gaze shot to the mirrors. "Roger that."

"What?" Mitch asked.

"The boys spotted some company. Way back. You can see lights bouncing now and then."

"Shit."

"Yeah," Ari said. "Not partygoers—not on this road or at this speed."

"Great." Mitch looked at Ian. "Better explain the complicated part."

Ian looked pained. "I had a deal with Salvadora— because we knew Lazaro was planning that fucked-up blood ceremony. If I could give her the opportunity to take out Lazaro, she'd go for it—because it would allow her to take over. Like, take power legitimately. In turn, she'd let me walk the fuck out of there, and she'd let Lucia do the same if she wanted."

"Who is Salvadora?"

Ian gave them the brief rundown of the old family feud.

"So why isn't she letting you walk now?"

"Because that guy Chief blew Guadalupe's brains out."

"And she was…?"

"I just told you. Salvadora's mother."

"Right," Mitch said. "But Guadalupe was trying to kill you. Why?"

"She saw me as a threat to Salvadora. If I was alive, I could steal power back from her."

Mitch was not getting it. "Why you? I mean, if you wanted out, why—"

"It's fucked up, dude." Ian sighed heavily. "I'm the only male heir to the family. A bastard, but blood."

Ari said, "Like a fucking soap opera."

"No," Ian said. "Way worse. More like *Game of Thrones.*"

Mitch had heard Salvadora's little speech after she'd knifed Lazaro. This wasn't about money for her—it was about power and revenge.

"So…" Mitch ran his hands through his hair. "We think this Salvadora now wants revenge on you for killing Mommy dearest."

"Yeah," Ian said. "She's got a temper and a mean streak, and…" He shook his head.

Mitch said, "And now she has an army of machine-gun-toting thugs at her beck and call."

Ian twisted in his seat, grimaced, and gave up. "Is she gaining on us?"

"Yeah, but barely," Ari said. "I can go faster, but the van can't, so for now…" He shrugged a shoulder. "We're getting close, though."

"To what?"

"To the bird that's gonna get you the hell outta here," Ari said. "Thank your daddy when you get home, kid."

It was hard to tell with the wind rushing in the cracked open window, but Mitch thought Ian's eyes got a little moist.

"A plane? We're going to an airfield?"

"Helicopter," Ari said. "Pretty much in the middle of nowhere."

"We can take Lucia for help, right? That's first?"

"Yeah." Ari checked the mirrors again. He glanced past Ian and caught Mitch's eye. "Numbers have changed."

A rock sprang up in Mitch's gut. He'd suspected as much and did some quick calculations. It was supposed to have been Ian, Mitch, Charlie, and the five on the spec ops team, plus the pilot, of course. He said, "So Ian, Lucia, Dia. What about the girls?"

Ari nodded. "Even collectively, they weigh nothing."

Mitch breathed a bit easier at that.

"What?" Ian said.

"Weight restrictions," Ari said. "It's full of cargo— we're not supposed to be on the thing at all."

Ian's eyes were panicky.

"It's okay," Mitch said.

"Who gets left behind?" Ian demanded.

"Me and Charlie," Mitch said. "The couple we came

with, Enrique and Conchita, the caterers. They weren't supposed to go anyway."

"No," Ian said. His head swiveled back and forth between Ari and Mitch. "No."

Mitch wanted to yell the same at the top of his lungs —*no!*—but it was what it was. There wasn't time to secure another bird or hatch another plan.

Ian said, "I'll stay. Charlie's small. Maybe you and…"

Mitch could see his mind racing.

"You and Charlie go," Ian said. He pointed his thumb at Ari. "One of these guys can stay with me. They're, like, super skilled, right? Like fucking magic—I'll be safe."

Ari shook his head slightly.

Mitch got it. They were hired for one thing and one thing only. Ian. Not Ian's shot-up mother, and not Ian's possibly soon-to-be-orphaned sisters. The team stayed with Ian and delivered him to his father—as a unit. They weren't going to split up and risk their lives beyond the mark. They'd survived service to their country. They weren't going to die now for a fat green banking deposit.

But Ari surprised him. "We discussed two of us staying, but the fact is we're overdue somewhere dicey, and it's gonna take all of us."

Mitch saw Ari's jaw clench in the light from the dash before he said, "I'm sorry, man. We'll do what we can to help from above."

Mitch nodded with a bit of a lump in his throat.

Ian said, "But…" But he couldn't think of anything either.

"It's okay. You're why we're all here. You're the most important piece," Mitch said. "Lucia's situation complicates things, and you wanted her not to be separated from her girls, right? Well, this is the way that happens. Your family goes with you. It's the only way."

Ian looked like he was deciding between hurling and bawling. "I am so fucking sick of deciding who lives and dies."

"This one's not your choice," Mitch said. "And we're not gonna die. Promise."

He leaned forward to look at Ari. "We can take the truck, right?" It was bulletproof to a degree, faster, and probably more reliable.

"Yeah, it's hot, though. Ditch it as soon as it's safe."

Mitch would think about that later. Right now he was busy deciding if there was anything in the van they couldn't live without.

Then, all of a sudden, the truck wrenched and lurched. "Shit." Ari gripped the wheel hard, pulling it back on course.

Mitch swore too. They'd just blown a tire. They'd have to take their chances in the van. This wasn't nearly over yet.

60

———

THEIR SMALL CARAVAN WAS STILL APPROACHING THE clearing when the helicopter touched down. Charlie held tight to the dash as they skidded to a stop just beyond the still-spinning rotors. Her pulse rate double-timed it and her leg throbbed and burned something awful.

The helicopter looked big, but Charlie knew the deal with the cargo. Only so many stowaways allowed. Not everybody was going to fit, period. And she'd also worked out, after hearing the argument between the spec ops team, that she and Mitch would need to be the ones to stay. Mitch being Mitch, he might try to force her to go, but she didn't see how.

She was okay with their staying. More than anything else, she wanted Ian safe, and his new family, too. Conchita and Enrique had a plan. And as long as Charlie and Mitch were together, they could sort something out.

The problem was that those vehicles following them were nearing fast. And that meant big trouble. Unless they suddenly decided to give up the chase, those who remained would either have to lose them or deal with them.

Losing them would be preferable. Dealing with them meant a gunfight, and her stomach turned over just from thinking about it. They'd rescued Ian, but they still needed to survive this.

"Lucia first!" she called as she jumped out of the van and stumbled when she had to put weight on that leg, but the spec ops guys were already on it.

She heard someone say, "Fireman's carry?"

"No!" Dia said. "Don't stretch her leg. I've finally slowed the bleeding."

By the time Charlie limped around the back of the van, they were halfway to the helicopter with Dia running alongside. They carried Lucia on the same tablecloth as before. Charlie swallowed hard. It was so saturated with blood that a steady stream trailed in the dirt.

"*Jesus*, Charlie."

She turned to find Mitch staring in horror. She looked down and saw she'd left a trail of blood herself. Her boot was drenched.

"It's okay. A nick."

"Fuck." His Adam's apple bobbed hard, and he'd gone white.

"Move, move, move!" Ren and Chief shouted. The men now carried the little girls, and Ari was shoving Ian toward the helicopter. Ian twisted, looking back at Charlie and Mitch. The rotors were picking up speed, and his black hair blew wildly.

Enrique had scrambled out of the van and pulled Charlie's arm. "Hurry."

Mitch burst into action, supporting her, even as she looked behind them to see how close those jeeps were.

Enrique pointed toward the passenger side. "My van. I'm driving."

Mitch lifted Charlie into the van, then climbed up and slammed the door. Enrique slammed the gas pedal to the floor, and they took off with a lurch.

The noise from the helicopter was deafening, but somehow Mitch was louder. "Conchita, the first-aid kit!"

"It's fine for now," Charlie shouted as she scrambled into the jump seat behind Enrique. "First things first." She tore down the tarp that separated front from back, but had to lean up and out to see out the small rear windows. Even through the dust the helicopter had risen, she could see the Valdez vehicles were gaining on them.

Conchita looked pale but resolute across from her. She had a death grip on the seat, trying not to bounce out.

There was a fork in the road, and Enrique took the right.

"Where are you headed?" Mitch asked.

"Back to Pase Viejo. If we can get to your car, they will have to choose. Us or you."

Charlie was horrified. "We can't bring this to town. They'll mow people down—either with the jeeps or bullets."

"We won't get that far anyway." Mitch, too, was focused on the gaining vehicles. And town had to be about an hour from here.

A burst of staccato noise came out of nowhere.

"Or maybe we will!" Mitch stuck his head out the

window and looked up. "Our pals in the sky are shooting at the Valdezes!"

Charlie craned around to look out the side windows. She couldn't see the cars behind them from here between the dark, the trees, and the curving roads, but she could catch glimpses of the cargo helicopter. The door was open and two of the guys were firing down. God, she hoped those children were strapped in. She hoped the team was strapped in too—but surely they'd had practice at this insanity.

An explosion rocked the earth, and she nearly flew out of her seat.

"They hit them!" Mitch said.

But the celebration was short-lived. Charlie saw sparks on the outside of the helicopter. That was bad. It hadn't occurred to her that if the team was in range for a gun fight, then so were the Valdezes.

Suddenly the helicopter made a sharp turn and veered off. She curled to bury her head in her lap. *Thank God.* She couldn't bear the thought of the helicopter with all those people on it being shot down.

"They're headed this way," Mitch shouted.

She sat up again. "Why?"

They started firing again—a constant barrage—and Charlie's heart jumped into her throat. It felt like they were aiming at the van. Was a jeep that close, then?

"They're firing at the trees! Trying to block the road!" Mitch's hair was completely windblown, his eyes alert, his expression tight. "Damn. Let's hope it works."

The engine was straining and the road was rough— every time they hit a bump, Charlie's leg throbbed worse.

Even her breasts hurt—there were no shocks whatsoever in this van.

The noise from the helicopter disappeared, and Charlie started to catch her breath.

Mitch kept checking the mirrors and sticking his head back out the window. "I see lights. They're still coming."

"Maybe it slowed them down," Enrique said.

They'd collapsed the shelving in the back, but it banged constantly. So did the now-empty pans that had been removed from the kitchens early on.

"What if," Charlie said, "when they get close enough, we throw the pans at them, and you shoot the tires out? Or the drivers." Mitch, she assumed, was the only one here who was skilled enough with a firearm to pull that off.

Mitch shook his head. "Opening those back doors and throwing pans opens us up to getting shot. They've got far more range on their guns than I do on this." He waved a handgun.

Conchita lifted a towel. "The men gave us these."

"Oh my God," Charlie said. "Mitch, there are two machine guns back here."

"The gifts just keep on coming." He looked almost hopeful. "Charlie—the gear bag, under the seat."

She bent, pulled it out, and rummaged through. Everything she and Mitch had brought was intact, and *yes* —grenades!

She pulled one out and held it up. "We're in business!"

"They need to get fairly close before those are any good to us." Mitch leaned into the space between the front seats and squinted at the rear windows. "First, we'll try to blow their tires out."

Charlie looked at Conchita. She had been stoic most of this insane day. Charlie had seen her fingering the rosary once or twice, and she was doing it again now.

A little more praying wouldn't hurt with the Valdezes still in pursuit. Charlie's faith was on shaky ground. This whole day felt like one step forward and two steps back.

"Conchita," Mitch said, "switch with me."

Conchita blinked and then rose, holding on tight to the back of the seat as she and Mitch squeezed around each other.

He parked his rear in the jump seat across from her and leaned forward. "Give me your foot."

"It's fine."

"We have time now. I need to know if you can run." He was already opening the first-aid kit, so she put her foot on his lap. It had been throbbing, but now she winced. The burning flared up again when she stretched into a different position. Still, she knew it wasn't serious. Not like Lucia's gunshot wound.

He tugged at her pant leg, but the bottom was stiff with drying blood. He didn't waste time, just sliced the fabric, pulled up the pant leg, and bent to the still-bleeding wound.

She hissed when he poured liquid antiseptic on it and fought a wave of lightheadedness when he pressed hard with a wad of gauze. Quickly he wrapped more gauze around and around before tearing the end with his teeth. Then it was tape, around and around.

He hadn't looked into her eyes once. "It'll do for now."

"I told you it was fine."

He ignored that, but she saw him wince. Okay, okay, she would be worried if he was bleeding, too. She reached out and grabbed his hand. "I promise I'm all right."

He looked her in the eye then, and she saw how tortured he was before he shuttered it and looked away.

Mitch peered again out the back window. Unlike Mitch, Charlie couldn't judge how fast they were gaining. It was too dark, and the headlights bounced in a sickening way. Her stomach rolled. She swallowed against it.

He made quick work of her pant leg, cutting off the bottom. She figured he probably didn't want it dirtying the dressing.

"If we…" He shook his head hard.

Charlie heard what he didn't say. *If we survive this…*

"You'll need to change pants before we get to town. No time now."

"Okay."

At that moment, she heard the distinctive noise of machine-gun fire and then a *ping, ping, ping* against the van.

Her breath came too fast all of a sudden and every muscle felt ready to run—except they were trapped. Pinned on this narrow dirt road, hills and trees and rocks on either side of them. Stuck in this tin can, a vehicle that was not reinforced by bulletproof anything and that could only go so fast. God willing, the old engine would keep up.

Okay, breathe. They'd made it this far against the odds, hadn't they?

Mitch grabbed a machine gun from the floor and

handed it to her. In one fluid motion, he scooped up the other and headed for the rear of the van. With the butt of the weapon, he smashed out the window on Charlie's side. "Stay out of sight," he said.

He smashed the other window as she pointed and squeezed from an awkward position. She recoiled at the force and the noise.

"*Don't* drop it," Mitch yelled. He fired. The noise they made in the back of the van battered Charlie's ears.

They couldn't stand upright, but Mitch, being taller, took a knee. Charlie braced herself as best she could. Enrique was weaving erratically, trying to dodge bullets, and she couldn't put enough weight on her injured leg.

Charlie winced every time the van was hit, but so far their tin can seemed to be holding its own.

Two minutes, three minutes. Charlie gasped—she'd hit a guard in the back seat. He tumbled over the back and under the next van. She clenched her jaw hard and just didn't let herself think about it.

The jeeps—three of the original four—were gaining steadily, too close. Plus, the swerving was maybe slowing them down.

She and Mitch kept firing.

"Conchita," Mitch yelled without turning around. "Bring me that bag."

"Okay!"

Charlie heard a thud and a "*dios*" and realized Conchita had been thrown into the wall.

Charlie risked a quick look and saw that now Conchita moved forward on hands and knees, sliding the backpack in front of her.

"There!" Conchita yelled. "By your foot."

Then, suddenly, it happened—Mitch took out a tire on the first jeep. It lurched left, and the driver overcorrected right. Off the road it went.

Charlie whooped. Only the pile-up she was hoping for didn't happen. The other two vehicles kept coming. *Shit.*

"Keep firing!" Mitch reached behind him for the backpack. He slung the gun strap over his shoulder, and next thing Charlie knew, he'd hurled a grenade. It bounced, rolled, bounced again—right off the road. It exploded just as both jeeps cleared it.

Mitch swore.

He pulled the pin on the other, and this time, Charlie saw, he only tossed it, letting it roll along the road. She stopped firing and held her breath. It came to a stop. The driver attempted to swerve, but—*yes!*—the jeep exploded off the ground in a giant ball of flame and roar of deafening noise.

Charlie and Mitch whooped and hollered. Enrique and Conchita added to the shouting—but that third jeep kept coming. They'd gained a bit of distance—the machine-gun fire was no longer hitting the van—but that meant their weapons were also ineffective. Charlie could see the girl in the gold dress.

She and Mitch ducked out of view and looked at each other. They were out of grenades.

Suddenly his eyes went wide and he started patting his leg.

Was he hit? "What?"

"The phone," he said. "Vibrating."

"The burner?"

The first phone he pulled out was his own, and he quickly dug for the other. He put it to his ear and covered the other ear with his hand. "Yeah." A pause. "Down to one." Another pause. "Okay. How far to town?" Mitch called to Enrique.

"Maybe ten minutes."

Mitch repeated that, nodded, and hung up.

"The police are coming."

Conchita twisted in her seat, her eyes wide with horror. "*Policía?*"

Around here, the police were notoriously corrupt, usually aiding the drug lords.

"It's okay," Mitch said. "Enrique, do *not* stop. They'll intercept the jeep before we reach town, if it's still with us."

And if they were still intact themselves. "Friends in high places?" Charlie asked.

Mitch had pocketed the phones and was repositioning the gun. "Friends with a shit-ton of money."

He pulled the trigger. They were in range again, the jeep's newer, more powerful engine closing the gap.

Bullets sprayed into the windows and hit the roof. Charlie gasped, swore, and prepped to pop up again. Yeah, they were taking fire. But they were giving it too.

Only another few miles.

61

A few more minutes and the road straightened out and grew wider. Sirens wailed and gained in volume as they raced toward Pase Viejo, replacing the noise Charlie and Mitch had been making when they were firing. Mitch squatted just behind the two front seats, a grip on both. Charlie slid into the jump seat behind Enrique. They'd shoved the machine guns under the towel just in case.

The police came straight down the road toward them but skidded to a stop ahead, sideways, making a blockade. The van lurched—Enrique must have laid off the gas pedal.

"No!" Mitch yelled. "Keep going. They left a gap. See?"

They surged forward, and Enrique prayed out loud. Conchita bowed her head and covered it with her arms.

Charlie held her breath. The doors of the police cars flew open. Officers jumped out and took cover, aiming at them—machine guns, plus some rifles.

Jesus. Three, two—

Another blast of machine-gun fire from behind. Charlie jumped and then jumped again at the sound of an explosion. Rear tire!

The van swerved, its tail end swiping the nose of the police car.

The officers fired—and Charlie nearly had a heart attack.

"God protect us!" Conchita cried over and over.

It took Charlie a few seconds, but then she realized: the officers had fired at the jeep, not at them! The van was off-kilter and slower, but still moving forward—*away* from gunfire.

"We're through," Mitch said. He put a hand on Conchita's shoulder and squeezed. She looked up and out the windshield and then behind and tears filled her eyes.

Charlie wanted to cry herself. Relief welled up with the force of a geyser.

Mitch shifted his hand to pound Enrique's shoulder. "Good driving, man."

Enrique shook his head in disbelief. In a minute he said, "Now what? Do I just drive right into town?"

"Yeah," Mitch said. "We've got to get our car. We can't keep driving this, but we've got to keep moving."

"We made it." Conchita reached over and squeezed Enrique's leg. She looked out the blown-out rear windows then swiveled back around. "But the Valdezes are still the Valdezes even without Lazaro. We cannot stay in town. We need a new plan."

"You'll come with us," Mitch said, even as Charlie opened her mouth to say the same. "Did you pack anything? Do we need to stop at your place?"

Enrique and Conchita exchanged a glance. He said, "The Valdezes will try to find us all. It is better, perhaps, if we split up."

Conchita nodded. "We can borrow a car."

They pulled into town, and Enrique asked, "Where is your car?"

"Just park behind your shop. We're getting too much attention."

Sure enough, people were staring. No surprise—not only were they driving with a flat tire, the van was literally riddled with bullet holes.

Enrique slowed further and then stopped the van half a block from the square where that young man was beaten only—what, about two weeks ago? The same square where the Rosaleses' son was burned to death.

Charlie asked, "Enrique?"

He looked at Conchita. "I will make an announcement."

"*Sí*," she said.

Mitch said, "We need to—"

"You go, friends." Enrique turned and clasped Mitch's hand in his. "Thank you. Thank you." He looked at Charlie and nodded once. Then he turned, pushed open his door, and hopped out.

"People of Pase Viejo. Follow me! There is news!" He strode toward the square and didn't look back.

Conchita hadn't moved, but Mitch was grabbing their bags, the weapons bag and the two backpacks with their clothes. He handed Charlie one, and she slung it on.

"Conchita," Charlie said, "you have our numbers.

Apply for asylum. We'll see if we can help—the same way we helped Chita."

Conchita smiled, a big, wide smile, tears in her eyes. She just might make it to see her daughter again. "We will. *Sí.*"

"But don't stay here," Mitch warned her. "That girl, Salvadora—"

"I know. We will move on just as soon as this is done." She gestured to the square, where Enrique was just arriving with a whole pack of townspeople converging.

She didn't smile, only looked at them with shining eyes. "Thank you. For everything."

Mitch shook his head. Charlie said, "Thank *you*. You and Enrique. We couldn't have done it without you."

Conchita hugged them both and then lumbered down from the van to join her husband.

"Let's get out of here. You can change later," Mitch said.

He went out the driver's-side door, as their car was parked in that direction. He turned to help Charlie down and then took her hand. Her leg hurt like hell, and she limped, but she'd do.

Charlie looked toward the square just in time to see Enrique raise his arms. He shouted names...one after another.

Just as Charlie and Mitch reached the alley, he called out, "Fernando Miguel Rosales Muñoz!" He paused, then shouted, "Now you rest in peace! Lazaro and Jorge Valdez are dead!"

The crowd erupted in shouts of other names—both male and female—who had been killed by the brothers and their long reach. Women embraced; men raised their arms to the heavens.

Charlie also saw some men slink off to the shadows. Did they work for the Valdezes? Or take news to other cartels? The reality was that today would not change things long term. Pase Viejo would not escape the drug trade. The residents would still lose their sons and daughters to crime and violence.

But for tonight, these people could mourn and celebrate knowing that, for once, the scale was tipped in their favor.

No one noticed two gringos limping away.

And by the time Charlie and Mitch hit the airport, they looked entirely different. Like any other American tourists, albeit maybe a little hungover from a raucous vacation.

62

———

Ian had passed out at some point during the helicopter ride, between the stress and the wound and the worry. God, he was just so tired from worrying about everyone: his little sisters falling to their deaths, Lucia hovering at death's door, Mitch and Charlie and that catering couple being chased by Salvadora…

When he woke, he was being wheeled into the Ronald Reagan UCLA Medical Center ER and greeted by beautifully flat American voices. He grinned despite the fiery pain in his side. He was really, truly in the States.

Now, he hissed and clenched and swore through the trimming of his skin and then all over again—worse—when the stitching commenced.

"Done with the muscle," the doc said.

"Christ." Ian was sweating and panting. "How many stitches am I getting?" They'd left that part out when they explained about suturing his six-inch gash.

The doc wore strange magnifying glasses and didn't

bother to look up. "That was twelve sub Q. There's about thirty-five to forty cutaneous to go."

"Hon, you should really—"

"No." Ian cut the attending nurse off. "No drugs. Just keep going."

He'd had to tell every single person—an entire parade of staff—over and over again: no drugs, no pain meds, no sedation. No, no, no.

By the time it was over, he was exhausted all over again and blacked right out.

He woke to his dad's voice coming from a long way away, muffled and faint. His first thought was that he must be dreaming and tried to stay asleep to enjoy it. He'd missed his dad.

Then he realized how badly his side hurt. Man, it hurt even to breathe, let alone move. He was so stiff and sore. How many hours had he slept?

He heard footsteps approaching—he wasn't in a real room, just in a curtained-off area. Probably still in the ER, then.

"Thank you. I—just…well, thank you."

It *was* his dad, right outside now. Ian felt such a rush of emotion—elation, relief, remorse. How would he ever explain what he'd done? His dad would never think of him the same.

A man said, "No need. It's our job, sir. How about I wait while you say hello, and then I'll take you down the hall."

The curtain parted with the swish of metal ball bearings, and Ian blinked. It really was his dad. And it wasn't a doctor with him, as Ian had assumed. It was one of the camo dudes—the one that had squirted saline in his wound on the helicopter and given him a temporary bandage. Davy, maybe?

Davy reached forward and closed the curtain, leaving Ian and his dad alone.

Stephen rushed forward. He reached to hug Ian and then stopped in his tracks with a jerk. "I don't want to hurt you."

"Dad." Ian reached out and clasped his father to him. He ignored the pain and closed his eyes as he sucked in a deep breath of steadfast familiarity—a feeling of safety under a classic spicy cologne. "I'm so glad you're here. That I'm here. That you got me here, I mean."

They both laughed, and Stephen put his hands on Ian's face and his forehead to his son's. Ian could see him trying not to bawl like a baby. His own tears fell.

"Don't cry. Don't cry," his dad said, much like he had when Ian was little. "It's okay now. You're home."

"I'm sorry, Dad, so sorry."

"You have nothing to apologize for. Nothing." Stephen's expression was fierce. He squeezed Ian's face with his hands before straightening.

His dad probably didn't know the half of it, but from Ian's perspective, yeah, okay. "How did you find me? How did you even know to look?"

Ian had run away before—willingly and willfully—a fact they were both all too aware of.

"I'll always look. Whether you want to be found or not."

"Okay," Ian said. "Okay. Good." Because for once, it felt like comfort instead of a threat.

"Excuse me, sir." The special ops medic—yeah, definitely Davy, Ian remembered—poked his head in. "Our transport is leaving soon. Want me to show you to Lucia's recovery room before I go?"

"Yes," Ian said, sitting up straight despite the hurt. "She's all right? Not dead?" Jesus. It should have been his first question.

Stephen said, "I don't know if you should—"

"I'm coming." Ian needed to apologize. Beg forgiveness. Tell her…what?

He swung his legs over the side of the bed. Luckily, he was still dressed beneath the waist. Even his shoes were still on. Just the top of him was in an open hospital gown.

His dad reached for his arm to steady him, but Ian waved him off.

"I'm okay. Let's go." He'd figure out what to say on the way.

Just as they neared the room, Davy called, "Hey!"

A figure popped out of a doorway—*Dia*. Thank God. Ian really, really needed to lay eyes on them all.

"You can't go in there," Davy said.

Wide-eyed, she clasped her hands behind her back. "I'm just looking."

"The rooms are private for a reason."

She hopped—literally hopped like a rabbit—over to him. "But I want to see how it all works."

He shook his head.

She gazed up at him with adoration. "You saved my mother's life. I want to know everything you know."

"*You* saved your mother's life, little doctor. Nice work."

"Lucia's daughter?" Stephen asked Ian quietly. He wore a strange look that Ian couldn't decipher.

Ian didn't have a chance to answer, because Dia finally realized Davy wasn't the only one in the hall. To Ian, she said, "I should punch you, but I'm too happy. You have to see this place. *Dios*, it's amazing!" She grabbed his arm and tugged him toward a doorway.

"Ouch." He winced.

"Look at this stuff!" She bounded along. "Just look!"

He heard Davy huff out a chuckle.

Ian turned to thank him, but it was too late. He was striding down the hall at a fast clip.

Ian froze at the site of Lucia. She was so pale. An enormous dressing on her propped-up leg. Oxygen tubes in her nose. Too many tubes coming from her arm. But she was awake and smiled at him.

"My God. I—" His voice cracked. "I'm sorry. I couldn't choose—I tried not to hurt you too much, but—"

"Shh, now. I'm fine."

He moved to the bed, took her hand, and bowed over it. "Can you ever forgive me?" His voice was a broken whisper.

"Always," she said. She settled her hand on his head and then smoothed his hair. He sobbed, and she smoothed.

Her hand stilled, and Ian figured she'd fallen asleep. He gulped and sniffed. Jesus, he had to get a grip. But when Ian looked up, Lucia's eyes were fixed on something behind him, and she wore a soft smile.

Stephen had moved into the room and stood stock-still staring at Lucia.

"He's amazing, Stephen," she said.

"Lucia."

One word, and holy crap—the emotion in this room. Ian squeezed Lucia's hand, then stood to move out from between them.

Dia had her face nearly plastered to Lucia's beeping monitor. Ian grabbed her arm—*oh damn*, reaching *really* hurt—and tugged her toward the door. "Let's give them a minute."

"What?"

"Dia." He squeezed her arm hard until she tore her gaze away and he knew she was listening. "Where are the girls?"

"Down the hall. A nurse took them to some family area. With coloring books."

"Show me."

She huffed, but followed him out the door and pointed in the direction of the family area.

She spun to return to Lucia's room, but he grabbed her arm. "Give them a minute. Go look at the monitors in the nurses' area."

She brightened and spun off.

Ian strode forward, the gown flapping wildly. He still couldn't believe he'd sent the girls out a window. They had considered the helicopter an adventure for a few minutes, but then they got a look at the shape Lucia was in, and he knew exactly how terrifying that was. He had to see them.

And then he did. Two little heads—their braids barely in place—bent over coloring books. Another, with her hands and nose pressed flat against the front of a vending machine. Had anyone fed them? He had no money, of course, but he could—

Wait? Three? Cat, Ana, Tierra…

"Ian!" said Ana.

Tierra turned to look at him and thrust her arm out with a finger pointed at his chest. Her eyes were wide.

"Just a small boo-boo with a big bandage," he said. "Where's Bebe?"

Tierra shifted her pointed finger to his right. He turned. Bebe was curled up half on the floor, half on top of a giant stuffed animal, her thumb in her mouth, fast asleep.

Ian bowed his head and heaved out a long breath.

Just then, he heard someone call out, "I've got him," and a nurse pushed through the door, shaking her head. "You can't just wander away from the ER. There's paperwork."

Ian put his finger to his lips and pointed to Bebe.

The nurse gave him a *well then, come on* look. Ian went, but mostly because she'd surely need his dad for the paperwork.

And Ian needed his dad to get food for the girls—his sisters—but first things first. He needed to find out about Charlie and Mitch and the catering couple. Had they survived Salvadora's fury?

63

———

WHEN THEY LANDED IN LOS ANGELES THE following evening, Mitch insisted the first order of business should be getting Charlie's leg real medical care. Charlie was more interested in seeing Ian, Stephen, Lucia, and the girls.

Mitch set his jaw and told the driver to go to the nearest hospital. He was worried about her wound splitting open, worried about infection, just—well, damn.

He'd nearly had a heart attack when he realized she'd been shot. He knew it wasn't life threatening, but still, he wanted it treated properly, and if they went to the hotel Cross had booked, she'd never get it taken care of.

Turned out she should have had stitches—however, because it was long past six hours since she'd been injured, they would just clean, secure, and dress the wound, as well as give her antibiotics.

"You want a recommendation for a plastic surgeon?" the doctor asked.

Charlie waved him off.

Satisfied, Mitch stepped out in the hall to call Henrietta, whom they hadn't talked to since before they set out for the Valdez compound. "We're safe and back in the States. So's Ian. Already reunited with his dad."

"Praise the Lord" was the hearty response.

He didn't tell her Charlie had been shot. No need to worry Henry after the fact.

His phone battery was nearly zapped, so he found a plug in the hallway and slid down the wall to a squat. Good thing there wasn't a chair, because he'd likely pass out.

He had several messages. Three calls from people with missing persons. One runaway, one spouse, and one caller didn't say—just begged him to call her back in a shaky voice.

Mitch would have to take it slow at first. He needed an office, equipment, and supplemental training.

He ran a hand over his hair, and then wiped it on his pants. *Ugh.* They needed showers.

He'd also need to hire someone to do office stuff. And maybe a partner—or at least somebody part time to help with surveillance.

He blew out a breath and leaned his head back against the wall. It couldn't be Charlie. If there was anything this first job had taught him, it was that she could probably handle the work—but he couldn't handle her in danger.

Granted, he didn't expect most jobs he took to be anywhere near as dangerous. Still, she was off the hook. She was free to pursue whatever career she decided on. They'd just date and be a normal couple. Well, maybe not normal, given it was Charlie. A smile broke his face—a wry one, but it felt good.

The fourth message was another number he didn't recognize. He hit play and held the phone to his ear.

"Hello, detective."

He frowned. The cultured voice was familiar, but the ER hallway was noisy. Mitch turned up the volume and started the message over.

"Hello, detective. You'll be glad to know I've healed nicely—or maybe you won't." The man chuckled softly.

Thomas Weihle. That *fucker*.

Mitch's skin heated, and he stood, every cell in his body wanting to hurl the phone across the room.

"My living accommodations leave something to be desired, of course, but all I have to do is think of the soft, oh-so-sensitive skin between sweet Laura's thighs and all's right with my world."

Mitch needed to smash something—preferably the phone so he didn't have to listen to this psycho. However, if Weihle was threatening Charlie, even from behind bars, Mitch needed to know.

"Please, tell her I'm thinking of her—always. I have *not* forgiven her. But she and I will straighten that out between us. I look forward to seeing you both soon."

That sick fuck! His voice made Mitch long for violence. His words made him want to explode.

He'd love to delete the message, except he needed to share it with the prosecutor. That bastard shouldn't have phone privileges—or access to a computer to dig for phone numbers. Mitch's wasn't hard to find. It'd be only a matter of time, though, before he found Charlie's.

Mitch stared at the phone, at the area code. My God —Weihle *did* have Charlie's number. All those calls she'd assumed were wrong numbers or hang-ups were from the prison. From Weihle. But Mitch had been too preoccupied with Ian's situation to realize.

He slammed his fist into the wall.

"Sir?" A nurse approached.

"Sorry. I'm fine. Really, I apologize." He swore under his breath as she finally turned away.

Unfortunately, Weihle would see them soon. The hearing Charlie had been dreading so much was coming up.

Mitch's next call was to the prosecutor, Gerty Kolacsko.

Charlie shouldn't have to lay eyes on her tormentor ever again. Weihle shouldn't have the freedom to make phone calls from jail.

As far as Mitch was concerned, the man shouldn't even have his life.

64

Cross had insisted on booking a room for Charlie and Mitch in the same hotel as his, near the hospital where Lucia was being treated. It was late when they arrived, so Charlie and Mitch showered and changed as quickly as possible.

Cross had secured a large suite on the top floor. When he opened the door, the look on his face was full of emotion. He opened his mouth, but ended up just shaking his head.

Charlie reached for his hand, and he grasped her tightly as her eyes welled with tears, at all the relief and joy she felt at bringing him and his son back together.

He shook Mitch's hand next, and his voice was shaky when he said, "Thank you."

Cross took a moment to wipe his eyes before he stepped back and said, "Come in. The girls are asleep in that room." He pointed to a closed doorway. "I wasn't comfortable separating any of them, so I'm sleeping with Ian. Which is fine; it's—"

He shook his head. Charlie understood. The poor man needed his son within reach. And it sounded like he needed to be near Lucia, too—otherwise he could have taken everybody home.

Cross told them he had somebody bring Ian pajamas, toiletries, and fresh clothes, and they'd all taken a trip to Target to get the same for the girls. Toys had made their way into the cart and now littered the suite. He'd even chosen some things for Lucia.

"Once she's discharged, we'll all go home."

Charlie smiled at that. Even Mitch smiled, and Charlie felt a rush of tenderness. He was tough and gruff and sometimes overbearing—but his soft side was just under the surface.

Stephen explained that the girls were still tired from the "adventure" but had perked up at the hotel, having never been in one before, or anywhere other than home. They tried the phone, flipped all the light switches, bounced on the beds, opened and closed the curtains, and squealed at how high up they were.

"I considered booking the neighboring rooms to save others from the noise." Cross chuckled. "Last night we ate at the hospital and fell into bed. But tonight, we ordered room service, and Dia took care of baths. All quiet now. Ian's really…very good with them." His eyes were a bit watery, and he blinked as if he was still unable to believe it all. Ian had half-sisters. *Five* of them.

"Is Ian asleep too?" Charlie asked.

Cross nodded. "He wanted to see you both, though. Go on in."

Ian bolted up as soon as they opened the door. "Jesus," he said, and shook his head as if to clear it. "Sorry."

Charlie's heart lurched. She knew well that when you'd lived on fear and dread, the effects didn't just disappear once you were safe.

He climbed out of bed and hugged her. "I still can't believe you came. I—"

He pulled back and pressed his lips together—probably to keep from crying.

"Thank Charlie," Mitch said. "I would have left your ass there." Ian snorted, and they pounded each other on the back as they embraced.

Ian had some questions. How the hell did they realize he'd been abducted? How had they found him? Mitch sprawled out in a big, cushy chair, while Charlie sat against the headboard next to Ian.

Eventually, Ian shook his head. "You shouldn't have come. You have no idea how dangerous Lazaro Valdez was."

Mitch said, "I'm sure we don't know everything, but we had a pretty good idea from the Rosaleses."

He looked at Charlie, and she knew he still would have chosen differently. He would have gone after Ian, but if he could have, he would have left her back.

Too bad. She couldn't say it hadn't been terrifying, but she wouldn't change it. She'd never be sorry they'd helped Ian and his dad, and it had taken all of them.

"There's a drink out there calling my name," Mitch said. "Need anything?"

Once he delivered them each a soda, he shut the door behind him so Charlie and Ian could talk.

"You know I've been through some serious shit, right?" Charlie asked.

He nodded.

"Everyone's going to push you to see a shrink. You probably should. But I'm good at keeping secrets if you need to unload."

He nodded.

"Want to watch TV? Or go back to sleep?"

"Stay? Pennsylvania is all the way across the country. Didn't think I'd ever see you again." He smiled, all teenage ribbing like when she'd met him at Glide.

"I still have my apartment above Henrietta's, you know."

"Cool." He reached for the remote control and scrolled through the choices, and then scrolled through them again.

Her eyes had begun to droop when he said, "You wanna know what the worst part was?"

It took hours, but Ian told her everything—everything he probably couldn't tell his father, maybe things he wouldn't even share with a professional. He must have sensed that Charlie wouldn't judge.

She wouldn't. She'd been there. Not there, exactly, but she'd been through much of the same. A whole lifetime of feeling trapped, controlled by other people. Made to do things against your will. Forced to make choices no one should ever—ever—have to make. Leaving the ones you loved. Hurting them. Abandoning them. Not because you wanted to, but because it was the only way to keep them safe from monsters.

When Ian finally slept—the deep, exhausted sleep of being in a safe place and finally unpacking some demons —Charlie wept. Sobbed hard into a pillow, like she'd never been able to for herself.

She didn't hear Mitch come in. He wiped her face and lifted her to standing. He led her past Stephen Cross, who was snoring on the couch, and through the hallway of the hotel to their own room. He undressed her down to t-shirt and panties, careful not to touch her wound, and then tucked her into him on blessedly clean sheets and fluffy pillows.

He stroked her hair and let out a long sigh.

"Yes," she said into his chest.

"Yes, what?"

She pulled back enough to look up at him. "I'll partner with you." He stared at her with concern, and she thought maybe he'd misheard her. "Retrieval, Inc. I'm saying yes."

Mitch pushed her head back down on his chest. "I retract that offer."

Oh no you don't. She levered onto her elbow, hooked her leg behind his, bandage and all, and squeezed to lock him in place. "You can't."

"You don't have to." He grimaced. "I shouldn't have pressured you."

"It was good this thing we did together." Good was totally inadequate. It was terrifying, exhilarating, important, and meaningful. She quirked her lip and said, "I might be hooked."

"I'm not sure I can take it." He traced the bandage

around her calf, then raised his eyes to search her face. "For real. I'm not sure it's a good idea anymore."

"I'm not going to take stupid risks. Ian's was…a special case."

He grunted.

"I get it," she said. "I was terribly scared that something would happen to you, too."

He smoothed his warm palm up and down her leg.

She almost didn't know when she'd decided on this, but once she saw Ian climb into that helicopter with his new family and fly away to safety, she'd been so… What was it? Moved? Stoked? Satisfied? Fulfilled? And when she saw Stephen Cross's face—well, there was maybe nothing like a parent's relief and the bone-deep joy she felt at seeing a family reunited.

"But it's better if we're together, isn't it?" She placed her palm on Mitch's still-stubbly cheek. "We'll keep each other from stupid risks. We can try to avoid jobs that look too dangerous. But if things get crazy, we'll have each other's backs, right?"

It felt like it took forever, but finally he swore softly. "Okay."

She kissed him on the mouth. "I didn't really need your approval, but since we're going to be partners…"

He shook his head. "You're going to be the death of me, you know."

"No," she said. "We make a good team."

He took a deep breath, the warm skin of his chest rising against her.

"We'll have plenty of business. There's a bunch of messages on my phone." A dark look crossed his face—

one she couldn't decipher—but he masked it quickly with a smile. "We have a benefactor, too."

"Cross?"

He nodded. "Rest now."

And Charlie allowed herself to sleep because, trapped in Mitch's strong arms, she believed herself safe.

ALSO IN THE RETRIEVAL, INC. SERIES

Thank you for reading *Trapped*! I hope you loved it and are already itching for the next Charlie and Mitch story—because *Blinded* is already in the works…

The most dangerous threats of all are those you are blind to…

Mitch and Charlie's new case triggers their biggest fears and compromises the Thomas Weihle trial. One way or another, Charlie's tormentor must be faced and put away forever. To make matters worse, Charlie is hiding a secret that will change everything. This time she can't run, but she'll be damned if she's trapped again. The trouble is, Mitch refuses to let her go.

Preorder BLINDED to read in early 2023!

———

And if you found *Trapped* before reading *Runaway*? Go read the story that started it all!

If she can't stay hidden, she must run—again.

While tracing his missing teenage sister, Detective Mitch Saunders uncovers a disturbing link to one of his old, and very cold, cases: Laura Macnamara, a young woman who walked out her backdoor and simply disappeared. Runaway, or victim? He never knew, but is about to find out. Because Laura—a sexy, grown woman now known as Charlie Hart—holds the key to his sister's safety. Except Charlie refuses to help him. Between her carefully guarded secrets and well-founded fears, too much is at stake to look back. Nor can she consider a future with Mitch—a man who will expose her to evil, if that's what it takes to bring his sister home. He leaves Charlie no choice but to run— again. Or is it already too late?

Read RUNAWAY now!

———

Turn the page for more heart-racing romance by JB!

Lives depend on keeping secrets buried. Eddie just started digging...

Marine Eddie Mackey knows his estranged wife's suicide was really murder. Videographer Miranda Hill knows more than she'll say. When she is attacked as a result of his investigation, Eddie swears to protect Miranda despite her secrets, his misgivings, and their undeniable attraction. In the end, there's only one choice: join forces to uncover evil —before anyone else winds up dead.

Read UNCOVERED now!

Maxine's inner circle hides a disturbed killer...

When Maxine Ricci discovers another brutally murdered model, she can no longer deny that a serial killer is targeting her agency. She has no choice but to enlist bodyguard Shane O'Rourke's protection. Of all people, he understands the unique demands and pitfalls of the fashion world. Unfortunately, Max was the one who ended his modeling career. Between the forced proximity to the sexy, grudge-holding Irishman and signs a twisted psycho is drawing too near, Max is coming undone. So, too, is the madman, whose ultimate obsession is her…

Read UNDONE now!

THANKS AND MORE

I'm so thrilled you found my books! Did you love *Trapped?* Kindly share your thoughts on your retailer, Bookbub, or Goodreads, and please tell a friend! Reviews and word of mouth are still the best way for readers to find books they love. I'm so grateful for the help!

I love to hear from readers, and these days there are so many ways for us to connect! The Finding JB page on my website has *all* the options—choose what works for you.

For the inside scoop, join my newsletter, which will come right to your email inbox. If you prefer *only* new release alerts, however, simply follow me on BookBub or Amazon.

ACKNOWLEDGMENTS

Huge thanks to my readers for loving Charlie and Mitch as much as I do! Sorry it took me so long to return to these characters. Hopefully it was well worth the wait!

Savannah Kade: how on earth you gave me such spot-on advice while slogging through such a messy draft, I'll never know! I owe you a critique (and so much more).

So many thanks to Paty García Peña for salvaging my sad attempt at Spanish with better word choices, proper spelling, and correct accent marks. Not only did you help out this author, you saved my readers from serious teeth grinding!

To my editing team: Trenda Lundin, Arran McNicol, Jen Coleman, please don't ever retire. I can't imagine launching a book into the world without you.

And going way back, a shout out to the incomparable Maureen Hansch. Upending Charlie and Mitch's happily-ever-after in *Runaway* paved the way for a much longer (and truer) character arc for this duo. More to come, my friends!

JB SCHROEDER, a graduate of Penn State University's creative writing program, crafts romance to make your heart race. Blessed with a mostly routine life, JB has no idea why her characters keep encountering danger—but she wouldn't have it any other way.

JB loves to connect with readers and can be reached through her website:
www.jbschroederauthor.com

* 9 7 8 1 9 4 3 5 6 1 1 7 9 *